How had Landen's father, wise King Veldon, renowned poet, generous, honest man, been overcome by a harsh aggressor like Kareed? How had justice been routed, and peace bled to death? Where had Bellandra gone wrong?

Veldon was a good man, but not a good warrior. He didn't know how to fight, didn't think he'd ever have to. Kareed won because he was the stronger warrior.

Landen didn't like it. He didn't like it, but knew it was true. In the Sword's chamber, it had been Kareed who knew how to pick up a weapon, and he had done it without hesitation, with power and with glee, while Landen faltered, wasting precious seconds.

Running now would lose him his chance to find out what made this king the victor in every conquest he undertook. If Landen left, it would be like handing Kareed the Sword all over again. No, he must not go. He had to stay, learn everything he could. Kareed had promised he would be trained; and though Kareed was a ruthless invader, Landen had heard that his word was true.

I'll hold you to your promise, King Kareed. And one day, I'll take the Sword from you. When I do, I'll know how to use it.

ALSO AVAILABLE IN DELL LAUREL-LEAF BOOKS:

WHO ARE YOU?, *Joan Lowery Nixon*
BURNING UP, *Caroline B. Cooney*
ONE THOUSAND PAPER CRANES, *Takayuki Ishii*
FOR MIKE, *Shelley Sykes*
HALINKA, *Mirjam Pressler*
TIME ENOUGH FOR DRUMS, *Ann Rinaldi*
CHECKERS, *John Marsden*
NOBODY ELSE HAS TO KNOW, *Ingrid Tomey*
TIES THAT BIND, TIES THAT BREAK, *Lensey Namioka*
CONDITIONS OF LOVE, *Ruth Pennebaker*

The
Seer
and the
Sword

Victoria Hanley

❖

Published by
Dell Laurel-Leaf
an imprint of
Random House Children's Books
a division of Random House, Inc.
New York

First published in the UK by Scholastic Ltd, 2000
The right of Victoria Hanley
to be indentified as the author of this work
has been asserted by her in accordance
with the Copyright, Design and Patents Act, 1988.

Visit us on the Web! www.randomhouse.com/teens

Educators and librarians, for a variety of teaching tools, visit us at
www.randomhouse.com/teachers

ISBN: 0-440-22977-4

Reprinted by arrangement with Holiday House

Printed in the United States of America

April 2003

10 9 8 7 6 5 4 3 2

OPM

to my children,
Emrys and
Rose

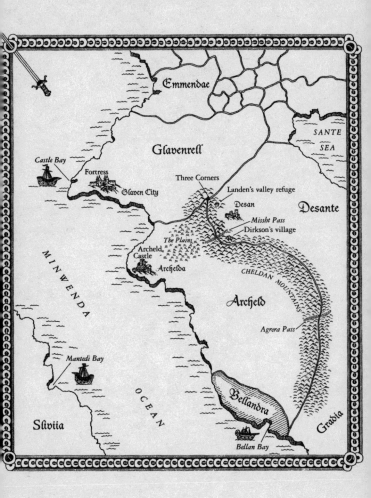

The
Seer
and the
Sword

Part One

Chapter 1

In the castle of Archeld, Queen Dreea sat at her loom. Her vibrant weavings were prized throughout the kingdoms. They revealed a quiet passion the queen never showed in face or voice.

Beside Dreea, curled on a rug, her daughter Torina stitched embroidery. Long, slender fingers pulled the needle back and forth, forming the pattern of a rising sun: the sign of the house of Kareed. Mirandae, the queen's close servant, spun wool, her wheel humming.

Torina stuck the needle crosswise in her spool and flexed her hands. "Enough sewing, Mamma! Let me go out and ride."

Dreea smiled patiently. "The sun is ready to set. You rode this morning."

"The boys are still out."

"And you are not a boy." Dreea paused to feed a thread of scarlet into the pattern of blue she worked.

"They have the chance to watch for King Kareed! He's my father—I should be the first to see him!" Wispy tendrils of Torina's red curls straggled free of their ribbons.

Dreea shifted, laying hands on her full belly, thinking with regret of how Kareed's nature goaded him to pit his strength against the might of other kingdoms. Once again, he was at war to extend his borders. Ever since he could swing a sword, the pride of warriorship had driven him to battle. Each time he prevailed, he drew his circle wider. Now his rule stretched north to Glavenrell, east to Desante, west to the sea, and south to Bellandra.

Bellandra, kingdom of peace, with a rich heritage of art and culture. Bellandra, whose citizens had enjoyed generations of harmony and prosperity. Dreea wondered, wistfully, what it would be like to live in such a land. It was said their magic Sword could stand against any foe. If that were so, what fate awaited Kareed?

Fear and hope struggled inside her. She'd seen Bellandra herself and loved the hospitable country. She didn't want its ancient beauty destroyed by war. Yet war was exactly what Kareed was determined to carry there. If he were the victor, he would force Bellandra into servitude to Archeld. And if the famous Sword defeated him, what would Dreea do? She loved Kareed with the enduring tenacity of a gentle heart. He filled all the landscape of her tender soul.

Now she feared Kareed had overreached destiny, and only sorrow could be the result. She had prayed and prayed that something good would come of this.

"Your father will be away a while longer," the queen told her restless daughter.

"I still want to ride!"

Dreea shook her head. Many had told her that a more unruly spirit than Torina's could not be found, even in the wild forests of Archeld.

When fiery King Kareed married Dreea, he passed

4

over many ladies of more obvious beauty and greater riches. She knew people wondered why he kept such a queen, who had no taste for war and never bore him an heir for Archeld. It had been nine years since the birth of their daughter, nine years and seven miscarriages. Sad that such a powerful king could not command something so simple as having a son. But with Dreea, and only with her, Kareed the mighty king could become Kareed the loving man. When they were together, he relaxed into warmth, telling her all the secrets of his life. She doubted anyone guessed how much she knew. She never passed on his confidences, guarding them as closely as she did her own.

And now, at last, her pregnancy was advanced; when the moon returned once more to fullness, she would deliver again. Perhaps this time, it would be a boy.

A small commotion at the door to the hall drew Torina's gaze. Her eyes, colored like the sea, lit with surprise as her comrade Zeon rushed in, face flushed.

"Torina!" his boyish voice announced. "We saw the king riding, beyond the first ridge!"

A guard pressed through the door, grabbing Zeon roughly. "That will be quite enough!" With Zeon wriggling in his grasp, the guard turned to Dreea. "Sorry, my lady, for the intrusion. If the boys can be believed, your husband will be here by sunset."

Dreea felt a strange leaping in her heart. Unthinking, she stood and took a step toward the door. She heard a crash and turned in surprise to see Mirandae rushing at her with outstretched arms. The room tilted oddly and the light went out, snuffed by a dark roar rising in her ears.

Torina was hardly aware of her mother swaying and Mirandae upsetting the spinning wheel in her haste to aid her mistress. All the young princess wanted was to beat Zeon through the door. Now, hair streaming behind her, she lay along her horse's neck, nudging Stina into a faster gallop. The westering sun caught the dust of a cloud of riders and glinted on the gold helmet of the king.

His amber-colored stallion charged ahead of his men. One large arm swept the princess off her horse, red beard mingling with red curls as they embraced.

"How's my princess! Out here, near dark, unattended? Did you escape again?"

"I wanted to meet you."

"And here I am."

"Did you win the war?"

He snorted. "Would I come home if I did not?"

She smiled, happy in her father's victory. They rode slowly, her horse trotting near. Kareed asked about her mother's health, and Torina answered that the queen was well. Beaming, the king leaned into his saddlebag.

"This is for you, all the way from Bellandra. Hold out your hand."

He put a crystal sphere in her palm. Her fingers barely fit around it. Torina held it up to the embers of the sun. Inside the crystal, light swam and brightened: a world of gold.

"How lovely." She nestled in the curve of her father's arm. Moments alone with the king, without soldiers or petitioners or servants, were few.

Hooves pounded toward them from the direction of the castle. The same guard who had interrupted Zeon galloped up.

"My lord," he breathed. "I'm sorry, my lord, about the princess. She slipped away."

"She's a true daughter of a king."

The guard bit his lip. "Sir . . . it seems the queen was taken early."

The king's indulgent smile changed to a frown.

"Vesputo!" he barked. From the horsemen following, a rider detached and sped forward. A dark mustache and heavy eyebrows marked a handsome face.

"Sir?"

"Take the child." Torina was handed into Vesputo's saddle, as if she wasn't grown up enough to get up and down herself. "When you've delivered her safely, ride back and see to it the troops are all accounted for."

"Yes, my lord."

"I can ride Stina, Papa!"

Not even looking at her, the king galloped away with the guard, their horses veiled in dust on the darkening plain.

Torina sat very still, sidesaddle on Vesputo's horse, clasping her new crystal and blinking.

"What did the guard mean about my mother?"

The soldier shrugged.

Torina stared at the crystal, rotating it in her hand. She brought it close to her face, then gasped as the dimming light congealed in its middle and began to form a face. It was her mother's. White, exhausted, lying on a pillow. Another face bent over her, a woman. Torina was somehow sure the woman was a midwife.

The midwife took the queen's hand and rubbed it. A voice came from her, echoing inside Torina's head as though mixed with the sound of surf.

"A son, my lady. Stillborn."

Dreea's face twisted into sobs.

"No!" Torina screamed, sliding down from Vesputo's saddle. She ran to Stina.

"What is it?" Vesputo called. Torina leaped on her horse and drove her heels into the flanks, heading for home.

❖   ❖   ❖

Outside the queen's rooms, a group of women stood, waiting for news. Into this small crowd, Torina burst like a quick flame trying to take hold on green wood. She almost made it through the door.

Though she flailed and kicked, the women surrounded her, their soft arms firm as trees. She cried and called for her mother. They would not let her pass. When her cries gave way to shrieks of indignant anguish, some of them carried her to her room and stayed immovably by her side.

❖   ❖   ❖

Dawn was beginning when Ancilla, Kareed's old mother, crept in to be with her granddaughter. The girl lay huddled in her carved bed, covered with blankets carefully worked by Dreea's patient hands.

Ancilla had borne only boys, and all had been killed in the Sliviite wars except Kareed, the son who arrived when she believed she was past the age for conceiving. Now she was older than anyone else, so old that wrinkles almost swallowed the delicate features that had once rallied kings. Yet her steps were still light, her eyes filled with the famous fire of the warrior line of Archeld.

She sat beside Torina, her bones barely dimpling the mattress. She smoothed the girl's wild hair. Torina's eyes fluttered open. She kissed Ancilla's withered fingers.

"Where's Mamma?"

"Resting."

"The baby?"

"A stillborn son." The old eyes misted.

Torina hugged her middle, staring as though impaled on some inner vision. The old queen followed her granddaughter's gaze and saw a pure crystal globe sitting on the bureau across from the bed.

"Stillborn!" the child cried, pointing. "Gramere, the crystal my father gave me told me that yesterday!"

Ancilla stared. Yesterday. The queen delivered this morning. How could the girl know? Was Torina a seer? Ah heaven, what a great and terrible gift, if she was.

Ancilla reached out to hold the shivering girl. Her thin voice quavered the ritual song of mourning. "One I love is taken from me . . ."

Torina joined her in broken, childish tones.

"We will never walk together over the fields of earth,
Never hear the birds in the morning.
Oh, I have lived with you and loved you
And now you are gone away.
Gone where I cannot follow
Until I have finished all my days."

❖ ❖ ❖

King Kareed leaned against the stone wall of the courtyard, looking out over the road where all travel from the plains must pass. The army was returning, and the king stood in silent review of his troops. The men rode in disciplined ranks, saluting as they went by. Later, when they reached their quarters or reunited with their families, there would be rejoicing. A great victory. Bellandra, the invincible, conquered. Bellandra's Sword taken. Yes, they would celebrate. But now, in the presence of the king, whose suit of mourning white proclaimed his latest loss, they were subdued.

At last, the rear contingent came into view. Vesputo, grim faced and dusty, turned his horse into the courtyard of the castle, followed by a small band of soldiers. The king went to meet them. He gripped Vesputo's hand as his liege man swung down.

"All accounted for?"

Vesputo nodded.

"Well done, Commander. Go refresh yourself. I know how well you deserve it."

Vesputo took a deep breath and spoke the formal words heard so many times during his five years serving King Kareed. "My spirit is saddened by the flight of your loved one."

Kareed put a hand to his chest, then let it drop. "May it be granted that at the end of my days we reunite." Kareed thought of the many battles fought side by side with Vesputo. "A son."

"Ah. Sir, I—"

"Next time, Commander, you'll stay here and guard my family."

The king stopped. Torina stood a few feet away, a mourning gown draped around her. How long had she been there? Her face was almost as white as her dress. He remembered he had not seen his daughter since she rode to meet him on the plains.

This stillbirth has changed us all.

He extended an arm. Her tentative fingers clasped his. Where was the eager child who had leaped into his arms only the day before?

Her small hand curled around the present he had given her. She held it out. "This came from Bellandra?"

He nodded.

"Who gave it to you?"

"I saw it and thought of you. I forget who gave it to me."

"Did you see my face in it?"

"Your face?" Kareed frowned in puzzlement.

"You've forgotten whose it was?" she persisted. Her voice sounded strained.

"Too many battles to remember all the places I've been."

But Kareed did remember. The disturbing woman, older than Ancilla, bent and wizened. He had burst into her room during the search for the Sword, when they were sacking Bellandra. She had looked up at him with ageless eyes, then down at the sparkling sphere in her lap. She smiled a twisted smile.

"Ah," she moaned, and kissed the crystal. She held it up to him. "For your red-haired daughter."

Then she collapsed in front of him. When he prodded her with a sword, she never moved. Kareed had stopped to pry the shining thing from her dead hand and slipped it into his pouch for Torina.

How had this old woman known he had a red-haired daughter? But then, he was a red-haired man.

My son! The pain possessed his soul again. He had seen the tiny, waxy blue, perfectly formed infant who would never draw breath. *If I rode slowly, would you have lived?*

He was sure Dreea would have no more children. Yet he could not bear to put aside his beloved wife for a younger, fertile woman. The king looked fondly down on Torina's shining head, bent over the crystal.

The last child in a long and formidable line.

Thinking of her that way made him remember the end of a different lineage.

"I brought you another present, Torina," he said, suddenly grim. "Vesputo! Fetch the boy."

The commander quickly returned. Before him walked the former prince of Bellandra. Dark, curling hair matted around his face; his features, under bruises and scrapes, were still. Dust and dirt had obliterated the elegant lines of his clothes. His legs, just beginning to lengthen toward manhood, were unsteady; his arms were tied behind his back.

Vesputo thrust the young prisoner forward. The boy stumbled and fell. Torina sprang to help him. Kareed saw the boy's eyes flicker wide for an instant as the king's daughter pulled him to his feet.

"Who is he?" Torina asked.

"The son of a king."

"Why are his hands tied?"

"He's a prisoner. And the son of a king no more. I brought him here for you, Torina. He will make a fine slave." Silently he added, *Yes, a slave. No matter that none of your other servants are slaves. This is different.*

Torina looked at the boy, at his heavy curling hair and wild, remote eyes.

"If he is my slave," she asked, "does that make him my own?"

"All your own."

"I can do whatever I want with him?"

The king nodded.

The princess shivered. "What is your name, son of a king?" she asked.

"Landen." The boy's manner, still that of a prince, contrasted oddly with his dusty rags and bruises.

"Vesputo," Torina said.

"Princess?"

"Cut his ropes, please."

The commander looked to his king, who inclined his head. A blade was drawn. Vesputo severed the ropes carelessly, trailing fresh blood. Landen rubbed his wrists as Torina stepped closer to him.

"My father fought your father." She said it very softly, speaking as if no king or soldiers looked on. For her, they must have been forgotten.

Landen looked at the ground. A pulse in his neck beat, like the heart of a newly hatched bird.

"Landen," she whispered. "I never had a slave."

The boy stood quietly.

"And I never will," she continued, lifting her chin. "Papa," her voice rose. "You gave him to me. I set him free."

Kareed's eyebrows billowed, a ferocious storm gathering. When Vesputo suggested making Landen a slave, it was to demean the spirit of Bellandra. King Veldon had strutted for too long behind his magic Sword, looking down his nose at warrior kings. Prince Landen of

Bellandra, King Veldon's only son, a slave to Kareed's daughter! That would finish the conquest.

Now she threw away this gift so dearly won. For a century, no one had dared attack Bellandra, but he, Kareed, had done it. The king felt the familiar battle rage rising. He wanted to strike Torina flat. There she was, standing small and white beside him. But there was something in the way she clasped her hands together; it was what her mother did when he told her he was going to war. Kareed remembered how Dreea had pleaded with him to spare Bellandra, to let them keep their ways. Women knew nothing of war. They knew nothing of battles, princes, and kings. He sighed, swallowing his anger. *Perhaps I've allowed this war to sully my judgment. Torina knows I don't keep slaves. And Bellandra's defeat is complete without this boy. After all, he's only thirteen—hardly more than a child.*

The king forced his face into a smile and pushed a laugh from his chest. "By my helmet!" he cried in his battle voice. "She's the true daughter of a king!"

A light wind picked up the collective sigh in the courtyard and carried it away. Men went about their business, taking horses to the stables, oiling weapons, and stacking leather armor.

Landen stood alone in the stream of activity. He rubbed his wrists with shaking hands, chest heaving. The girl near him pretended not to notice, looking past him to the distant mountains. Vesputo had gone. The young princess spoke affectionately to King Kareed, calling him to her side.

Landen's knees trembled as his father's killer approached. He remembered that cruel fist batting him down, in the chamber of the Sword.

"Landen." The king's rough voice held no animosity.

"Sir." The word felt like a betrayal.

"You are now a member of my household. You'll receive warrior training with the other boys."

The exiled prince felt faint. His father's dying words rang in his ears. *"Find someone who can teach you to fight."*

Kareed shifted his feet. "I bear you no ill will. The past is buried."

Not for me. My father is buried.

"Torina," the king said. "Attend to this boy. See he's fed, and get him washed." Kareed turned and left them.

Landen felt a small, confiding hand touch his arm.

"This way." The red-haired girl led him into the castle. She moved with assurance through the halls, to a private room. There she gave him a soft chair, then went out into the hallway.

Landen scanned the room. It was the first time he'd been out of bonds or cages since Bellandra fell. If he ran, would anyone stop him? He was a fast runner. He could get away, steal a horse, make his way back to Bellandra.

But what about the Sword? His father had told him to get the Sword. And what about learning to fight?

He heard the red-haired girl speaking imperiously to someone, ordering a bath, steaming hot. Landen's filthy, blood-scabbed skin cried out for the relief of a soaking. The girl came back.

"Your bath will be ready in moments," she told him, and there was kindness in her haughty voice.

He nodded, not trusting himself to speak, ashamed of the weakness that made him shiver.

"My name's Torina," she volunteered.

He mumbled her name. He knew he should thank her: for setting him free from slavery, for having the good nature to tend him. He couldn't bring himself to do it.

He looked at the furniture. It was rich, well placed, well polished. This was the castle of the most powerful king on the continent, if the soldiers were to be believed, and he was inside it. How had Kareed gained so much wealth and influence? Not by justice or compassion. Not by kindness.

How had Landen's father, wise King Veldon, renowned poet, generous, honest man, been overcome by a harsh aggressor like Kareed? How had justice been routed, and peace bled to death? Where had Bellandra gone wrong?

Veldon was a good man, but not a good warrior. He didn't know how to fight, didn't think he'd ever have to. Kareed won because he was the stronger warrior.

Landen didn't like it. He didn't like it, but knew it was true. In the Sword's chamber, it had been Kareed who knew how to pick up a weapon, and he had done it without hesitation, with power and with glee, while Landen faltered, wasting precious seconds.

Running now would lose him his chance to find out what made this king the victor in every conquest he undertook. If Landen left, it would be like handing Kareed the Sword all over again. No, he must not go. He had to stay, learn everything he could. Kareed had promised he would be trained; and though Kareed was a ruthless invader, Landen had heard that his word was true.

I'll hold you to your promise, King Kareed. And one day, I'll take the Sword from you. When I do, I'll know how to use it.

A tap on the open door, and a large woman appeared. Torina took Landen's hand again, as if he were a small child, and he allowed her to lead him. They followed the woman down a hallway to a luxurious private bath.

The boy bathed without thought of modesty, nearly weeping with gratitude for the water's heat and the fine soap. He was so tired it was a valiant effort to towel himself dry and step into the clothes Torina thoughtfully brought him. Sturdy, working clothes, they fit, more or less. His ragged, stained Bellandran garments were gone.

She took him back to the other room and had food and water fetched. As he ate and drank, she watched quietly. The bath, and coming to a decision to stay in Archeld, had washed away his tremors. He was glad.

Torina went to get more food, and he felt himself slipping into sleep, only dreamily aware when she returned. He was never sure if he imagined it, but as sleep claimed him, he thought he felt her light finger tracing the features of his face.

Chapter 2

In the bowels of the castle of Archeld stood an ancient door, cut in stone. Kareed, carrying a torch, fit a key into the lock. Beside him, Vesputo held a long wooden box. The door opened with a creak of disuse.

The dank smell of close air greeted them as they entered the vault. A bare dirt floor and stone walls housed boxes covered with dusty cloths. In the center of the room was a large, pyramid-shaped steel box. Kareed bent to open it. Taking the long box from Vesputo, Kareed set it down. He lifted its lid, revealing the Sword of Bellandra. The blade shimmered pale and sharp in the torchlight. It was so resplendent that a stab of reproach hit the king as he closed the Sword into the pyramid. He shot bolts and fastened locks on the pyramid's sides.

"Old Talsed counseled me that this pyramid of steel will disguise the Sword of Bellandra and mute its power," Kareed said. "And he knows more than he ought to about enchantments."

"Forgive me, my lord, but why not carry it yourself, as a token of your victory?"

"Ah, my friend, I dare not. There's said to be a mighty

curse on anyone who lifts this Sword for conquest. Who knows if it's true; it may not be. Certainly, the weapon turned out to be useless to Bellandra, for all its reputation of invincible magic. But there's no call to invite a curse. I don't have any need of this Sword; I'm strong enough without it."

"True indeed. If you don't intend to wear it, why not get rid of it?"

"My advisers tell me it cannot be destroyed. There *is* an enchantment on it, though of what sort I can't tell. Perhaps it's losing power. It hasn't been raised in battle since King Landen the First fought off hundreds of invaders, all of them warriors of note, and that was many generations ago."

"Strange that Veldon never tried to use it."

Kareed shrugged his massive shoulders. "Stupid. Stupid to remain complacent after the message I sent him. Stupid not to post scouts or send spies. And stupid to try to parley his way out of war when we arrived to do battle. After the warnings I gave, did he think I wouldn't keep my word? He was a fool to ignore me."

Vesputo nodded. "Who can account for it?"

"At any rate, this weapon holds the spirit of his people and must not be set free."

"Ah. Then you want to keep the Sword in this vault so it doesn't fall into anyone else's hands?"

The king assented, making sure all the locks were secure. "You and I will keep this secret. If anyone asks what became of it, say the Sword was destroyed."

❖   ❖   ❖

Before she went to bed, Torina slipped into the small room where she had left the strange boy. He was still fast asleep. Should she wake him? Take him somewhere? Her father said he was now a member of the household. All the boys in training lived in a barracks on the far side of the king's house, near the practice field. Zeon had told her about it; they slept in bunks, took their meals, and practiced the arts of war, all under the fierce eye of Emid, the trainer.

Should this boy be with them? If he woke, would he wonder what to do? She would not like to be alone at night in a strange house in a far land. Her father had called him the son of a king. King Veldon ruled Bellandra, so King Veldon must be Landen's father. What happened to kings who lost the war? His mother was Queen Anise. She died before this. But what about his father? Where was his father now?

Torina went to Gramere with her problem. The sharp old eyes watched closely.

"Veldon's son, Landen," she murmured. "Sad those two men fought—your father and King Veldon. I always hoped they would keep the peace. Torina, my dear, my son takes no prisoners among rulers. Landen's father is dead."

Torina felt a cold shudder. How dreadful that when kings fought, one of them must die.

"What'll I do, Gramere? No one else is helping him. I think they forgot him."

"Go to bed, child. I'll send Maude to be with the boy. If he wakes up, she'll let him know to stay in the room. In the morning, come to me and we'll take him to the barracks."

Torina walked through the familiar halls of the castle, her mind sad. What would it mean to her, to sleep alone in a foreign country, with her parents dead? All those bruises and cuts she'd seen; why had the soldiers been so unkind?

❖ ❖ ❖

As soon as dawn filtered in, Torina was awake. She bounced into her clothes. She found Gramere snoozing in the great carved bed of her ancestors. The old queen was instantly awake at Torina's touch. Together they went to Landen. Ancilla dismissed her servant as the boy stirred. He stretched guardedly, looking at them with large, doubtful eyes.

"I knew your father," Ancilla said. "Long ago. He was a fine man. None better."

Landen sat up. He looked at the floor.

"Come, young man, there's no cause to be ashamed of grieving a good man who died too soon."

He gave her a darting glance. She sat beside him and spoke firmly.

"I am Ancilla, mother to King Kareed. I say what I please in this house, though I may not choose to say it to everyone. You've lost your father, and your country. It will not be easy for you—not for a long time. But remember, you can still be the son your father would be proud of."

Landen said nothing, but his shoulders relaxed.

"You've met my grandchild, Princess Torina. We'll take you to the barracks now. That's where you'll live until you're grown. Now help me up, and I'll show you where to pass your water."

Fascinated, Torina saw Landen get to his feet and

21

bend to Ancilla. He lifted her grandmother with graceful ease. This boy had been raised a prince in a fabled country. A little while ago, before her father went to Bellandra, Landen was going to be a king. King of Bellandra.

Torina had heard stories of that mystical land. Her mother had been there. Dreea had been friends with Queen Anise, years before. When Anise died, Dreea lit candles for her. Dreea said that in Bellandra people did the work they most loved. All the children wore bright colors. Every building was beautiful. The sky filled with rainbow sights whether it had been raining or not. And no wars . . .

No wars.

Torina had learned to be proud that her father always won the wars. Now, looking at the bruised and haunted face of a dead man's son, she was seized with shame. Her father should not have brought war to Bellandra. Why had he done it? There must have been a good reason. But what if there hadn't? What if King Kareed only wanted to fight? What if he killed a good man (he must be good, Gramere had called him good), killed him just because he wanted his kingdom?

She wanted to curl up and never move. Gramere's eyes bathed her with tenderness. The tightness in her stomach eased.

Outside, the world shimmered under a spell of dew. The old queen led the way over the grounds behind the castle. Close behind came the captive boy.

Trees dripped on either side as they went, while gold rays of new sun shot through here and there. Torina wondered if she'd see inside the barracks at last. After hiking for perhaps a quarter hour, a large wooden building sprang into view. It was built simply and sturdily, left unpainted.

Marching to the front door, Ancilla rapped sharply. They could hear boys inside. Eric, a tall young man, opened the door and squinted at them. Torina spoke up eagerly.

"Eric, would you fetch the trainer?"

Eric disappeared inside, while other boys grouped themselves in the doorway, the young ones staring.

Soon Emid, the trainer, stood there. Torina had seen Emid about the grounds since she could remember. His fierce face never scared her. She knew he was there to protect her.

Emid rotated his great shoulders. "You called, my queen?"

Ancilla gestured toward Landen. "Emid, the king has left word that this boy is to be brought up in his household."

"The prisoner from Bellandra?" Emid made a sweep of his arm to scatter the gawking boys surrounding him and stepped out of the barracks. The door shut behind him.

"You are telling me to train this boy, madam?"

"My dear Emid, the orders do not come from me. Keep in mind, this child should not be answerable for the actions of my warmongering son." She looked every bit as ferocious as the trainer. "Let him grow up here. In time, Archeld will become his home. He has no other now."

Emid shook his head. "Child he may be, but he won't forget."

"Give him something else to remember."

Emid turned on Landen. "Boy—"

"His name is Landen," Ancilla interrupted.

Emid sighed. "Landen. Can you live here in Archeld, forgetting the past? Obeying my orders?"

The boy's voice was clear and ringing, without being loud. "You said yourself I wouldn't forget," he answered.

"I said it. I meant it."

"Then why do you ask if I'll forget?"

All four stood silent a moment, while Emid gnawed his lip.

"Ah," he said. "I want to know if you can live here and obey my orders."

"I will."

Emid shook the boy's hand. "Very well. Landen, come inside and we'll find a place for you."

That was all. Landen disappeared through the doorway, and Torina walked away with Ancilla.

Chapter 3

Dreea returned to her weaving, very pale, even quieter than before. Sometimes the king sat beside her and they talked, apart from everyone. Then Dreea's eyes glowed and her movements quickened.

Torina hovered near her mother till Dreea begged her to walk outside and amuse herself.

In the courtyard, Torina climbed the low wall and sat with legs dangling. Below she could see the training field. She decided to watch the boys go through their exercises.

Emid was conducting seltec, the tests that determined the level of warriorship for each boy. During the test, every soldier in training paired with someone of his size and fought with a variety of weapons. When they had done seltec for a few weeks in practice, the final championships would be public games, with crowds gathered to watch. Those who excelled in any field would receive the most comprehensive training—they would become members of Archeld's warrior elite.

Today they were practicing hand-to-hand combat. Torina saw Zeon best another boy and strut to the sidelines. She picked out Landen, off to one side, away from the knot of boys and young men. The trainer called out two names, and Eric and Beron came to the center.

Torina was fond of Eric and disliked Beron, a large young man who often used his size to bully the younger children. She watched avidly as the boys circled each other, throwing punches. They seemed well matched, and neither could land a hit. Then Beron said something. Eric looked behind him. Beron's fist was swift and vicious. Eric spun around and lunged for Beron, giving him a blow that sent Beron to his knees. Eric followed up with a brutal chop to the back. Emid pushed in to declare Eric the victor.

Torina squealed with satisfaction. Feeling a soft weight on her shoulder, she turned to see Ancilla's hand. Impulsively, she pulled her grandmother to the stairway from the courtyard that led to the practice field.

When the field was in close view, they could see Landen and Jolten fighting. Landen was easily beaten.

"Gramere, he's a prince! He should be best of all."

"Ah, child, war was never something King Veldon planned for his son. Landen was raised to be a fair man and a gentle-minded king."

"But everyone knows kings have to fight if they want to keep their lands."

"Not everyone."

The combat test closed. Emid gave the call for archery. The old queen and young princess sat on a nearby boulder as the boys took turns aiming for a target thirty yards away.

Torina watched anxiously as Landen took his place. It seemed to her he was as bruised as when he arrived. Yes, those were fresh marks on his face and arms. When he stepped up to shoot, scattered gibes were heard. No one spoke up for him.

Each boy was allowed four arrows. As Landen lifted the bow and pulled it taut, Torina called out, "Hit the center!"

Landen glanced at her and released the arrow. It went wide, grazing the outer rim of the target. Jeers sounded as he fit another arrow. He shot quickly. The shaft lodged in the bull's-eye. The shouting died away as Landen repeated this feat twice more. A few boys grinned. Most stared open-mouthed. Torina tried to smile at Landen, but he didn't look her way as he walked to the sidelines.

Clearly, Veldon's son had been trained well in one art of war.

The older boys shot, and though some surpassed Landen because his first arrow counted, none but Beron were better archers.

Emid ordered regular target practice. Six lines of boys ranged in front of straw-backed targets. Torina had often watched archery from the courtyard, but never this near. She hurried to Emid.

"I want to learn to shoot a bow."

Emid met Ancilla's gaze. The old queen shrugged.

"Zeon, let the princess have your bow. You shot well today. Teach her how to pull a bowstring."

Zeon, puffed with pride, demonstrated. Torina tried the bow and found it awkward. The string was tight, hard to pull. The arrow landed two feet to the left of her target. She fit another shaft, and this time the arrow fell to the other side. As she reached for another arrow, the bow was seized from her hand. Turning, she saw her father. His color was high and his eyes blazed.

"Papa," she faltered.

"A practice field is no place for a princess."

She wanted to tell him she could shoot as well as any of them if he would let her practice. Wanted to yell out loud that, because of men like him, she must learn to defend her kingdom.

"Leave at once." His tone left no room to argue.

She took Ancilla's hand. They followed a track to the meadow, where wildflowers grew. There the girl threw herself on the ground among fragrant blossoms.

"I want to learn to shoot!" she burst out.

Ancilla carefully lowered herself to the grass.

"My little Torina. There will always be warriors. Be glad you don't have to be one of them."

Torina sniffed. "How will I keep my kingdom if I don't know how to fight?"

Ancilla sighed. "You know, my dear, that I'm very old?"

"I know."

"For all my years, what have I learned? That there will always be enough killers. Leave the killing to them. Wherever you find something good, help it grow."

Torina caressed a flower with her finger. She brought her face near the beautiful, fragile thing.

"I wish I could take these flowers home and help them grow. But they don't need me."

Her grandmother smiled. "When the seeds fall in a few weeks, we'll gather some. You can have a flower garden."

"Gramere, if I were a boy, they would train me to keep my kingdom. They must believe someone else will rule."

"Yes. The man you marry."

Torina bent her eyes on the flowers, thinking of her mother. Dreea was always quietly occupied and seldom tried to influence what happened. In her mind, Torina tried on such a life. She saw herself in her mother's place, weaving patiently, watching and waiting for a king.

She could never live that way.

❖ ❖ ❖

The grand seltec competition was scheduled. Several days of archery, knife throwing, and matched combat, attended by crowds of Archeldans who would feast, relax, and cheer their favorites.

Landen wrestled with the knowledge that his public humiliation would be great. He could hardly beat even the youngest boys in combat. All his early training went against it: he'd been taught to be compassionate and thoughtful, to give everyone a chance. And though he was determined to break his old habits, the maxim of his childhood, *Do no one harm*, echoed in his mind when he stood opposite an opponent.

He was utterly ignorant of how to use a staff. Fencing was something he'd learned as an art, using delicate foils. In Archeld, the boys fought all-out battles with heavy wooden swords. Landen had never been taught how to throw a dagger. Though naturally fleet of foot, the toll of his captivity had slowed him. He could handle a horse as well as anyone, yet Archeldan customs in horsemanship confused him.

One late afternoon during the time the boys were excused for rest or chores, Landen sought Emid. He walked the now familiar paths from barracks to practice field, taking pleasure in the cool shade.

As he moved into the glare of the practice field, he saw Emid sitting alone, feathering arrows. The trainer's deep frown made him appear forbidding. Emid was gruff at the best of times. His shouts could pierce some hollow core in every boy. But Emid was fair. There were even moments when Landen believed this fierce man, who trained the fearsome fighting force of Archeld, actually liked him.

Landen consciously slowed his breathing as he approached Emid, reminding himself what his father had taught him: *The moment is vast.*

"What is it?" Emid asked, expertly testing a feather.

"I've come to ask if I can be excused from the seltec."

Emid's frown intensified. "Why?"

"I never learned to fight."

Emid glared. "Every man should learn to fight."

"True," Landen agreed. "I want to learn, and I will. But, as you see, I wasn't taught before: nothing but archery and fencing and how to ride. It was never serious, never in order to overcome someone."

The trainer sighed, his face softening. "Young man, many boys have come to me over the years to ask exclusion. I've never granted it." He paused, waiting for a reply. Landen only looked at him. "I suggest you find someone willing to help teach you. You can have use of practice items at any time. But you *must* attend the seltec."

One glance at the trainer's face told Landen it was useless to argue.

Someone willing. Landen thought of the other boys. All were too young, too hostile, or too indifferent.

"Yes, sir," he said.

❖ ❖ ❖

As he neared the bunkhouse, Landen saw a familiar knot of boys. His stomach clenched. Beron and his young followers, about five who tagged along. Landen could have turned then, skirted the woods, and gone in by the front way, but they had seen him. He did his best to keep his pace even, face expressionless.

They moved in.

"So, the Belly Lander." It was Beron's name for him, deriving from the Archeldan word for weakling, and a sarcastic play on his homeland. Landen kept walking.

They stepped in front of and beside him.

"What were you talking to Emid about, Belly?" Beron's face thrust close. The older boy's eyebrows, heavy and thick, stretched from temple to temple. His fist jabbed Landen in the chest. "Feel that, Belly?"

Landen knew if he hit back, Beron would maul him again. If he did nothing, he'd be punched and humiliated and allowed to go.

"Go on, Belly, tell me what you were saying. Did you want to get out of the seltec?" Beron jabbed again. "Eh?"

Landen looked round. There was a good tree with a wide trunk where he might put his back. . . .

"I told him the rules don't do justice to your fighting style."

Beron's eyes narrowed. "What?"

"If Emid wanted to know what a warrior you are, he should hold a seltec where you could be matched with boys younger and weaker than you."

31

Beron's heavy fist sent Landen to his knees. No time to get to the tree. Blows dropped on him like rocks. Landen curled over, arms protecting his head.

❖ ❖ ❖

Eric Aldon sauntered through the trees toward the barracks, idly chopping branches with his fist as he went. He didn't feel easy in his mind. Up until a few weeks ago, he'd known exactly what life was. It was always the same: getting up early, scrambling into his clothes, eating breakfast with the other boys in the noisy hall lined with benches. Spending the day practicing arts of war, coaching youngsters, playing games: preparing for the day when he took his place in the fighting force of Archeld. That day was less than a year away for him. He was seventeen: tall and strong and a credit to his trainers.

During his years in the barracks, there had been rivalries: mini-wars between ever-changing factions of boys. Alliances formed, were broken, formed again. Friends became friendly enemies; enemies turned into wary friends. Some boys he genuinely liked; he and Phillt were almost always on the same side when they could be, and young Zeon tagged after them whenever they let him. There were those he disliked, Beron chief among them. But Emid had drummed into all the boys that they were linked indivisibly by the most important of bonds: they served Archeld, King Kareed, Queen Dreea, and Princess Torina. On the battlefield, they would be brother soldiers, loyal to one another, with animosities forgotten.

Emid was renowned throughout the kingdoms for the

fighters he and his trainers produced. It was an honor to gain a place under his guidance. New boys were always being added to the mix: Archeldan boys whose families had petitioned or finagled or otherwise earned their place in the barracks near Archeld's castle, where the best warriors were drilled.

Now a different sort of newcomer had been thrown into their midst: a stranger, the son of a conquered pacifist. And Eric was uneasy.

He didn't know what to think as he watched Landen subjected to shameless bullying by Beron and his followers. Landen was tormented every day, from the time he woke till the time he slept. His food was stolen, pieces of his clothing filched, and his searches for missing shoes or shirts followed by derisive laughter. His name and homeland were held up to constant abuse; his lack of fighting skills endlessly mocked.

At first, it had been a matter of indifference to Eric. Bellandra had been stupid, Landen was lucky to be alive, and abominably lucky to be under Kareed's protection, getting training many eager applicants were denied. None of the boys understood what such a weakling was doing among them, and no one much cared. The rumors about Bellandra, that it was a whole country of milksops, must have been true. Otherwise, why wouldn't the boy—who was supposed to become their future king—know how to fight better?

So Eric thought for a while, and his friends shared his outlook. They dismissed the exile as a foolish coward, son of a dead foolish coward. His problems were no one's business but his own.

But lately Eric was troubled. He'd seen instances of bullying that sank beneath the common norm. Beron, in particular, seemed to outright enjoy giving Landen bad bruises, then ridiculing him for them. In Eric's mind, there were too many younger boys influenced by Beron. He began to watch Landen and reluctantly discovered that this stranger was neither weak nor foolish. In fact, Landen seemed to be learning very quickly; Eric had seen him successfully use a move on a larger boy that usually took a long time to master. During Emid's demonstrations, Landen watched avidly, even when others seemed bored or tired. And he wasn't clumsy: his archery, the one martial art he'd learned in Bellandra, far surpassed other boys of his age. He could handle a horse, Eric admitted, better than Eric could himself. Though still young, and therefore not big, especially compared to Beron's bulk, Landen was strong and would be tall when he was full grown.

Clearly, Landen could have put an end to some of the annoyances done to him by smaller boys. All it would take were a few moves, moves that Landen knew. The more Eric watched, the more the forbearance Landen showed his young tormentors began to seem noble instead of cowardly.

Once he saw Landen in a different light, Eric couldn't go back to dismissing the former prince as a nobody. He began to consider what fortitude Landen showed, staying among them and enduring without complaint the taunts and beatings that had become his lot.

For he could have escaped. The boys weren't guarded. It was understood that to be a member of this barracks was a privilege. Anyone half-witted enough to leave simply lost his place. So yes, Landen could run away. But he didn't.

Eric had broached the subject with Phillt—maybe someone should teach Beron a lesson.

Phillt had shrugged, grinning. "You're the only one who can beat Beron, Eric. It ain't worth the bruises to me."

Beron had gone too far. He was turning the barracks into a place Eric was ashamed of. It was time someone stood up to him.

Scornful voices were raised, not far off. Eric quickened his pace.

As he tried to make himself smaller, huddling in a ball, Landen was afraid. He'd provoked Beron; what would the larger boy do now? Not only was Beron strong, he was also well trained and intent on inflicting damage. Who would really care if Landen were maimed or killed? He had no friends here. No one thought well of him, except possibly Princess Torina, and he never saw her.

There was a shout and running footsteps. The boys were scattering.

Gasping with the effort not to sob, Landen tried to get up. Eric squatted beside him.

"Stop trying to get up. It will pass more quickly," Eric said.

Landen wondered how Eric would know that. Did all Archeldan boys go through beatings? He obeyed his rescuer and sat, reminding himself that the moment was vast.

Eric's chiseled, even features were set in angry lines. He was panting. "Sorry I did nothing sooner," he said. Quiet, dark eyes looked at Landen with cautious friendship.

35

Landen didn't know anything to say, so he concentrated on breathing.

"So," Eric said. "You want to learn to fight?"

Wearily, Landen nodded.

"Good. I'll teach you. You can help me improve in archery."

For the first time since Bellandra fell, Landen smiled.

❖   ❖   ❖

The next morning when Landen woke to the gong and reached for his clothes, nothing was missing from his sparse wardrobe. He didn't have to waste time looking for a "lost" shirt or shoe. He walked to the eating hall in peace.

Beron strutted up and made a show of sitting next to Landen.

"Not hungry, are you, Belly?" Beron slid Landen's bowl in front of himself.

Landen shrugged, prepared to forego the meal. Then Eric took the seat across from him. Eric's arm flashed out from the opposite bench. The bowl reappeared in its original place.

"Keep out of this," Beron growled.

"No. You keep out. And stay out." Eric's contemptuous words rang through the room.

Beron pushed his own food at Eric. Eric's quick hand blocked the bowl. "Thank you," he said calmly. "As you haven't taken a bite, this food is fit to eat." He put his spoon in Beron's portion.

Beron's big hands lifted the edge of the long table as he sprang to his feet. The table tipped and all the bowls slid toward the floor. Eric's strong forearms crashed down, righting the bowls before they fell. Beron flung himself across the table. Yells erupted all around, as Eric jerked Beron's head back and aimed a blow at his stomach. Beron reflexively curled his torso. Eric slammed a fist down on his head.

Boys gathered into an immediate circle, egging on the contenders with cheers and gibes. Landen got out of the way, surprised at how many voiced support for Eric.

The two fighters went at each other, breaking all the rules of hand combat: going for the eyes, using teeth, kicking below the belt. Afraid they'd kill one another, Landen tried to elbow his way closer, ready to defend his friend.

The door flew open. Emid strode in, shouting in his great voice. It took him no time at all to hurl Eric and Beron apart. They stood glaring and unrepentant, bruises beginning on their faces. Beron's lip was swelling, and Eric's left eye turning purple. The crowd of boys stood in rigid silence, as though a huge hand had gagged the room.

"What's the meaning of this?" Emid asked, full of menace. "I've told you before, you both serve Archeld. That means you may fight, but only to develop the skills you need in order to be soldiers! I won't tolerate battles like this between fellow soldiers!" His yell was frightening. "Now come with me."

Eric and Beron were marched out. Boys quickly returned to their places at the benches. Landen knew neither combatant would be allowed meals until they did whatever atonement Emid set forth. He sat, with a space across from him and beside him, avoiding the stares of the other boys.

❖ ❖ ❖

In the weeks leading up to the public seltec, Eric shadowed Landen. The beatings and covert attacks ceased.

Landen noticed signs that the barracks was dividing into two camps, headed by the oldest boys, Eric and Beron. Eric had more adherents, but they were quieter. Beron's followers continued to throw taunts at Landen, calling him "Prince Belly" and "King of Cowards."

Gradually, Landen's weakness and stiffness healed, and Eric's black eye faded. Landen began to feel he'd survive his time of training. Eric was happy to accept his coaching in archery, and Landen was glad of the chance to repay his new friend. As he handled the sharp, deadly arrows of Archeld, he remembered ruefully the blunted arrows and pretty targets of Bellandra.

The former prince began to learn the customs of Archeld. Here, contests of physical prowess were taken most seriously; they were the marks by which boys earned respect. Compassion and gentleness were neither cultivated nor admired. Landen realized why he'd been treated with such disdain and without mercy: he practiced kindness before aggression, fairness before trying to win. In Archeld, these were unforgivable offenses, indications of weakness. As he understood this, desire grew in his heart to prove himself and his lost kingdom. He wanted to show these barbarians he was worthy.

Father, you had me trained to shoot a graceful arrow, but never to fight. Now the king who murdered you has given me the means to learn. Emid will never have a better student than the prince who was reared in peace.

The day of the competition dawned gleaming and fresh. Emid led his trainees out to the fields set aside for the seltec. These had been carefully cultivated, with green turf as smooth as scythes could make it. Gaily dressed people thronged the stands, laughing and chatting. It was the day for archery. Targets stood at intervals. A champion's platform crowned the range.

Landen thought of the festivals in Bellandra, with contests presided over by King Veldon, where courtesy overcame the drama of competition, and no blood was ever seen.

Emid dispersed the boys to three groups, according to age. While they stood in the heat, King Kareed and Queen Dreea, with Princess Torina between them, walked to the royal seats next to the fields. Flowers were thrown their way and cheers greeted them. As Landen watched Torina's carefree step, his heart ached. Not long ago, he had lived as a prince, walking with dignity beside his father, never guessing how swiftly and terribly that life would end.

Kareed raised his arms for silence. Landen was thrown back in memory, to when he stood on a shining marble floor, reaching for the Sword of Bellandra. The pain of defeat and loss throbbed in his heart. *One moment more and I would have held the Sword.*

"Let the seltec begin!" Kareed roared.

Onlookers tossed scarves and caps in the air, whistling, yelling, and clapping, while Landen struggled to hold his grief. Emid called out the rules in his loud voice. Each boy would shoot four arrows. The three best from each of the three age groups would shoot again. Out of these, the champions would be found.

Landen watched as the youngsters, aged eight to eleven, shot. The scores were meticulously logged. Zeon, Westol, and Frin were asked to stay, while the others left the field. Landen saw Eric flash Zeon a "well done!" signal. Westol and Frin both belonged to Beron's camp.

The sun was strong. Tormented by memories, Landen felt a wave of faintness. He banished it.

Now it was his group's turn. Emid gave out the bows. Landen ran his hands over the wood, fingers seeking defects. Finding none, he let the bow rest on the ground. Dark spots swam across his vision. The earth and sky seemed mixed up, whirling together. He took a deep breath. *The present moment is everything. The moment is vast.*

The remorseless sun shone, too hot to bear. Landen kept seeing the moment when Bellandra's Sword was taken, when Kareed put an end to his peaceful homeland. He gripped his bow and forced himself to regulate his breath. Still it came short and shallow.

Jolten, the boy ahead of him, moved forward in long strides. Jolten's muscles tensed, released, tensed again, released again.

Landen received an arrow from a young boy's hand. He wiped his dripping forehead. The target looked far and dim. He aimed, pulled, released. His arm tried to shake but he wouldn't let it. He shot again, three times. Zeon beamed at him. All four arrows were close to the center.

The boys in line behind him still had to shoot. Landen joined Jolten in his place, fighting dizziness. He searched his mind for something calm and steady. He recalled the words of old Queen Ancilla. *Remember, you can still be the son your father would be proud of.*

He looked around at the utterly foreign land he stood in. Realization dawned. *Kareed took the Sword and killed my father. But his daughter gave me my freedom. I must take hold of this life that belongs to me. Bellandra lives as long as I do.*

He turned to the field and saw that half the older boys had shot and he was now standing beside two other archers from his group, the rest having gone to the sidelines. He was one of the three finalists.

It was Eric's turn. He did well, better than he would have earlier in the season, though not well enough to be among the top three. As expected, when the winners were announced among the older boys, Beron proved to be one of them.

Next came the interlude for lunch. While the crowd picnicked in colorful groups of laughing enjoyment, the boys were fed seated on the archery field. Steady-handed soldiers held cloth umbrellas over them. There was no stinting on portions. Looking at the food, Landen realized he hadn't felt hungry since Bellandra fell. During his captivity under Vesputo, and afterwards on the nightmarish ride to Archeld, he'd passively eaten what they gave him, hardly seeing it. Then came arrival, and the weeks of torment at Beron's hands. And now . . . Landen smiled. Now he was hungry.

The food was excellent: tender, flavorful cheeses; flaky, tasty breads and crackers; delicious soups bursting with herbs; stuffed hens simmered in their own juices. Landen ate with a kind of ecstasy, savoring everything. He looked about him eagerly, as if he had just arrived.

The colorful clothes of the massed spectators blended like an enormous banner. Garlands of flowers decked heads and necks, spreading perfume. Everywhere were smiles and happy chatter. Musicians roved, filling the air with festive notes. The sky made a glorious canopy.

The king signaled for the last round. The championships for archery would be awarded, then the rest of the daylight hours used for dancing and feasting.

Zeon, Westol, and Frin, nervous and proud, took their turns again with the bows. Zeon was the clear victor and Emid declared him so. The youngster stood alone on the champion's platform, radiant and flushed, waiting to be joined by two more.

When his turn came, Landen shot calmly. Two of his arrows landed so close that, from a distance, they appeared one; all four fell in the bull's-eye. He won the contest for his age group convincingly. Emid announced his victory, and he joined Zeon amid a buzz of surprise from the stands.

Next, the three older boys competed: Beron, Phillt, and Bendes. Landen knew Eric wanted Phillt to win, but it was not to be. A stray wind caught the archer by surprise, and one of his arrows barely made the target. Beron lodged all arrows in the bull's-eye, aiming slowly and deliberately with each. Grinning arrogantly, he added himself to the winner's circle.

Emid announced that now, for the sport and pleasure of it, these three champions would compete against one another.

Zeon went first and did his best shooting of the day.

He stood beside Landen then, fairly dancing with happiness, buoyed by cheers.

Landen felt light and sure as he took up his first arrow. It flew true and landed in the center of the bull's-eye. In quick succession, he sent three more after it. All landed in a tight quadrangle. The people in the stands burst into excited applause, a spontaneous roar of approval for his skill. Archeldans liked nothing better than to see proficiency in the arts of war.

Landen wondered if the people watching him knew he was a foreigner from the "country of cowards," as Beron had dubbed Bellandra. If they knew, would they care? Or would their traditional careless generosity and appreciation of skill win out?

Glowering, Beron took long and careful aim. His first arrow lodged in the exact center. The cheers were wild. He fit another arrow. Landen heard Zeon breathing loudly and gritting his teeth.

It seemed an age that Beron stood with the bow flexed, squinting at the target, muscles bunched in his back. When at last he let go, the arrow winged to land right next to the first. The crowd erupted with admiration.

Beron repeated his slow aim, and the third arrow fit neatly into the first two. Landen took a deep breath. In Bellandra, archery was judged on three counts: accuracy, swiftness of aim, and manners. Apparently the second two weren't categories in Archeld, for Beron was frowning and taking so long.

The fourth arrow flew, hitting just outside the bull's-eye. Beron tossed his bow on the ground. Groans of disappointment ran through the stands.

Zeon jumped up and down beside Landen, pumping his arm. Landen spotted Princess Torina waving and smiling, while Kareed and Queen Dreea clapped their hands. The grand winner hardly heard the crowd's applause. It didn't matter to him if the watching adults ever knew his name. It was enough that he'd given Eric reason to be proud of befriending him. He'd redeemed his homeland, at least among the boys. This way, he could hold up his head even if he made a poor showing in hand combat.

Kareed presented the three champions with garlands, commending them for their diligence and talent. Landen kept his eyes down except when the king gave him a ritual handshake. As those fiery green eyes bored into him, he swallowed hard, wondering if he'd made a mistake by putting himself in the foreground this way. But Kareed seemed to be ungrudging, his congratulations sincere.

There was a gentle touch on his arm. Torina, close on her father's heels, reached for Landen's hand. He pressed her palm, accepting her smile.

Kareed raised his arms. "Let the dancing begin!"

People rushed from the stands, plumes waving, voices calling, bearing the princess away in their tide.

Elated and tired, Landen felt Eric's slap on his back. He shook his friend's hand. Then Eric moved off to meet Phillt and a cluster of other boys, urging Landen to join them.

But Landen wanted only to be alone. As he wove slowly through the throng, strangers stopped him to find out who he was. He thanked them for their interest and told them his name. When they asked who his parents were, he merely said he was an orphan, courteously detaching himself and drifting away.

Wearily he sought the trees that surrounded the festival. Once inside the protection of their branches, he headed for the sea, enjoying the sweet, dancing shadows of leaves. The path felt good under his feet; the songs of birds filled his ears. The moment was vast, truthfully this time. He thought of all his father's patient teaching.

I was groomed to grow into a king, years from now. The future my father planned no longer exists. Now I am only myself. He came out of the trees to where the ground was level and rocky. He took pleasure in the sun glinting on mica in the stones as he walked on toward the cliffs. *No kingdom will show me the way.*

He came to the cliff's edge and gazed out on the water, remembering the waves on the beaches of Bellan Bay. Lifting his eyes to the blue that arched overhead, he felt limitless as the sky, full of motion like the waves crashing far below. He looked down at the turbulent water rushing in from far away to spray the sheer rock of the cliff. It occurred to him that just as his life had changed once, it could change again. His thoughts absorbed him so completely that he didn't hear Beron coming up behind him.

Torina sat beside Ancilla on a blanket, sipping water, getting ready for more dancing. She loved to dance. As her breath settled down, the water cooling her throat, she became aware of an uneasiness she couldn't name. It troubled her, like a biting insect too small to be caught. She searched her surroundings for anything wrong. Everyone seemed to be enjoying the festival. Restlessly she fingered the crystal in her pocket. It seemed to pulse in her hand. She brought it out.

In the crystal, she saw an ocean cliff, steep and high. Tiny rainbows shot up from the rocky shore where waves crashed in a riot of spray. Landen appeared, clinging to the face of the cliff by small handholds in its sheer surface, which stretched high above and far below him. His white, perspiring face contorted with the effort of gripping the rock. Then his fingers lost their hold. He fell.

Torina, watching, knew he would not survive that fall. She glanced at Ancilla's peaceful face. Slipping the crystal into her pocket, she stood and walked rapidly away.

As soon as the trees bordering the seltec fields covered her, she ran hard. A stitch cramped her side. She ignored it, racing on to the king's stables.

Inside the stables, a forlorn soldier, Bant, lolled on bales of hay. He jumped to his feet as she entered.

Torina spotted a long rope coiled on a high nail.

"Bant! Fetch me that rope." She pointed. He stretched a pitchfork toward it.

Torina went to Amber, the king's horse, opening his stall.

"Help me saddle this horse."

"Is the king to ride then?" Bant gaped at her.

"Hurry!" was her answer. Bant hefted an enormous saddle. He cinched it on the great stallion. Torina slung the coil of rope over the saddlehorn. She led Amber from the stable, calling thanks over her shoulder.

She leaped on the biggest horse her father owned and galloped away.

❖ ❖ ❖

Beron ran through the trees as if the king's dogs were after him. There seemed to be footsteps behind him, many footsteps, pursuing, gaining. His ears roared. He was consumed with only one thought. He had to get back to the festival before he was missed.

The branches of trees caught at him as he ran straight through raw undergrowth. Twigs whipped his face and arms and tore his clothes. He pounded on till he staggered, breath loud as a storm wind.

He could see the lighter air ahead where the clearing began. He aimed himself at it. That bright unshaded sun seemed like the assurance of salvation. He would make it. No one saw him leave, he made sure. No one had been there when he pushed Landen over the cliff. No one.

He stopped running just short of the clearing and hung on a sapling, gasping.

"Training for the races tomorrow?" A cool, deep voice nearby startled him.

There was Commander Vesputo, quiet and unruffled, examining him as if Beron were an amusing toy. The young man tried vainly to slow his heartbeat and calm his lungs.

"What's wrong, champion? Did you run too hard and fast?" Vesputo took a few steps toward him.

Beron tried to call back his ebbing strength. Vesputo had seen. He was sure of it. The commander had watched him leave, known what he meant to do. Now he would be brought to justice for breaking the first and last code of a soldier: he had killed a fellow soldier. *But he wasn't my*

fellow! We fought Bellandra and Bellandra fell. He's the enemy!
Sweat poured down Beron's face. He panted helplessly.

"Come," Vesputo said. "Perhaps you stood too long in the sun today. Allow me to guide you."

A strong grip steadied him. Perhaps Vesputo was not going to execute him. Beron stammered his thanks.

"Not at all."

They emerged into the clearing. Vesputo helped him through the crowds to the water barrel. Everyone seemed to be laughing, singing, or dancing. Vesputo dipped for Beron. The young man guzzled the water.

"Beron, you're nearly ready for a troop. I'm recruiting for mine. Will you serve with me? I like to have champions riding at my side."

Beron turned a face of worship on the commander. Vesputo's troop was second to none.

"Yes, yes," he managed to croak. "Yes, I'll serve with you."

❖ ❖ ❖

Landen squeezed his eyes shut, straining with every screaming muscle to embrace the cliff.

It was not enough. He would soon fall. His strength was nearly gone, and only Beron knew where he was. Why not let go? The pain of hitting the rocks would be brief.

He opened his eyes. The beautiful sweep of sky, relentless wall of the cliff, and insistent pounding of the surf all seemed callous to his plight.

How can it be, that I would end here, today?

The immediate sounds around him faded, replaced by a rushing in his ears. A spot in the sky thickened and swirled. It shaped itself into an image of his father, King Veldon, holding the Sword of Bellandra. Looking apprehensively at the vision, Landen was filled with the agony of failure. He had survived to live with the conqueror and still knew nothing about where the Sword might be hidden. And now he was going to die.

"No," he heard. "Don't let go."

Landen clenched his teeth till his jaws spasmed. His legs shook.

"Landen!" A female voice this time, clear and childish, pierced the roaring in his head. He licked dry lips.

"Here!" he croaked, ready to break grip with the cliff, sure the voice he heard was supernatural.

"Landen!" The call came again, urgent and corporeal.

He cleared his throat. "Down here!" he cried, and looked up.

High on the cliff, fifty yards up from where he clung, Princess Torina's face peered down.

"Hold on!" Her face disappeared.

Landen's whole body trembled. His breath rasped.

She reappeared above him. "I'm throwing down a rope."

The rope, knotted into a loop at one end, hurtled toward him.

"It's tied to my horse," she called. "Can you get it around your chest?"

He grasped the rope with one hand. "I'll climb it!"

"No!" she yelled. "That way you'll die. Let the horse pull you!"

With the dregs of his strength, he pushed first one shoulder and then the other through the loop. The slip-knot tightened around his chest as his feet swung free of their toeholds. He grabbed for the rope, but his hands flexed convulsively and slid off the coarse fibers to hang slack at his sides.

The rope cut into his chest and dragged him up the cliff. His body scraped and banged against the rock wall. At last, he was over the top. Looking ahead, he could see Torina's small figure leading a great stallion. Landen began to be pulled along level ground.

"Stop!" he called. Torina whirled around, checking the horse. She ran back to where Landen lay. She knelt beside him as he tried to loosen the biting knot. Together they tugged at the stubborn rope until it came free.

"There." She sat back on her heels, looking at his shredded clothes, which seeped blood from the cuts and scrapes the cliff had made. "I'm sorry you got scraped. I didn't know what else to do."

"I'm alive. That's more than I expected." Landen raised himself painfully on one elbow. "How did you happen to be here, with this horse—the king's horse?"

"I saw you," she said.

He sat up. "You saw me?"

She nodded.

"How did you see me?"

She pulled something out of her pocket. A round crystal of exceptional purity. "I saw you in this."

He touched the crystal with a frozen finger and remembered Marla, the old one. It had been said she might live forever. What became of her when Bellandra fell?

"This crystal reminds me of one I've seen before," he said. "With a very old seer in Bellandra." He stroked the smooth globe. "Wait. You saw me in this? Where were you?"

"At the seltec festival."

"You saw me, from the festival, in this?" He tapped the crystal.

"Yes. I see things in it."

"Things?"

"Things that have happened. Things that are going to happen." She touched his cheek softly. "This is the first time it hasn't come true."

He frowned. "You said you saw me."

"I did. But I saw you fall."

He stared at her, all the horror of the previous hour returning. He had been going to die. Somehow this child had intervened. Strange that she would be *his* daughter.

"A seer," he breathed, his mind reeling. "You're a seer."

"Is a seer someone who sees what will happen?"

"Yes. Don't you have seers in Archeld?"

She shook her head. "I never heard of any."

He caught himself panting. What wild absurdity, that this gifted child had no inkling of the enormity of her gift, and that he, a foreigner, would be the one to enlighten her. He remembered the great Bellandran School of Sight, where seers were sent to develop their art. "In Bellandra, there were many. Marla, the old one, told me a great seer is born once every fifth generation, and only one for all the kingdoms." He paused thoughtfully. "Marla was our great seer. She tried to warn my father . . ." He stopped, seeing her eyes.

The silence was painful.

Finally she spoke. "How long did you hang there?"

"Forever," Landen sighed. "Why didn't you send men?"

"I didn't want to tell them about the crystal. And if they didn't believe me . . ."

"I see." He touched the crystal again. "Who else knows you can see?"

"My grandmother knows."

He stretched his arms. He was beginning to feel the sting of all the cuts and scrapes.

"Perhaps," he said gently, "it would be best to keep it a secret." Even in Bellandra, seers lived in protected seclusion, for if they didn't, they were hounded endlessly by people desperate for knowledge of the future.

She nodded. "Then you won't tell?"

"I won't tell."

"How did this happen?" she asked, looking pointedly at the nearby cliff.

Landen shrugged. "I lost my footing."

Her face went still and took on a listening look as she bent a little over her lap. Landen watched, fascinated, feeling as if he observed something that shouldn't be seen. Seers kept their visions private.

Torina's silence was short. Her eyes narrowed as she put the crystal back in her pocket.

"Beron."

Landen looked closely at this girl, thinking of how she had known it was wrong for him to be given to her as a slave. She'd used spirit and wit to save his life just now. Untrained, she could accurately see the past as well as the future, which he knew was extremely rare, even among the greatest of seers.

And she was still just a child, with a child's innocent face. Beautiful sea-colored eyes, flushed cheeks, and hair like an amber fire.

"Princess," he said. "Thank you for saving my life. Please, as a favor to me, say nothing to anyone."

A bewildered frown puckered her forehead. "But—"

Landen managed to grin at her. "When he sees me alive, let him wonder."

"What if he tries to kill you again?"

"I'll be on my guard."

"I'm glad you're not dead."

"And I."

"Can you get on Amber now?"

He shook his head, amused. "It wouldn't do for me to be seen on the king's horse, and they could be looking for you by now. No, Princess, I'll walk."

"But you can't even stand up!"

He summoned his will and stood. He looked into her guileless eyes and thought of how, only one short season ago, he too had been innocent and unafraid. Stiff and sore, he bent and coiled the rope, hanging it over the saddlehorn. "Time for you to be on your way."

"You can get home alone?"

"Yes."

She climbed onto Amber. "Then I'll go back, before they miss me."

He watched her canter into the trees. When she was out of sight, he collapsed on the ground, shaking in every muscle.

Torina returned the horse without comment. She made her way back to the festival and sat beside Ancilla. She was grateful that her grandmother neither questioned nor

53

scolded. She fingered the crystal in her pocket, thinking of Landen's lost kingdom.

A seer, he had said. So this happened to other people too. But why not here, in Archeld? *I've never heard of a seer, yet I am one. How did I get to be one? Why did I have the vision of Landen? Would he really have died if I hadn't gone to him?*

What about the old seer he had talked about? Where was she now? Landen said the crystal reminded him of one he saw in Bellandra, and Papa had brought this from Bellandra. Was it stolen? Should she give it to Landen, tell him it belonged to him and not to her?

She shivered at the idea of giving it up. Inside her pocket, it fit smoothly in her palm, pulsing in rhythm with her heart. She took it out and gazed.

The curving sides turned gold as a picture swam into view. An ancient woman, with more wrinkles than Gramere, long snowy hair, and eyes that seemed to go on forever. She was holding the crystal and kissing it. An eerie certainty crept on Torina that the woman was Marla, and the crystal the same one she now held.

Her father appeared, dressed in armor and looking ferocious. He came close to the woman. She held the crystal up to him. "For your red-haired daughter," Torina heard her whisper.

Gradually the old face washed from the crystal till it was clear as water. Torina sat clasping it, filled with joy and heartache. Joy that it was hers: Marla gave it to her father for her. She could keep it and not worry about it belonging to someone else. Pain, as she had glimpsed through Marla's eyes the great world of struggling futures and the end of peace for Bellandra.

The yearly seltec competition ended with Landen watching events from the stands. Emid had declared him exempt from the competition, due to injuries sustained in a bad fall. He had the satisfaction of seeing Eric named champion in hand combat, and Phillt for footraces. Landen believed he could have carried off the horsemanship, but cheered the winner wholeheartedly.

In the ensuing months, the tensions that had divided the barracks dissipated as Beron strictly avoided the captive prince, sneaking sideways glances at him.

Landen taught Eric all he knew of archery, the one martial art Bellandra had not forgotten. Their friendship flourished as Eric returned the favor with coaching in hand combat.

Landen wanted to do something for Torina, to thank her for saving his life. He wanted it to be special, a thing no one else could give her. He knew it wouldn't be easy because, being a princess and an only child, she was spoiled. He pondered the question in his bunk at night and finally came up with an idea.

All Bellandrans, princes included, were expected to practice at least one form of art. Some chose painting, singing, dancing; some weaving or dyeing, jewelry-making, carpentry, or poetry. Landen loved wood and was good with his hands. He'd been taught how to make things. His favorite art was crafting elegant bows.

Torina wanted to learn archery, but her father had forbidden it. Good. Landen would make her a bow. He'd give her something exciting and secret, defying Kareed in the process.

55

Landen went to Emid and told him he could make weapons. Did the trainer have need for any new bows? Emid gruffly assented, and Landen was given use of all the tools he asked for. He turned out several well-made bows, working at odd hours in a shed, sometimes watched by a herd of smaller boys, often alone. Soon no one questioned his comings and goings with wood.

Chapter 4

By early autumn, a weak sun shone through gray skies. A cape covered Torina's dress as she bent to scatter seeds in shallow furrows she'd dug herself. The girl felt she couldn't wait through the long winter to see blossoms in her garden. Gramere had promised the snow would seal the seeds they'd gathered, and the spring melt would germinate her flowers.

Gramere sat on a bench nearby, propped with cushions and bundled in shawls, asleep. Torina looked at her with affection. No one else knew how often she slept these days. If they found out, they'd probably assign someone else to watch over the princess.

She looked at the cleared beds she'd labored over. Ancilla believed nothing was better for health than exercise in the open air, claiming that her own long life was due to the outdoors. But Gramere was not the only one with a say in the way her granddaughter spent her days. Torina thought of the dark winter evenings approaching, with nothing to do but sew. No more digging in the meadows and gardens or riding Stina after dinner.

A pebble landed in front of her. She looked up. Standing in the ruddy leaves bordering her garden,

Landen beckoned her. She glanced at Ancilla and stepped over the dark brown earth into the trees.

"Landen." She smiled at him, thinking he looked healthy and strong. Dark hair curled around high cheekbones and large eyes.

"Hello, Princess," he said, as if sharing a secret. "I have something for you."

"For me?"

He reached into a bush and pulled out a small bow and a cluster of feathered arrows.

Torina took the bow and stroked its silky wood. The grain had been cut to look like a bird's wing.

"How beautiful. Where did you get it?" She hefted it lightly.

"I made it."

"You made it! But how can I keep it? My father won't let me have a bow."

"Keep it in the woods. It has a leather case to protect it from the weather."

"Oh! I could hide it!"

"Yes. And if you want to meet me sometimes, I could teach you archery."

He would teach her! He'd won the seltec over everyone else. He must know a great deal.

Torina and her grandmother had a picnic planned for the next day by the great pine in the meadow. Eagerly she asked if he could be there. He agreed, then turned to go.

"Good-bye then. Thank you! But Landen, how did you know I wanted a bow?" she called to him.

"How did you know I was hanging from the cliff?" he threw over his shoulder. In a moment, the leaves swallowed him.

❖   ❖   ❖

One spring evening, Emid took a walk to the soldiers' quarters and asked to speak to Eric. The young man had joined Commander Franton's troop, a division serving directly under King Kareed. As the air was warm and the sky clear, Emid proposed a walk.

"I want to ask you a question, Eric. It's about your friend Landen."

Eric raised an eyebrow. "Landen? What trouble is he in now? He certainly learned how to defend himself well, I thought . . ."

"It's nothing like that. No. A disciplinary problem."

"Problem?" Eric stifled a grin.

"He goes his own way, at least twice a month. He leaves without permission and refuses to account for himself."

"Ah. Is there a schedule?"

"No. I've deprived him of supper, barred him from games, and forced him to extra hours of practice. Nothing makes a difference. Landen takes his punishment without resentment. Then he goes his own way again."

Eric's smile broke out. "Doesn't say where he goes?"

"He answers 'out hunting' and sometimes brings small game back with him."

"Have you had him shadowed?"

"I've made it a tracking exercise." Emid shrugged.

"What's the trouble with this?" Eric grew serious.

Emid sighed. "I've been charged to train this lad. He's just a boy, true, and good hearted. But he's the only son of a conquered king. He was once groomed to be a ruler. I begin to believe he'll never obey orders without question. This innocent hunting may be more than it appears."

Eric's face was guarded now. "Why do you come to me?"

"You're his friend. Has he ever said anything to you?"

"No."

"And if he did?"

"You wonder which would be stronger, my loyalty to my friend or my loyalty to my king?"

Emid's mouth was dry. "I suppose that's it."

"I'm sorry you doubt me, Emid. My training comes from you. I'm sorry you doubt Landen. He's my friend and I stand by him. But he could never make me forget my duty."

Emid decided to trail Landen himself.

His chance came the following day. He led the boys on a grueling hike and asked them to get in groups and find their own way back. He watched as the clusters formed. Landen neither joined nor led any of the rest. Emid started off in cautious pursuit.

He was surprised at how fast the boy gained distance from the appointed direction. Emid had to use all his skill as Landen performed expert doubling maneuvers. Once Emid almost lost the trail. Only dogged tracking allowed the chase to go on.

Landen hurried to an obscure meadow, deep in the trees but not far from the king's castle. Emid was startled to see old Queen Ancilla, sound asleep in the new spring grass.

Everyone knew the ancient mother of the king loved to take walks with her grandchild. Emid often met the two on their outings. The old woman was strong and lively enough to take short hikes in any direction. But alone?

Puzzled and wary, Emid went past the meadow and followed Landen's tracks into the forest. He soon saw other, smaller footprints leading in the same direction. His heart beat fiercely. Landen and Princess Torina? What could they have to do with each other? They didn't know each other well—what could bring them to meet? Or was it a meeting? Had the princess simply noticed the boy and wandered after him?

Emid inched his way on through thick trees. Tender spring leaves gave cover. The sound of carefree children's laughter soared toward him like a rush of birds. He slithered forward on his stomach to see.

A small glade in the trees. There stood Torina, face shining, eyes sparkling, hair wild, with a bow in her hand. She looked at Landen with trust and enjoyment. He smiled at her with familiar friendship.

"But why do you want me to shoot left-handed?" Emid heard her ask.

"Because you're too good with your right and I can't beat you."

"Liar! You always beat me!"

"You need to be able to shoot with both. What if someone hurts your right hand?"

"No one would do that."

"No one would do that because you're a princess? You say you want to protect your kingdom."

Protect her kingdom! Emid's chest tightened with outrage. She had soldiers to do that. What was this troublesome boy up to? Princess Torina should not be taught to fear.

A thought struck the trainer. Living as a prince in Bellandra, Landen had probably not been taught to fear.

Indeed, before Kareed's bold attack, Bellandra was considered invincible. The reputation of its legendary Sword had deterred invaders for generations. What had it cost the boy to go undefended? Emid knew the answer. It had cost him everything but his life.

How did these two come together? And what would come of it? It was innocent enough now, Landen teaching the young girl archery. But later, when they were no longer children? What about when they became man and woman?

Emid watched the entire lesson, struck with the degree of their camaraderie and amazed at the prowess displayed. They must have met many times for Torina to gain so much expertise and for both children to treat the other with unguarded ease. How odd it was to watch Landen here in the woods, laughing and teasing like a normal youngster. Gone was the quiet reserve Emid had come to think of as Landen's nature.

The longer he observed, the more uncomfortable Emid became. He knew already, of course, that Torina often found comrades among the boys. Emid had encouraged this. These boys he trained would lead the fighting forces of Archeld. If their allegiance to Torina was personal as well as dutiful, so much the better.

But this. This was a full-fledged friendship on an equal footing. Landen didn't try to be a prince for a princess. He didn't have to try.

In less than an hour, it was Landen who remembered the time. Emid listened to them arrange another meeting. Both scampered off as if they had no cares.

The trainer stretched his stiff muscles and made his way back to the practice field.

What am I to do? King Kareed would never condone his daughter taking archery lessons, let alone from the son of a former enemy. If he learned about this, the boy would be sent away, perhaps killed. And Torina? She'd be restricted to the castle and her embroidery.

Emid envisioned Torina, pale and listless, sitting by the hearth with her needle. Then came the memory of her standing in the trees, color high, eyes bright as she bent the bow.

Emid sent the boys back to the barracks and remained alone on the practice field, pacing distractedly. *If I tell the king, I destroy this boy I've come to respect and like. And the princess will pine away. If I keep it from the king, do I forfeit my vow to serve the royal family?*

Back and forth, back and forth, Emid paced. Kareed had taken in an eaglet and had it carelessly fostered as if it were no more than a clipped chicken. Was it possible the king didn't expect his captive's heritage to show? It was said that when Kareed's legions arrived in Bellandra, they were met by gentle soldiers, interested in negotiating rather than battling. Did Kareed so despise Bellandra's weakness that he assumed the Bellandran prince would never be a fighter?

To Emid, it was obvious every day that Landen was a king's son. He was mastering every bit of information taught. He'd grow up to be a dangerous warrior.

What was better for the house of Archeld? Send Landen away, kill him? Or try to make him a commander in Archeld's army? The boy would not only be skillful in battle, but a brilliant strategist as well. But could he offer unquestioning loyalty to the land that had destroyed his own? Could anything truly bind Landen to Archeld?

Again Emid saw the glade in his inner vision. This time, he focused on Landen looking at Torina, all the fervor of true friendship shining in his eyes.

Landen would never feel loyalty to Kareed, but for Torina, he already felt it. Torina was the future of Archeld. The princess had unknowingly converted what could have been her country's worst foe into an ally. How had it happened?

Emid suspected he never would find out. He drew a long breath. He had made up his mind. The boy did not deserve to die for befriending Kareed's daughter. His friendship was a protection on her future. Emid would say nothing.

He knew it was possible someone else would discover them. He hoped they would be crafty.

Chapter 5

A few days after Torina's twelfth birthday, Landen met her by the great pine. It was only the fourth time in three years they'd used that particular spot.

Her ocean-colored eyes were wet. "I escaped my chaperones, Landen. They say Gramere is too old to look after me. They'll be guarding me always now. I pleaded with them, but they don't care: 'You are becoming a young woman and must conduct yourself as such.' They have no ears when I tell them I don't *want* to conduct myself as such."

Landen's heart squeezed in sudden pain. The secret meetings with Torina had put life into his exile. What had begun as archery lessons had become much more. Not only could Torina shoot remarkably well, she was his dearest companion. For years, at least twice a week, they'd found a way to meet, playing and talking together as only equal friends can do.

For she was his equal. Not because she was born and raised royal: in fact, he found her imperious bearing tiresome. It was something about Torina herself. Landen admired the girl's vivacious flaming spirit, so like her hair. With him, she often forgot to be an arrogant princess, showing innate kindness and a keen sense of honor. Buoyantly she shared confidences, trusting him with her many triumphs and defeats, telling him of her mischievous little rebellions. She was guileless. He felt able to ask her anything in the world.

There was one thing, though, he'd never inquired of her, though he often thought of doing so. He hadn't asked her to look in the crystal and find the Sword of Bellandra. Oh, how he wanted to know! He'd heard the rumors that it was destroyed, melted down in a careful ritual. But he didn't know. Before he put it out of his mind forever, he wanted to be sure.

Torina could tell him. She'd made him the confidante of all her visions. He was amazed at the truth of her sight, the extent of her gift. Oh yes, she could tell him what had become of the Sword. A thousand times, the question was on his lips. Then he'd look into her innocent eyes, and something would stop him.

"I hate being a princess!" she stormed, sliding to the ground and covering her face to cry. Landen knelt beside her, whispering the only comfort he felt.

"I'm glad I know you."

She nodded, making small, choked sounds.

He stroked her hair. "Torina, I'll always be your friend."

"Yes," she said. "My dearest friend."

What could be more precious than hearing her say that?

"One day, you'll have the power to do as you please."

She gathered a handful of pine needles in one hand, large tears gliding over her flushed cheeks.

"Yes, some day. And until then, I'll remember you." She reached out to him.

Embracing her was something he'd never done. It felt easy and right to hold her.

"I must go," she said, after a few moments. "They'll be looking for me."

He opened his arms. He could hear her muffled sniffs as she ran off. Landen sat propped against the huge pine, feeling a swift sense of loss. As he looked across his life, he saw Archeld again the way it had seemed when he first arrived: fearsome, barbaric, devoid of justice.

His mind drifted back to Bellandra and images of boyhood. For years, he'd put such thoughts aside as too painful to bear. Now he remembered.

He recalled the way muted rainbows would touch the clouds at any hour of the day. The dazzling glint of sun on the surf of Bellan Bay. The bursting, creative joy of careful artistry practiced everywhere. Farmers in love with the land. Musicians enthralled with their instruments. Inspired dancers. Healers: bloodless surgeons, herbal masters, touch healers, spirit walkers who guided the passage of death.

Marla, the old one. Wise, sad eyes looking at him, not speaking.

The peace that soothed and brightened the air of Bellandra—until Kareed tore it away. Here in Archeld, peace did not light the way. Instead, war and fighting were all the glory.

And now I am a warrior. My training is nearly complete. If I found the Sword, I could wield it.

For a moment, Landen allowed himself to daydream about gripping the mighty Sword of Bellandra, its invincible power an extension of his arm. With the Sword, he could vindicate his ancestors, avenge his father, and restore Bellandra to freedom.

But that vision was vain and disregarded the truth. The Sword probably *had* been destroyed, just as the whispers claimed. And now he had lost his chance to ask Torina what she knew of it.

Landen sat, baffled and sorrowful. With the Sword hidden or gone, and Torina isolated from him, perhaps it was time for him to leave Archeld. He could do it. It would be easy to steal a horse by night. He was sixteen now, nearly a man. There were other kingdoms where he could make his way. Stories circulated about Glavenrell, the kingdom north of Archeld. Glavenrell's new young king, Dahmis, was working to forge peaceful alliances with his neighbors.

Perhaps that's where I belong.

The boy closed his eyes. He yearned to be part of an effort for strengthening peaceful ties among countries. How weary he was of the sparse, stringent life of a soldier in training. The only chance he got to be artistic was in making bows from time to time. His weapons were sought for their quality.

Like the rest of Bellandran craft, he thought bitterly. Everyone said Bellandra, swallowed into a province of Archeld, had descended into a land of greedy merchants, selling off their heritage of beauty.

How tempting it was, the thought of going away!

But then he thought of Torina. *My dearest friend,* she'd said. Landen was overwhelmed with tenderness for her. Would a friend abandon her? Once he left, returning would be difficult. He might never see her again, and that would be unbearable.

Landen arrived late for the mid-afternoon training session, feeling years older than he'd been in the morning. When Emid barked at him, the words didn't penetrate his gloom. He expected harsh punishment, but none came. Instead, Emid looked at him compassionately, as if the trainer knew his sorrow. On his bunk that night, Landen lay sleepless. He resolved to stay in Archeld a while longer.

After that day, Landen found it impossible to get near Torina. His time was almost entirely taken up with advanced training, and she didn't come near the practice fields. Though he haunted her periphery whenever he found a spare moment, not once did he get close enough to speak a private word to her. Surrounded by attendants wherever she went, her life was more and more taken up with royal functions. She was being groomed to be a king's wife. Landen chafed at the barriers of protocol, wondering how Torina, who adored adventure and prized freedom above all things, could bear her virtual imprisonment.

Sometimes, when he went on solitary rides, he met chagrined soldiers who would ask him if he'd seen the princess, for she'd escaped her attendants. Then Landen would look for her, hoping to snatch a conversation. But her bouts of freedom were few and short, and he never chanced to share them.

Gradually, elapsing time wedged itself between them. At the beginning of their separation, if she saw him hovering outside her circle, Torina gave Landen a glowing smile. But when six months had come and gone, she stopped meeting his eyes with any special recognition. After the first year, her manner toward him became one of friendly courtesy, the same stance she took with everyone.

She was young. To her, a year must be a long while. But to Landen, it was not. His affection for her lay bright and shining in his heart, untarnished by distance, time, or neglect.

Landen didn't like large groups or gatherings but forced himself to endure them in order to get glimpses of Torina. He soon discovered that he was not alone— someone else was trying to get close to the princess.

At first, it seemed a wicked coincidence that each time Landen sought out Torina, he saw Vesputo. Soon, however, it was plain to him that Vesputo was trying to snare the king's daughter. The thought of such a courtship horrified Landen.

Commander Vesputo's authority had steadily risen till it was second only to King Kareed's. Archeld was enjoying a period of peace: the provinces had ceased challenging Kareed's right to rule. Prosperity governed. Vesputo was a rich, privileged man. When he wasn't fulfilling administrative duties assigned by his king, his time was his own, and he chose to spend it being very charming, especially to the princess.

Of course. He wants the crown, and she's the way to get it.

Sometimes Vesputo was the one to review Emid's training exercises. He'd stand watching the boys, relaxed and collected, while Landen shuddered.

Vesputo seemed to have forgotten that Landen was once the prince of Bellandra; indeed, everyone in Archeld treated Landen as if he'd been raised among them. It didn't matter. Landen remembered the cruelty just beneath Vesputo's surface. Vesputo was evil, in a way Kareed could never be. Kareed did what he did out of pride and strategic need. Thus, Kareed had murdered Veldon as a commonplace act of war, then taken in Veldon's son and treated him with casual generosity.

Vesputo would never have done so. Vesputo would have kept me a slave and taken pleasure in it.

How dreadful to see Vesputo's charming smile bent on Torina! To watch him act deferential and considerate, as if he cared. Landen prayed that Torina would be wise enough to see through Vesputo. But what could she know of his vicious, inhuman side? She'd never ridden with him to war, never been his captive. To the soldiers of Archeld, Vesputo was a legend. It was said dust parted for him. He never lost a battle. He was treated with the utmost respect, and people vied for his attention. How was she to know his real character?

Landen redoubled his efforts to get near enough to talk with Torina. But the months passed, and she was always out of range. He thought of sending her a note. But a note in the wrong hands could get him killed.

He began to spy on Vesputo, putting himself in danger to do so. Several times, he was nearly caught but managed to elude his pursuers. Over time, Landen became extremely stealthy, able to come and go noiseless and unseen. While others confided in him, he kept all his own secrets with unbending resolve. And he discovered Vesputo's weakness: women. The commander always kept at least one lady, secretly. Deceit was something he readily engaged in. It was as if a dark enchantment allowed Vesputo to dupe men and women while he constantly ascended in power and prestige.

Chapter 6

Late in the afternoon on a clear day, Torina sat on her horse at a favorite lookout among the high rocks, gazing down into the valley. She was now fifteen years old. The simple lines of her soft green dress set off the curves of her body; its color brought out highlights in her eyes and hair. The hair, still rebellious, straggled out in curling streams.

Though she tried continually to find new ways of being alone, she wasn't often successful. But today she'd given her attendants the slip and ridden up the ridge by herself.

She recognized Vesputo's helmet from far away and hugged herself at the prospect of seeing him again. So strong, noble, handsome, and adoring! His cool eyes always warmed when she was near. And his kiss! How he thrilled her. Torina was happy to be in love with the one man capable of ruling after her father. The king often remarked on how indispensable Vesputo had become. He could be trusted, Kareed said, with the most precious secrets and valuable objects in the realm. And, just as important, he could be counted on to wage victorious campaigns whenever needed.

At first, when the commander smiled on her, Torina thought he was only being kind.

Slowly, with steady devotion and a hundred considerate attentions, Vesputo took hold of her heart. His love was powerful and devoted. In a private moment, he confessed that he'd loved her since she was twelve.

His unwavering ardor honored her. With all he'd seen and done, and with all the women in Archeld making eyes at him, he'd chosen her. Whenever she came near, his handsome face lit with gladness. And he was still young enough: not yet thirty. When he kissed her, she never thought of his years.

Now they were pledged to be married. And Vesputo was bringing horses laden with rare Bellandran goods as a token of his love, to show everyone how much he cared for her.

Torina kneed her horse to turn into the adjacent trees, ready to take the trail down to the castle. As she turned from the lookout, another horse blocked her way. A big, gray stallion, with Landen on his back.

Landen. Their paths hardly ever crossed. When they did meet, it was always in the presence of many other people, with no chance to really speak. Her memories of their friendship had grown hazy. Sometimes she envied him when she caught glimpses of his solitary rides. He'd grown tall and broad-shouldered and earned a reputation as an unbeatable fighter. Emid had recommended him for command training when he left the barracks. Now he sat his horse with easy grace.

"Afternoon, Landen."

"Hello, Princess. Out alone?"

She smiled happily. There was no answering smile as he gestured at the plain.

"Vesputo has returned."

Torina let her joy show. "Yes." With a flick of the reins, she let him know she was ready to head down the narrow track.

He continued to block her.

"Please," she told him, still smiling, "let me by."

"What a noble plunderer he is." Landen ignored her request. "Are you to be sold for what a few horses can carry?"

She laughed in surprise. "The horses mean nothing to me! I love him."

Landen leaned in. "You love him?"

"Yes. Of course I love him. We're to be married! I've known for a while that he will be king. I have seen it."

She urged her horse forward. Landen maneuvered so as not to give ground.

"Did you tell him about the crystal?"

Torina blushed, recalling that as a child she'd told this young man many secrets. Why was he asking her about it now? But then, when had she last seen him alone? She tried to remember.

"No. No one knows about the crystal, except my grandmother, and . . ." She felt uneasy and wondered why.

"I see. You haven't told him. Then perhaps you know."

"Know? Know what?"

"He's not the man you think him."

"Let me pass."

Landen's intense stare cut into her happy glow. "He's not who you think he is."

Heat flooded her body. "You know his heart better than I?" she flared.

"I see more than you."

"This is hardly gallant, sir." She took refuge in cold courtesy.

"He cares nothing for you, Princess," the relentless voice continued.

"He loves me!"

"He loves the crown you will one day wear."

"How dare you! Be off!"

Landen grabbed her bridle. "King Kareed will never have a son. Whoever marries you will be the king!"

"I told you—I know Vesputo will be king. I saw it. Now get away from me. I want to meet my love."

"He wants the crown, only that!"

"Liar! My crystal would have told me."

"Your crystal might not tell you what you can see with your own eyes if you would open them!"

Torina felt suddenly weak. How could Landen have guessed that she never saw her own future? And that the crystal seemed to abide by a stubborn ethic, refusing to show her what she ought to see by virtue of her own perception, as though it were afraid of fostering laziness of mind.

"There's nothing to see." She was desperate for him to be gone.

Dizzy with anguish, she clutched the saddlehorn like a novice rider. She fumbled for her dagger, brandishing it with shaking hands. Landen dropped her bridle and backed away.

"If I wanted to tell lies, they wouldn't be the kind to earn your anger, Princess."

He wheeled his horse, leaving Torina looking at the dagger trembling in her fist.

"I won't believe it," she whispered to the trees.

Torina stayed sheltered until the sky was streaked with rose. When she emerged, she took the direct path home, knowing they'd be looking for her, probably searching everywhere but the common trails she never used. By riding openly, she managed to avoid the servants out beating the woods for a glimpse of her.

She left her horse near the stable and decided to go in one of the back entrances. The one she chose was reached through a long, open walkway of stone, with small intimate benches set in pillared recesses looking out on the formal gardens. When the season cooled, as now, it was rarely used and the rosebushes stood drooping and brown. Ornamental lanterns, kept lit in warmer months, hung empty and dark, the walkway very dim. Torina walked with the rapid, silent step practiced since childhood during play with Landen. She went past dusty benches that a few weeks earlier had held laughing couples, remembering the times Vesputo met her here. The way he looked at her then, the words he spoke, surely they were true? What man could *pretend* such devotion?

Soft sighs of lovers nearby caught her ears. She shrank into a recess, not wanting to be discovered here now, with her face tear-streaked.

"I couldn't wait to see you alone," someone whispered.

"But we must be careful, my love." A strong, quiet

voice, and Torina's heart thudded like galloping hooves on the plains.

It was Vesputo.

She forced herself to breathe shallow and quiet, though her lungs wanted to explode in screams. *My love!* Who was he calling his love? Hidden huddled against a stone pillar, Torina listened to their kisses.

"You're the queen of my heart," she heard.

"What about her?" A female voice floated down the walkway.

Torina strained to catch the soft tones.

"A spoiled child, who'll learn what it means to obey her husband."

There was a giggle. "Vesputo, there's something about her I know that you don't."

That silly, flirtatious laugh. Count Madis's daughter, Irene.

"What's that, darling?" Vesputo's voice was detached, cool as frost.

"I heard about it from Eva, who serves the old queen."

"Queen Ancilla?"

"Yes. Eva was in the next room, and she heard the old queen talking with Torina. Eva says Torina has a magic crystal that tells the future."

"Indeed?" There was heat now, in his tones.

"That's what Eva says."

Landen sat on his horse at a cliff overlooking the sea, remembering the day a girl-child saved his life. The surf pounded as forcefully as ever, beating tiny grains out of the great rocks. He watched the waves for a long time, sitting still and morose.

Torina had taken his words very hard. He'd no idea how deeply Vesputo had invaded her passionate heart. He kept seeing her furious, denying eyes.

Faith battling with truth. Whichever wins, I have killed her innocence. And what now? She has seen Vesputo crowned.

Landen knew enough about her abilities to believe that vision would come to pass—unless she acted to prevent it. Would she stop Vesputo? Remembering her stricken face, Landen doubted it. She'd give her beloved a chance to vindicate himself. Vesputo would play the part of doting suitor perfectly.

If she denounced him, how would she do it? Would she sound like a foolish child? And would Kareed, if asked to choose between the commander he'd prepared for kingship and the wayward daughter he loved, erupt in rage? *And then there are those other, dangerous rumors, and no way to fight them.*

He slapped the reins in frustration. The gray horse trotted on. He rode slowly back toward the castle. Once he was stopped by a patrol that asked if he'd seen the princess. No, he answered.

Sunset found him in the little glade next to her garden. He dismounted and squatted at the edge of the late, lush flowerbeds. This place bore the stamp of her exuberant spirit: the carefully set rocks and riotous surging colors created an atmosphere of delightful tangles. Like her hair, he thought sadly. She always managed to gather blossoms, long after other gardens went to sleep for the year.

The sound of running footsteps urged him into the bordering trees. Red colors from the sky ran over the mass of flowers like a trail of blood, as Torina ran into the garden alone. She was crying. At the sight of the dagger in her hand, Landen almost came out of the woods. But she didn't turn the blade against herself. Instead, she began to slash at her precious plants, hacking flowers to pieces and shredding delicate leaves. Landen watched, transfixed, as her wild grief destroyed the garden.

Finally, surrounded by mangled petals and shoots, she crumpled to the ground, tears streaming. She took out her crystal and stared at it.

"Why?" Landen heard her sob. "Why not tell me?"

She must know. But how? Surely Vesputo would try anything to soothe her fears? Unless she chanced upon Vesputo and his latest lady.

And how am I brought here to see this? If she knew I watched her, would she hate me? I'm watching a tender young girl die. What strange, wild woman will take her place?

She was looking hard at the crystal. Her face went still.

"No," she spoke. "No, no. Not her. Not Gramere. Please, please, please, not Gramere. Not her."

She stood. A wind picked up some of the scattered flower petals and whirled them around her as she drew back her arm and threw the crystal. It flew in a shimmering arc. She didn't stop to see where it fell. She raced for the castle.

Landen hunted for the crystal in the torn beds. The light was dimming rapidly as, down on his hands and knees, he searched the ground. The crystal eluded him. No sparkle, no glimmer showed, and the sun didn't wait for him to find it. Soon dusk fell, and then true night. Still he sifted through bleak, curling petals and cut leaves. He wouldn't leave her cherished seer's eye buried in the remains of the garden she'd nurtured for years. He groped on doggedly in the dark.

❖ ❖ ❖

Torina took a side entrance, the nearest one, into the castle. She tore through hallways at a run, oblivious of servants going to and fro. They would spread the word she was home and call off the searchers. She wasn't thinking of that. She could think only of her grandmother.

Ancilla's rooms were at the end of the west wing. There, the flurry of activity common in the main part of the castle slowed to nothing. Torina's footsteps echoed in deserted halls. She hurried on to Ancilla's bedroom.

A single serving-woman attended the old queen, who lay on the great bed of her ancestors, withered hands clasped on her frail chest. The servant looked up from sewing.

"Princess. Is something wrong?"

"I must speak with my grandmother. Alone."

The woman gathered up her sewing and left. Torina went to sit on the bed, bending over Ancilla with anguished concern.

"Why isn't my mother with you? And the king—has he been sent for?"

A gentle smile flitted over Ancilla's face. One hand slipped into Torina's. The hand was so shrunken it seemed nothing but bones and ropy veins, the skin translucent.

"My dear, to the others, today is only one more day."

"Please." Torina put her young cheek next to the parchment of her grandmother's face, willing her own throbbing life-force into the ancient husk. "Not now. I need you."

"Dearest child," Ancilla spoke faintly. "They call me. If I fight them, I'll die fighting. If I listen, I'll die at peace."

"Can you stay just a little longer?"

"Oh, my dear, I've lived so long . . . seen so much."

Torina raised her head and looked into the faded, kind eyes. "I suppose you saw my death in your crystal, child?"

The girl nodded, tears flowing again.

"Ah."

"Shall I get the others, Gramere?"

"No. No time. Stay with me. I have something to tell you."

"Is it about Vesputo?"

"No, not him. This gift of yours. My love, whenever something rare is handed out, you must know it's borrowed from something greater than yourself. While you have it, remember it belongs to more than you. Use it to benefit others . . . always."

Ancilla sighed, and the light went down in her eyes.

"My life is ended," she whispered. "My love for you will never end."

Torina was alone with the empty shell of Ancilla's body. She buried her head in the worn-out bosom.

Oh Gramere. You are the one I could always talk to, the one who understood. You loved me without any thought of a crown. I need you now. I never had a chance to ask you what to do about Vesputo. I never asked you, and you're the one who would know what to do and how to talk to my father.

Too exhausted for anything else, she lay beside the

body and watched candlelight flicker on the walls. The future, which had been so joyous and whole in the morning, now gaped at her like an ugly wound.

Dreea arrived.

"Torina," she said, arms around her daughter. "I know how you must feel this."

No. No one knows. None of you knew her like I did.

"Papa?" she croaked through dry lips.

"Messengers have been sent to tell him of his mother's death."

Death.

"The funeral must be tomorrow," Dreea said. "There is too much else planned to wait. She kept so much to herself these last years—not many will be there."

Oh Gramere. No time, even for your burial. These last few years . . . what about all the years before? You lived so long, and now I'm the only one who will miss you.

Unable to respond, Torina lay back on the bed, aching all over.

"Don't let them take her yet," she whispered. Dreea nodded, drawing a chair close.

The queen kept vigil all night with her wakeful, grieving daughter, sitting silent beside her through the long time till dawn.

In late afternoon of the following day, Torina sat alone under a gloomy sky beside Ancilla's grave. Flowers were heaped over the fresh earth near the simple headstone. Simple, as Ancilla had wanted. She had chosen her own epitaph. *Life is long and goes quickly.*

Torina had stayed when the other mourners left. Her perpetual attendants were absent; the king's entire household seemed caught up in a great bustle of preparation for something, but Torina only vaguely noticed. Lost in a fog of grief, she hadn't talked with anyone during the short funeral service. Kareed and Dreea had left once the eulogy was spoken.

Torina sat rocking herself as a wind tugged at the bouquets left for the dead. Though very tired, sleep didn't beckon her.

Maybe I'll never sleep again.

Life seemed to stretch far in front of her, into a wasteland of broken hopes.

I'm fifteen, and what if I live as long as my grandmother did? How will I bear the coming days, weeks, years?

When she thought of Vesputo, her heart felt like a dry, cold stone. If Gramere were here, she would have found something to say to break up the harsh rock inside.

I have lived with you and loved you, and now you are gone. Gone where I cannot follow, until I have finished all my days. She looked at the bowl of sky, gray and bleak, spreading up and up, on and on. Where was Ancilla now?

She closed her eyes and tried to find her grandmother. She caught a glimmer of the love that had touched her at the moment of death. For a moment, she sensed unity with her grandmother. Gramere was there. She would always be there. She had promised that her love would never end.

Torina opened her eyes and started at the sight of

Mirandae staring down at her. The lovely feeling fled. She shut her eyes again, trying to call it back.

Mirandae stooped and put an arm around her. "Come, Princess. Rest yourself."

Straining to regain her grandmother, Torina shook her head.

"It's best, dear. You must prepare yourself for the feasting now. The king and Vesputo will be toasting your coming marriage."

Her coming marriage! Surely they did not expect . . . but she had told no one. Through all the weary night hours, she'd never spoken to her mother, had not felt as if she could talk at all.

She pulled away from the encircling arm. "I won't be there," she said hoarsely.

"You must be there," Mirandae insisted. "Everyone expects you."

"I want to be here," Torina answered, each word an effort. "I want to be with Gramere."

"Now isn't the time to spend with the dead. You're about to be married."

"There can be no marriage now, Mirandae."

"No marriage! What are you talking of? What am I to do with you?"

Torina's eyes, puffed with crying, narrowed to slits. "Leave me," she said, using her royal voice.

Mirandae turned on her heel. Torina stared after her, rage blasting her mind. Not the time! Her grandmother had loved her patiently, wisely, and always. Did they all expect her to be forgotten in one day?

She gazed at the gravestone. *Life is long and goes quickly.*

Another figure was coming into view. Torina recognized Landen, dressed in a heavy cape and wearing weapons. He approached and sat beside her.

"I'm sorry," he said. "I know how you loved her."

Somehow his quiet sincerity released her tears again.

"You look very unwell, Princess. Shall I take you in?"

She shook her head, feeling unable to talk. He stayed beside her, saying nothing. She felt a kerchief prodded into her hand. Gratefully, she mopped her face.

"Princess, about yesterday. I—it wasn't—"

"I know."

"I know how bad the grief is. I'm sorry to come to you now. But I wanted to say good-bye, and now is all the time I have."

"Good-bye?" She looked up, puzzled.

"Will you be glad to hear I'm leaving your kingdom?"

"Leaving Archeld? Why?"

He took her hand, rubbing the fingers. "Because there are rumors that say I'll kill the king."

Shock cleared her head. "Kill my father? Why?"

Landen's chest heaved. "To avenge Bellandra."

"But Landen," she said. "That was so long ago."

"I haven't forgotten."

He spoke calmly, but the heat in his eyes frightened her. She jumped to her feet, backing away.

"You mean to kill him?"

He rose, closing the distance between them in two steps.

"No, Princess. It won't be me. Vesputo wants him dead."

Landen's hand kept her from slumping to the ground. She held on to him, as if he were the only land in a wild sea. The years of separation between them seemed to vanish, and he was her trusted comrade again.

"You think him a murderer?"

He shrugged. "He's used to killing. His heart is loyal only to himself."

A chill filled Torina from inside. Landen's arm went around her.

"Let me take you in."

He began to walk her through the cemetery. The wind rose, sweeping petals from the grave across their path.

"My father! I must go to him!"

She hurried forward, too tired to run, too agitated even to know which direction would be fastest. Landen steered her.

"You don't have to leave, Landen. I'll tell them the truth."

"Please do. But I won't gamble my life on the truth. It didn't save my father."

She had nothing to say, only quickened her step. He matched her, pointing to the walls of the castle, now in sight as they crested a small hill beyond the cemetery.

"If Vesputo strikes, you'll be at his mercy." His face was full of concern.

"If you believe this, why have you left him free to harm the king?"

"King Kareed isn't my father," he answered evenly. "And he's blind to Vesputo, just as you were. Should I do Kareed's killing for him?"

She bit her lip. "No, no. I see now, Landen. I see."

They hurried along. "You intend to denounce Vesputo?" he asked.

"Yes, of course."

"Be careful. Treachery is never the work of one man. Who can say what promises he's made to his followers?"

Oh, Papa. This is our kingdom! We have made doorways for betrayal.

"Who are his followers?"

"Beron, for one. Watch where you place your trust, Princess." His clear voice, lowered to almost a whisper, rang ominously.

"What about you? May I trust you?"

"You know you can. Though once I'm gone, many will tell you I'm your greatest enemy."

"Who else knows you're going away?"

"No one, though the friends who warned me guessed it would be soon."

They neared the place where the cemetery path met the main road. The road was filled with people moving in streams to the banquet hall. Landen guided her away, into the trees behind the castle.

"Why do you tell me?" she asked.

His hand rested lightly on her elbow. "Because we were children together," he said.

She pondered for a moment. "You're ready to live exiled?"

He gave her a dry glance. "I've lived exiled since I was a boy."

He lost everything so young. But I still have my parents. My father! I have to talk to him.

"Take your stallion," she urged. "I give him to you."

Landen smiled. "Thank you. I will." He stopped where the trees thinned. "There. You can go in the back way."

She rushed past where he stood, then stopped. "When are you going?"

"As soon as I make a visit to the stable."

She doubled back to him, drawing a small gold ring from her finger. It was set with a tiny crystal globe. Ancilla had had it made for her, and she cherished it. She didn't know what made her hold it out to him.

"Please. Take it and keep it."

Landen slipped it into a pocket, then felt inside his cape. "Thank you. I have something for you, too."

He pulled out her crystal. As she took it, he held her hands, the crystal inside both their palms. There seemed to be a question in his eyes. But he only raised her hands to his lips.

"Good-bye, Princess."

As he walked away, Torina stared after him.

"Good-bye," she said, as if he could still hear her.

She gripped the crystal, gazing into it. She had wanted to put the seer's gift behind her, and it had found her again, given back by Landen. How had he come to have it? It still held the warmth of his body.

In the crystal, small dark rainbows floated across a paneled room. Torina recognized it as a favorite refuge of her father's, one he used when he wanted privacy, a place to sort out the issues that came to him for decision.

Her father appeared. He stood alone, bareheaded, looking into the fire burning in the hearth. His head swiveled as the door opened and Vesputo came in. Torina heard the door close behind Vesputo with a soft echoing thud. The king motioned him forward, then turned back to the fire.

No, Papa! She screamed inwardly, filled with horror. Vesputo's face showed single-minded, emotionless determination. She stretched out a hand, as if she could stop him.

He advanced to stand behind the king. He pulled a small stiletto from his belt.

No! She called to Kareed, and as if in response, his head came around. But it was too late. Vesputo plunged the stiletto into the king's back, and the crystal went black.

Torina reached for Landen's retreating figure, just visible beyond the trees. She gasped, forming his name soundlessly, trying to call him back. But Landen disappeared around a hill.

In a spacious room near the banquet hall, Vesputo stood with Dreea, regally dressed, looking, he was sure, every inch a king. Tonight it would all come together, everything he'd worked for. A sumptuous feast was ready, and Kareed had withdrawn to his private haven to prepare for the festivities that would set the marriage in motion.

There had been times over the past two years when Vesputo doubted Torina would ever be persuaded to marry him. But he'd watched her from the time she was a child, carefully storing away all her habits and delights. It had paid to do so. Now she was his. She had accepted his suit, and he'd seen in her eyes all the testimony he needed that she loved him.

Dreea had told him the girl was grief-stricken. Knowing Torina as he did, Vesputo expected the old queen's death to affect her deeply. He chafed at the inconvenience of the timing, hoping it wouldn't lead to delays. He was anxious to see Torina. She'd been inaccessible since his return. He'd meant to meet her at the funeral.

But Kareed had turned urgent matters over to Vesputo in order to attend the burial. Of course, Vesputo could not refuse the royal request.

A tap on the door announced Mirandae. Her puckered forehead mirrored Dreea's worried look.

"Madam, we've searched everywhere."

"Poor child. So distraught. Who was last to see her?" the queen asked in her gentle way.

"I believe I was," Mirandae answered. "When I went back for her at the grave."

Dreea turned to Vesputo, who watched with misgivings.

"I ought to have stayed beside her, but I thought she would come in with the rest of us. While you were away, Vesputo, all she talked of was you. Now that her grandmother has died, she can think of nothing but her grief."

Vesputo addressed Mirandae. "Madam, you spoke with her at the graveside?"

"Yes, sir."

"Tell me what she said," he probed, trying to modulate his voice to reflect a lover's concern.

Mirandae threw up her hands. "Said there could be no wedding! Said she wanted to be with her grandmother!"

Vesputo's fists clenched. He hid them behind his back. "My dear queen," he said. "I must excuse myself to do what I can in this."

"Oh yes, Vesputo. You're the best one to help her. Please, tell us instantly if you get any word."

Vesputo bowed and let himself out of the room. His palms were cold and damp as he hurried along the corridors.

What if Irene heard true? Could Torina have seen something . . .

Vesputo ground his teeth. It was the only explanation for her avoidance of him. Ordinarily she would have run to meet him. He had carelessly construed Ancilla's death as the reason she shut herself away. Now he recalled she'd been missing for many hours before that last visit to her grandmother.

His fists opened and closed furiously. If she had seen what he planned, then he couldn't wait. She was too headstrong. Not even her father could make her marry if she refused.

What if she was with the king now? Vesputo doubted they'd looked for her in Kareed's sanctuary.

The commander forced his features into their usual mask of calm, striding through the halls to the king's rooms.

King Kareed stood alone in the private room that had become his haven over the years. The walls were paneled with polished oak cut from his native forests, the hearth made of stone from the quarry where he played as a boy. Three tapestries hung where he could see them from his chair, all worked by his wife's charmed fingers. One was a wreath of flowers encircling two clasped hands, made for their wedding day. Another showed rays of a rising sun, against the familiar ridge of the Cheldan Mountains. The third, she had only recently finished. Torina, standing in her garden, red hair flowing free, a riot of blossoms around her. It was uncanny in its lifelike quality. The eyes seemed to follow him, the lips ready to speak.

A fire the king had lit himself burned on the hearth. Warmed by its blaze, he gazed at the woven portrait of his daughter. A procession of memories drifted before him.

He saw the face of his wife, radiant with love, as the baby girl was placed in his arms. When the newborn gripped his finger, the strength of her tiny hand filled him with ecstasy. They thought then, and for many years, that more children would follow.

He recalled the small, fire-headed toddler, following him about whenever she could. And later the prattling child, eager to tell him everything she'd seen and done, as if to introduce him to the world afresh. Then the mischievous young girl, with her endless escapades.

Such love she had given him. Powerful, innocent love. Her face would light brighter than a hundred chandeliers when he was near. And then . . .

Somehow, she had grown up. Others were her confidantes. He saw her frequently, of course, and always felt an aching pride in her. Yet she was reticent with him now. Hesitant, a little formal, distant in an unthought politeness that tore his heart.

He longed to lift her up and hear her laughter again, ask her of her day and have her tell him all she felt. He wanted to hear her feet running to him, wanted to convey to her his life—all he had done, and all he wished undone. But he was constrained. He felt the bricks of his absences and misdeeds, mortared together by his remote affairs of state into a wall too high to come down.

And Vesputo? Was he the man to entrust her to?

Vesputo the promising commander had become Vesputo the powerful right-hand man. His ambition led him to undertake great risks.

Ambition! I wish I could be certain that affection rules him when it comes to Torina. He seems to care, but if she were not the king's daughter? If only I could be sure he loves her!

And if he did not? Too late to train another king. Why these doubts? Kareed had fought beside Vesputo, trusted him with the gravest secrets of kingship. Rejoiced in and encouraged this match.

The door opened without a knock. Annoyed, Kareed turned.

Torina was running to him.

She wore an outdoor cape. Dead leaves clung to it. She came right up to him and put both hands on his chest, panting, shaking. He folded his fingers over hers. She lifted a blanched face to him. There were purple smudges under the wide, frightened eyes.

Alarmed, the king guided her to his chair. She collapsed into it. He pulled another chair close and she reached for his hand.

She had come to him! She had a problem and had come to him.

"Torina, what is it, my dear?"

"Oh Papa!" She spoke through pale, trembling lips.

"What is it, my Torina? What's the matter?"

"Papa, you must—listen to me!" She sounded breathless.

"Tell me what has happened."

"Not what has happened. What will happen."

He smiled. "Cold feet over marriage? Is that the trouble? Torina, I promise you—"

"No!" She surprised him with her vehemence.

"What then?"

"Papa, do you remember the crystal you brought back from Bellandra?"

"Crystal?" He frowned. "Bellandra? Torina, there are things I regret . . ." He drew back his hand. She snatched it, clung to it.

"The crystal! You gave it to me. Remember?" Her voice quivered.

"I . . . vaguely recall something."

"Papa, I can see the future in it."

"The future?"

"Believe me, Papa. I've seen many things and all were true." She seemed to choke on emotion, her eyes imploring him. She was shivering, though covered with a wool cape and sitting near the fire.

"Oh!" she cried. "If only I had told you before. Now, when you need to believe me, you—"

"Believe you!"

"Papa, I have seen," she swallowed. "I have seen—"

"Steady, girl. What are you talking of?"

"I have seen Vesputo." She seemed to be strangling again.

"Vesputo. Yes?" The king chafed her wrists.

"Papa, I love you."

"And I love you, my dear."

Again, the door swung open without a knock. Vesputo stood framed in the doorway for a moment before it closed behind him.

Kareed rose, prying himself loose from Torina's nervous grasp. He heard her trying to choke out a word.

"Vesputo."

"My king." Vesputo was calm, deferential. He strode forward, eyes on Torina. He was dressed well, moving with his normal, smooth, unfaltering gait.

The king coughed. "Excuse me. My daughter and I have things to discuss."

"Ah," Vesputo answered, but did not break step. His eyes looked very dark as he kept coming. "This will only take a moment. Sorry to intrude. There's something I must ask you."

"Very well," Kareed allowed. "What is it?"

Behind him, Torina called to him. "No, Papa! Don't let him near you!"

Vesputo was at his side, clapping him on the back. Pain filled him in a rush and then burst. He tried to whirl on the traitor, but staggered forward instead, inexorable agony gripping his chest.

The warrior king fought to find his enemy, but could see nothing. He reached for his battle voice. No sound obeyed. His mighty arms, which had slain so many, refused his will.

His world darkened and went out.

Chapter 7

A piece of cloth gagged Torina's mouth. Cords bound her ankles, fixed her arms behind her back, and tied her waist to a chair. She was in her own bedroom. Candelabra were lit. A massive man she remembered seeing with Vesputo stood in front of her. Her head ached and a strange, bitter taste was in her mouth. Next to her, Vesputo caressed her hair.

"Awake, my dear?"

She glared at him.

"Thank you, Toban. I'll speak privately with the princess now."

The guard left Torina alone with Vesputo.

"Sorry they were rough with you, darling." He held up a menacing finger. "I'm going to cut your gag now. Since you never learned to keep your silence, I must be your teacher. From this hour, any word you speak against me will send someone dear to you to the grave. Take care."

He sliced through the gag with his dagger. The quiet in the room seemed very loud.

"Grieving the death of your grandmother and your father, you are completely unable to hold festivities. I've taken the liberty of sending your guests away."

"Too late," she mourned. "I was too late."

"Never mind, darling. We all make mistakes."

She shivered under his cold eyes.

"You." Her voice dripped with loathing. "You killed your king."

"Not I, dear Torina. An assassin. The Bellandran orphan, regrettably left alive all these years."

"What new lie is this? You hope to blame your crime on—Landen? Don't pretend with me, Vesputo! I saw what I saw!"

"You saw through the lens of madness. I hope you'll recover soon."

"Madness? Yes. I was mad. To think I once loved you!"

"Once loved me. Will love me."

"I suppose you mean to kill me. It doesn't matter. Go ahead with it."

"No, no, sweet princess. Quite the contrary. When your wild mourning period has passed, we will marry. Archeld needs a new king."

He slung a chair in front of her, his face inches from hers. She shrank from him, wishing he would untie her hands. She wanted to see if the crystal was still there in a pocket of her dress.

"The kingdom won't ever be yours through me," she answered, trembling. "If you want it, you'll have to take it by force."

He pursed his lips as if annoyed by a petty irritant. "The loss of life would be dreadful. No, Torina. Everyone knows we love each other. You love me so dearly, I'm the only one you'll agree to see. You refuse even your mother."

She gasped. "You're not the king! You can't keep us apart!"

"Certainly I can. Your mind is disordered. You insist on shutting yourself away. I know you love our dear queen too much to want to risk her life."

"You wouldn't kill Dreea! She's never hurt anyone!"

"Ah! Please, my dear, don't weary me with your childishness."

Torina paused. Vesputo's calm, handsome face made her mind stagger. This was the man she had kissed!

"Very well," she said. "I won't see her. I'll send her away if she asks to speak to me."

"Good! You learn quickly, my love, when you have a worthy teacher." He reached into his shirt, pulling out the crystal.

He extended it so that it rested in front of her eyes. Torina wanted to grab it from him, feeling its purity would be contaminated by such a conscienceless man. But she was tied. Her heart thumped in powerless rebellion.

"Now, Torina," he said. "I have questions. You shouldn't have secrets from me, my love. Why didn't you tell me about this lovely stone?"

Tears fought their way into her eyes. "I haven't told anyone about it except my grandmother."

"No one else?"

"No one," she lied.

"Why keep it such a secret?"

"I don't know."

"Ah. Don't you? Where did you get it?"

"My father gave it to me."

"And where did he get it?"

"You should have left him alive, so you could ask him."

"How long have you had it?"

"Since I was a child."

"And it shows you the future?"

"Sometimes. Please! Untie me, Vesputo. There's nowhere to go; I'm sure you've seen to that."

Now that Vesputo knew her powers, what if he tried to force her to tell him about her visions?

He freed her hands. She wiped her streaming eyes.

"Better?" Vesputo asked, holding up the crystal again. "Now tell me, how do you get this stone to tell the future?"

A tiny door of hope chinked in Torina's mind. Vesputo thought she *did* something to get the crystal to work. Good! It would be easy to reinforce his mistake.

"I don't know completely. It doesn't work when I'm tired." Torina still tasted the bitter flavor in her mouth, and the edges of her mind felt smudged. She knew it wasn't only grief. Someone had drugged her.

"Ah." He put the crystal back in his shirt. "Then now isn't the time." He stood up. "You have two months to grieve. Then, we marry as planned."

"Marry you! I never want to look at you again." *At least he doesn't know I can change the future sometimes, if I act quickly enough. But not this time! Oh Papa, I failed you.*

His eyes darkened. "It doesn't matter what you want, my dear. You will learn to do exactly as I say." He went to the door. "I count the minutes till we meet again, my beautiful bride-to-be."

Torina wanted to yell with all her might, but her throat closed. Vesputo would kill her friends, as he had threatened. She stared at the wall.

A woman entered, dressed in an ornate gown of pale yellow silk, her long blonde braid extending below an embroidered cap, a light veil covering her face. She lifted the veil.

"Irene is here to provide you with a woman's care," Vesputo said over his shoulder as he left.

This fresh outrage frayed Torina even more. Irene undid the rest of the ropes, asking if she wanted anything to eat or drink. Torina refused. Her stomach signaled no hunger. She lay down, silently begging sleep to take her away.

As Landen directed his horse toward Missht Pass in the Cheldan Mountains, he was glad of the chance to be utterly alone. Here, even nature was foreign: cold and desolate, filled with nothing but stones and bone-aching wind. He was heading for Desante, Archeld's neighbor to the east. He knew little about Desante beyond the rudiments of geography, which reported thick forests and vast farmlands. And he knew the name of her king: Ardesen.

Desante was bordered by the Cheldan Mountains, and Missht Pass was the most treacherous crossing point. Far to the south, the mountains were less steep: Angrera Pass was much more hospitable, but probably well guarded. Landen hoped that by choosing this lonely path, he could skirt any outposts guarding the border and shake any pursuers. The Missht landscape was so forbidding, there was only one thin track. The harsh environment seemed a fitting companion for Landen's heart as he sped on his way.

Time was everything, and Landen wasted none of it. He rode without stopping, filled with a hundred emotions that all seemed to return to one thing—the impossibility of staying near Torina when she faced a ruthless enemy. His sadness and danger fueled the long, sleepless ride.

What did he take with him to start life in another foreign land? His mind, his aching heart, his skilled hands. He must sell the horse that knew him like a friend and get rid of the thick hooded cloak that allowed him to weather the pass.

"Along with everything else that belongs to my life in Archeld," he said to a twisted pine clinging to boulders above the tree line.

Sorrowfully, he surveyed Archeld one last time from the summit. The view let him see a long way in every direction.

North was Glavenrell, where King Dahmis had grown into a powerful peacemaker seeking broad alliances. The northern kings honored him as the high king in disputes over boundaries or trade. Landen still wanted to serve Dahmis. But depending on when Vesputo struck, he might already be a hunted man. He didn't want to present himself to King Dahmis with nothing to offer but a price on his head. If Vesputo struck down Kareed, Landen knew he was the chosen scapegoat.

He pondered the strangeness of life, which brought him to hope Kareed would live into old age. So it was: he prayed for a reprieve for Veldon's murderer, the despoiler of Bellandra, the destroyer of Bellandra's Sword. As long as the invader lived, Torina would be protected.

Southwest lay the province of Archeld that had once

been Bellandra. Landen no longer felt drawn to go there. Every bit of knowledge he'd been able to gain about his former homeland told him it was nothing like the place of his boyhood. Oh, there were still artisans at work there: Bellandran pottery brought a high price in the markets, and Bellandran weaving was all the fashion. But greed seemed to be the new ruler. People reportedly fought hard for the right to control wealth. And all the mystic healers and seers had disappeared. It was whispered they'd vanished as soon as Bellandra fell. There were even rumors that they'd never truly existed.

King Veldon's face drifted vaguely across Landen's inner vision. Veldon's last words had been about Bellandra's Sword. "*Landen. The Sword of Bellandra. Take it and hide. Find someone to teach you . . . to fight.*" But the young man could hardly remember his father's features. The wondrous Sword still shone, deep in the heart of Bellandra's prince, but only when he looked inward far enough, and he seldom looked any more. The Sword hadn't saved Bellandra, and everyone agreed it was destroyed, its mystery and magic a thing of the past.

When he turned his horse, he could pinpoint the location of the garrison guarding the Desantian border. From his vantage, he picked out a way to go around it. A cold rain began. Landen ordered images of Torina to leave him and started down the mountain to Desante.

Vesputo sat in a large carved chair in the king's rooms, flanked by Beron and Toban, his partners in treachery.

Toban was a valuable man. Not only was he formidably strong, he also understood plants very well. Dreea had dropped from exhausted grief and anxiety, helped into sleep by a strong potion he had mixed.

There was a tap on the door. Irene entered, swishing her skirts. Vesputo smiled.

"What news?"

"She's asleep. The door is locked."

Vesputo nodded to Toban, and the large man left the room. He would stand guard over Torina's door.

"Come close, Irene, I want to show you something," Vesputo said.

She rubbed against him, smiling. He kissed her, savoring her lips.

"What did you want to show me?"

From a drawer near his chair, he took Torina's crystal, handing it to Irene. "Look into it, my love. Do you see anything?"

She held the glittering sphere in her lap, staring into it. This was the stone that had changed all his plans. Vesputo waited curiously, wondering if the crystal's magic would work for Irene. He'd already tried looking himself, without success. Perhaps it only performed for females.

Irene looked up at him. "It's blank as glass, my lord."

Disappointed, Vesputo reached for the crystal. She held on to it, smiling at him.

"If you let me have it, I might learn to use it. Then I could see the future for you, my lord."

"Hmmm. Interesting, my love. I'll consider your request. Perhaps. You might want to see what you can find out from Torina, as you'll be looking after her."

❖ ❖ ❖

In the cemetery where Ancilla had been buried only a few days before, a great crowd of mourners gathered for the funeral of their king. A large marble headstone displayed his epitaph: *Kareed Archelda, mighty king, beloved husband and father.*

Vesputo stood beside the priest, head solemnly bowed. Beside him, Queen Dreea wept. Torina was conspicuously absent.

The priest gave an eloquent eulogy. He spoke of Kareed's many victories, prosperous kingdom, wise judgments. Vesputo grew restless as the minutes dragged on, though not a quiver betrayed him. At last, the service was complete, the prayers delivered, the flowers laid out. Vesputo moved closer to Dreea and took her hand.

"Torina's door is still barred to me," she sobbed, her face ravaged. Vesputo was pleased. There were people watching. The news would travel quickly. "When I knock, her voice tells me to go away. If I didn't hear her myself, I couldn't believe it. Not to pay her respects to her father! Torina loved him."

"She is distraught, madam."

Dreea cried harder. "Yet she will see you."

"I give what comfort I can."

"Tonight I'll have her door broken down. She can't remain alone!"

"My dear queen, I know your heart is aching. Still, I would not advise breaking down the door. Her reason is too fragile now."

"Oh! My king! My only child!" Dreea buried her face in her hands.

❖ ❖ ❖

Torina lay miserably in her private prison. Oh, why hadn't she been wiser? She'd failed herself, failed her kingdom, and failed her father.

Irene prattled at Torina constantly, reporting every bit of vicious gossip in the castle. Did Torina know everyone thought she was mad? Had she heard how soldiers were combing the land for Landen, and that he wouldn't get far?

Torina's heart pounded in fury at the thought of Landen taking the blame for Vesputo's crime. At the same time, an angry voice berated him for deserting her, just when he was needed most. Why didn't he warn her sooner? It was all too late. Too late.

She wanted her grandmother desperately, and the only solace she found was that at least with Gramere there had been time to say good-bye. But that always brought her father to mind. She kept seeing him in front of her, waiting for her words. How terrible was the finality of death. Not even to see his face one last time!

And her mother. Every day, Dreea came to her door begging to be allowed in. Every day, Torina forced herself to send the queen away, listened to her weeping cries, and hated Vesputo more.

He visited often, bringing the crystal. She played the part of the flustered, inept female trying to coax visions from a recalcitrant stone. She did everything she could to convince him the crystal only gave her occasional images and that most of the time what she saw confused her.

"What has it told you of your own future?" he once asked.

"I've never seen my own future," she told him, hoping that mixing an honest answer in with half-lies would give the ring of truth to all she said.

"No? What about mine?"

"All I've seen of you is the crown on your head."

There was a glint of triumph in his eye. "Ah." She could see her answer pleased him. "Tell me why you were with Kareed in his study that day."

That day. The day he died. The day everything changed.

"I wanted to tell him I wouldn't marry you."

"Why? Why didn't you see me when I returned?"

"Because I heard about Irene."

"You didn't see Irene in the crystal?"

"No."

"Who told you?"

"I don't remember."

"You lie."

"And you, Vesputo. You don't even know what the truth is."

He gave her a half-amused, deprecating stare. "Perhaps it's best this way, my love."

He stood, and she was glad. It meant he would soon leave, and she'd rather listen to Irene's vapid chatter than spend time with Vesputo. "Your mourning period is almost up. Soon we'll be man and wife, and then you can have your crystal back. You'll learn to use it better and tell me everything it tells you."

Later that evening, Irene couldn't do enough for Torina. She hovered around, smiling and sweet.

"I believe I'll go to bed, Irene."

"Oh! Yes. Would you like me to brush your hair? It's so beautiful, especially in the firelight."

"No, thank you."

"Torina, I wonder if you would answer a little question for me?"

"What is it?"

"What makes the crystal work?"

Torina smiled inside. "Don't tell Vesputo, but only a woman can make it tell the future."

Irene nodded eagerly. "I won't tell."

"You have to take it out during the full moon, and then again when the moon is dark. You have to be all alone when you do it. That part was ever so hard for me. Then it will start showing you visions, Irene."

Landen had no trouble evading the garrison that guarded the border. When he reached Desante, he rode for a half-day without stopping, to distance himself from the edges of Archeld. Then he chose a prosperous, secluded farm to trade his stallion for a less valuable Desantian mare and some money.

He made his way to a bustling village not far from the main city of Desan. After examining passers-by, he searched the shops and bought warm black pants, a flowing shirt of dark red, sturdy boots, and a quilted jacket. Most Desantian men had short beards. Landen was glad he'd let his grow since leaving Archeld. In a few days, his thick whiskers would pass for native. He gave his Archeldan clothes to a beggar, trusting dirt and deprivation to erase their foreign lines and help lose his trail. He was bound to be tracked, but he would hide his footsteps wherever he could. His next move was to sell all the weapons he'd brought with him, down to the bow made with his own hands.

He watched as an aging shopkeeper stowed his bow and sword out of sight and handed him some coins in return.

"Beautiful workmanship, that," the man remarked, eyeing him curiously.

"Aye. Down on my luck or I wouldn't sell," Landen answered.

"Can you use them?" The shopkeeper jerked his head at an array of swords and bows hung on his wall.

Landen nodded.

"Seems like a young, strong man like yourself, with knowledge of weapons, should enlist."

"Are they taking soldiers, then?"

"Oh, very particular, but the king always needs men at the ready."

"Particular?"

"Well, if you have your own weapons and know the business, you stand a chance." The man's gaze went back to his display.

"How much for a plain sword and bow?"

The man stroked his chin. "Well, I've a customer will buy everything you've sold me, so I can make you a rare deal."

"Indeed?"

"We seldom get the Archeldan swords, and truth be known they're better metal. And that bow, why, a master craftsman made it."

Landen swallowed and didn't contradict. The man seemed in no doubt of where the sword was made.

Wearing Desantian weapons, he rode on to the city of Desan. The wide road leading to its gates had been fortified with pebbles; still it was muddy. Streams of boisterous bearded men, women with bright scarves on their heads, and laden animals passed through the gates into the city. Guards barely glanced at Landen's unremarkable horse and clothes. They were occupied detaining a ragged band of minstrels ten paces ahead of him.

The exile entered the city and followed the flow of crowds, looking keenly about him. Narrow streets were lined with simple, well-made buildings of wood and stone. The bustling, rowdy people were friendly with one another, jostling good-naturedly. Landen kept to the main road, listening to the patterns of speech he heard.

"Desante and Archeld must have the same mother," he muttered to himself, glad to find that the languages and accents weren't far apart. The common people spoke with a rough, oddly clipped slur. But when he heard nobles talk, they sounded much like he did himself.

He stopped occasionally to buy food from cart vendors. Desantian bread was fragrant and robust. By early afternoon, he reached the market square, which led into several thoroughfares dense with public inns and taverns. He took a room for the night and found the groom.

"Going to see the fight?" the man asked.

"Indeed," Landen answered, certain that to ask "what fight" would mark him a foreigner.

"Best hurry then. The mare's in good hands with me."

The young man stepped into the street, guided by the direction of the busy crowd. Just ahead of him, a boy hurried along by the side of an older man. Landen picked out their conversation.

"Is Tamand going to win?" the boy asked.

"Aye, he may, for the soldier gets to wear leather armor, and the criminal none."

"They both get swords, don't they?"

"Aye. And if Tamand kills the criminal, he gets twenty rashoes in gold. You and me won't see that much till we've worked twenty years with no quitting. You can see why the soldiers fight."

"Tamand is strong, ain't he, Papa?"

"So they say. The criminal he's to fight is main burly too."

"What does the criminal get if he wins?"

"He most never does, seeing he has no armor, and he can't win without killing. But if he kills, he gets full pardon and can hire for mercenary."

"Full pardon for killing a soldier?" The boy's wide-eyed question echoed Landen's thoughts.

"Ah, they won't fight if they've nothing to gain. No one's making the soldier do it. Just look at the crowd here. Each one paying their end wage to see. This way, the king can pay his troops, and they say there's wars again soon."

"Jern told me there's another rule, where neither one gets killed."

"Bah! No one's used that in half a century. Aye, it's there, but Tamand won't do that. No point getting to where he could kill, then sparing the criminal's life and walking away with nothing."

"Then why's the rule there?"

"They say in the old days, if the soldier felt honor for the man he fought, he'd let him off. Nah, don't think about that, son. Won't happen today."

111

As the father and son quickened their pace, Landen walked in their wake, shaking his head with disgusted admiration. So, King Ardesen sponsored blood sports, a sort of entertainment tax on his citizens, to pay the troops that protected their borders! No doubt he ran a tight hold on such interests. Horrible ingenuity, whereby a poor soldier could fight his way to riches by killing one of the kingdom's criminals, and a desperate prisoner could purchase freedom by besting a soldier! And whoever died, Ardesen's wealth would grow, for here were rushing swarms of Desantians: men, women, and children, eager to witness the coming fight, undaunted by the chill of autumn.

Did the king attend these gory spectacles? Did he hand out the prizes himself? And how many times a year were these battles enacted?

Though he had no heart to watch, Landen paid his fare and entered the huge stone amphitheater, crowded with tiered benches. Below was a round walled courtyard, perhaps thirty paces in diameter. It was empty. Landen found a seat and waited as new throngs made their way in. The roar of humanity was loud. There was no sign of King Ardesen.

The sun was westering but still strong when a man appeared in the courtyard. He carried himself with authority. When he spread his arms, the multitude grew quiet. He raised a hand and another man, dressed in leather armor and carrying a bright sword, danced out to the center of the courtyard. The crowd cheered him with fierce hurrahs. He kissed his hands to the people and smiled, bowing as if he'd just finished a great performance. Tamand was graceful and cocky. Landen feared it was a foolish stance for a man about to fight for his life.

A third man rushed into the courtyard. He too carried a sword, but wore only a loincloth. Landen recognized the agile strength of a wrestler in this man: those arms and legs, though smaller than Tamand's, would be supple and deceptively mighty.

Tamand's attention was still taken by the crowd as his opponent charged. The people yelled a warning. At the last instant, Tamand turned to meet the appalling ferocity of a sword-thrust. Though he leaped away, the sword caught him in the thigh. Blood spurted over the stones of the courtyard. Tamand stared aghast, crying out.

The other man didn't wait. He struck again, this time to the heart. Then he stood warily, watching while the soldier died. Before the spectators could take in what had happened, guards emerged and escorted the criminal off, presumably to freedom.

Landen gazed mistily at the body on stone below. It lay as though flung, one twisted arm still gripping the sword, blood pooling around it. The people in the stands sat in gaping silence for a few moments.

Then a rumble of disappointment traveled around the tiers. They had paid to see a fight. Now it was over and their favorite had died without striking a single blow, died protesting the reality of his wounds.

Abruptly, soldiers were thick among the benches, meeting the grumbling crowd. The people were herded through the gates into the street, Landen among them.

As he watched the taverns swell with disgruntled citizens, he guessed many would seek the outlet of frustrated men, fighting each other in alleys, damaging themselves with heated punches and raw booze. It would not be a night to make friends without paying the price of split lips, broken noses, or worse. Still, the friends made at such times often stuck together for life. Landen hesitated, listening to voices already raised in anger. He ached to do something himself, to forget the laughing young soldier who had underestimated death. He lingered in the street as the sun met the horizon, drawn to join noisy Desantians at the door of a tavern.

No, the timing was wrong. Tomorrow he meant to enlist in the king's forces if they would take him; he didn't want to present himself with bruises. He returned to his inn to spend the evening alone. He passed the time thinking of a new name to go with his Desantian life.

In the morning, the groom told him where to enlist. He rode out among the bleary-eyed populace, to the training grounds of the king's army.

Here I am, exiled again, with ambitions to become a soldier in the service of a king I feel no allegiance to.

His sword and bow gained him an immediate interview with a captain. Required to display proficiency with a variety of weapons, he easily demonstrated his usefulness. When they asked his name, it was no effort to answer "Bellanes." The chosen alias seemed to belong to him as much as the name that had once been given to a king's son. He claimed to be from Guelhan, an outer province of Desante, far enough away to account for being unknown.

They told him it was peacetime. King Ardesen had just signed a broad treaty with King Dahmis, the powerful leader of Glavenrell whom men called the high king.

As a soldier, his skills would be used to keep the peace, unless war broke out. Pay was one rasho a year, doled out in monthly stipends, plus room and board. He was issued leather armor and given a place in a contingent led by

Captain Hadnell, a decent man who reminded him of Emid. There he entered training to apprehend criminals and protect citizens.

A few days later, Landen stood in morning review exercise, a cold wind blowing his hair. Captain Hadnell looked over the rows of soldiers.

"I have news," he announced, "that may affect our kingdom."

The men stood erect, waiting. Their captain was not given to overstatement.

"As you know, across the mountains to the west is our neighbor, Archeld," Hadnell continued. Landen braced himself. "Ten days ago, King Kareed, her ruler, was murdered with a poison-tipped stiletto."

So soon! For a short moment, Landen felt a child's bursting, painful exultation, to hear this poetic justice. His father's murderer finally dead! Kareed's life cut short, just as he'd cut short the lives of so many.

Then he remembered that Kareed had trained him to meet a world he must now live in. Without that training, he'd be lost. And Kareed was *her* father. If he was dead, that meant Vesputo was alive. How did she bear it? He recalled her grieving face the last time he had seen her.

"The killer escaped, no one knows where," the captain went on. "His description might fit many of you!" His eyes narrowed, and he shrugged. "Young, tall man with dark hair, good with weapons and horses." There was a collective chuckle. "It's believed this young man may try to set up as a bow maker." Landen blessed the foresight that had ordered him to relinquish his craft.

"His name is Landen. Rumor says he's the dispossessed prince of that fabled land, Bellandra, conquered

115

by Kareed six years ago." Hearing his name, Landen struggled for calm. It was no more than he had expected. Yet it was official now. He was a hunted man.

"Each new entry to the city will be carefully searched and questioned. All new mercenary hires will be examined. He was riding a gray stallion and wearing Archeldan weapons and clothes. If you find this man, he's to be turned over to the king, alive."

Chapter 8

Torina asked for hot water. She bathed, soaking away the traces of her grief. She arranged her hair in a single neat braid and dressed herself with care. Then she sent for Vesputo.

"Irene says you wanted to see me?" His voice was smooth as oil.

"Yes."

"Are you through with your mourning?"

"Even if I grieve for the rest of my life, you won't see it and I won't speak of it." Her face was expressionless. "I'm ready to marry you."

"Wise decision. The people will rejoice."

"They must see, as I do, that you're the one man capable of governing my father's kingdom. You lead the army. You know the laws. It's best for Archeld."

Vesputo took both her hands and clenched them in his large fists.

"I lead the army—something for you to remember always," he said. "As queen, you will follow in your mother's footsteps. Your habits will be domestic and pious. You will leave the affairs of the kingdom to my judgment. You will look in the crystal each day and tell me all the visions you have."

She bowed her head. "It's what I want."

He dropped her hands. "Then we're in perfect agreement." His smile reminded her of a predator's grin, a predator who knows its kill is sure. "Tomorrow evening, we celebrate the wedding. At noon, you will see your mother and tell her of your joy." His arms went around her, pulling her into a fierce kiss. Torina submitted.

"Remember, one word against me—"

"Don't concern yourself, my lord," she replied, letting him see her fear. He seemed to relax, moving to the door.

"Now we must rest, in preparation."

She reached out to him. He raised an eyebrow. "May I have a sleeping draught tonight?" she said. "My sleep has been fitful."

"Ah. Certainly. Irene will bring it."

He left, trailed by Irene. Torina heard the key grinding. She stared at the door and thought of her mother. For the first time in weeks, she let her tears fall.

Irene, dressed in one of her favorite gowns, the soft green one with lace at the collar and sleeves, swished through the halls of Archeld's castle, carrying a tray with a goblet on it. Her hair was in a single braid down her back. Many women envied her that hair, she knew, so long and thick and golden.

She had to remind herself that this time she was going

to Torina's room. Usually, when she carried a goblet, it meant the queen.

The goblet the queen drank every evening made her sleep long and deeply; it took her until noon to be roused each day. Then she would go to Torina's door to plead with her daughter. Torina always played her part, sending her mother away. The queen would be carried back to her rooms to mourn and cry. *Will I start bringing the princess a goblet every night, now that she's going to be queen?*

Torina was so quiet, never any trouble. She just mooned around, listless and slow. Vesputo still planned to marry her and expected her to look in the crystal for him, to tell him what was in store. *Not if I can stop it.* Irene fingered the pocket of her silk dress, feeling the weight of Torina's crystal. Tonight the moon was full. When she told Vesputo what Torina said about how to see the future, he agreed she could keep the stone till morning. *Once I can see visions, Vesputo will keep me with him, always. I'll be the queen of his heart forever.*

Toban leaned casually against the wall by Torina's door. He had orders never to look as if he were standing guard. If anyone inquired, he was there in case the mad princess needed anything or anyone. Irene smiled at him, even though she knew her veil made it hard to see her face. He glanced both ways down the hall and opened the door. Yawning as he waved her through, he pinched her as she passed. He always pinched or squeezed, and Irene let him. She could tell Vesputo, but what was the harm? Toban was handsome.

She entered the room and heard the sound of the key behind her. Torina was in bed, dressed in a nightgown, hair over her shoulder in a red braid, covers pulled halfway up.

Her hair is as thick and long as mine; I wonder if Vesputo likes it? Her face is strange though. She used to be beautiful. Now she's far too pale.

Irene stooped to set the tray down by the bedside. As she did, Torina flashed off the covers and sprang up, a dagger bright in her hand. Irene felt her braid grabbed from behind, her head tilted back. She gasped as steel was laid against the skin of her neck.

"One sound and I'll kill you," Torina hissed. Irene whimpered. The knife dug into her neck. She froze.

"Drink it," Torina ordered. Irene's thoughts spun wildly, panicked by the pricking steel.

"Drink it," she heard again, and realized Torina meant the goblet. She lifted the sleeping potion and set it to her lips. She drained it, a few drops dribbling on her chin.

"Good. Now sit." Torina yanked on her braid, steering her. Irene's knees gave and the bed caught her. Torina let go of her hair. The knife left her neck, but the princess remained in front of her, dagger poised, eyes burning.

"Wh-what are you going to do?"

"In a few minutes, you won't know what I do, or care, until tomorrow."

Tomorrow! Then she would not be killed. She was only being put to sleep. Torina must intend something desperate, but she, Irene, would not be harmed. Vesputo would be angry, but what could she do? She'd been taken by surprise. How could she know that the docile girl would turn dangerous?

Torina stood over her, watching every breath she took. Irene looked down at her hands, captivated by the pattern of lace on her sleeves. Her breathing changed, getting slow and heavy. Her eyelids drooped beyond the call of her will. The lace glimmered oddly. She sank onto the pillow.

❖ ❖ ❖

Dagger ready, Torina examined the sleeping girl. She lifted Irene's arms and let them fall back limp. The drugs, whatever they were, had taken full effect. Good. Irene wouldn't be able to tell anyone anything until morning.

She set to work. Grabbing Irene's long blonde braid, she cut it off with her dagger and tossed it on the bed. Closing her eyes, she reached behind and severed her own braid. She took off Irene's lace cap and carefully pinned the yellow hair inside it.

"How fortunate that you wear those foolish little veils," she said to the sleeping figure on the bed. She bent to undress Irene.

Faint sounds from the hall hammered at her heart. Soon she stood by the bed, adjusting her own simple nightcap on Irene's head. Pinned to it was the red braid. Only the curve of Irene's cheek was visible. Torina hurriedly got into the other woman's elaborate dress, deft fingers nervously buttoning and lacing.

In the skirts of the gown, her hand found a pocket weighted with some object. Her fingers recognized the crystal! Drawing it out, she clasped it.

She fastened Irene's cap on her own head, dropping the veil over her face.

She pulled a stone from the hearth. It concealed a recess she'd hollowed out as a child, playing games of secret intrigue suggested by Landen. Here, long ago, she'd placed the little dagger and a small velvet bag of rubies. She remembered his solemn eyes the day he told her, "You never know when your life will change." She'd laughed then, believing nothing could disrupt her secure future. Still, she'd enjoyed playing at preparing for evil times, storing secret treasures against some distant, dark day.

That day had come. She slipped the crystal into the bag of rubies. She gave a last tug to the blankets over Irene, picked up the tray with its empty goblet, and went to the door.

She tapped out Irene's series of knocks. She knew them perfectly. The door opened. Toban peered in, looked at the bed, nodded absently. He squeezed her waist as she went past him. Torina's heart jumped. What would Irene do? Sweat trickled down her back under the silk. She took her cue from the man, who touched her as if out of habit, and pretended not to notice.

"Good night," he said. She waved two fingers at him as she sashayed away. She knew it was one of Irene's favorite gestures.

Eric Aldon paced out his duty in front of the great stables. He liked the stable post better than watching the castle or grounds. In King Kareed's day, there had been few sentries: King Kareed took his safety for granted when he was at home. Now the place teemed with active soldiers.

Yes, the stables were better. Here, at least, he was

alone, now that the early evening guard had left for the night. He could walk to relieve the tedium of the long hours, the view was pleasant, and soft nickers soothed him far more than human conversation. He was free to ponder in solitude, though his thoughts gave him no peace.

It seemed to Eric that his twenty-four years shouldn't be enough to make him feel old. Yet old was how he felt, and sad, when he looked at what the kingdom had become in two short months.

It was as if all of Archeld had darkened. People neither laughed as much nor talked as loud as they once had. It was strange to have Vesputo behaving like a king, when he'd never been crowned, and people scrambling to serve him, as if it were an honor. He was going to marry Princess Torina, everyone knew, but . . .

Eric missed the princess. Oh, she'd led him on many a goose chase over the years. In the old days, whoever was on duty might find himself looking for her. Now it was a pity. Everyone said she was half-mad. Never let anyone near her but Vesputo.

And the queen? No one saw her any more either. She kept to her rooms, and there were rumors.

Eric's thoughts broke mid-branch at the sound of soft, hurrying footsteps. He knew his orders. He was supposed to hail whoever it was, loud enough for the other guards to hear. Instead, he stepped back into the shadow of the stable and watched to see who was coming.

It was a woman. Eric knew her. That veil, that hair. Only Irene dressed and walked that way.

She sauntered up to him, all silk and lace. "I need the

king's horse. Vesputo commands it." Her voice sounded strained.

Eric felt anger welling. "You get no horse just by saying Vesputo. Do you carry his ring?" He folded his arms. "Besides," he continued, "he's not king yet. And you are no princess."

He thought she was breathing very hard. Too hard. He stared at her, annoyed at the way the veil kept her face from him, puzzled that she wore no cape in the chilly air.

She reached her hands to the veil as if it was something heavy to lift and pulled up the gossamer fabric.

The princess! It was she. But her face was all changed. Thin and white. Her face had always reminded him of a rose. Smooth and pink and full of sweet life. She used to have a joyful glow. That was gone. Now she looked like something was hunting her that she wanted to kill.

"Now will you give me a horse?" she asked.

"Princess!"

"I need a horse. Please. If you ever loved your king or me."

"Where are you going?"

"Away." She looked at him with unwavering eyes, and no smile. She always used to smile, at least a little, when she talked.

"You've gone mad, just as they say!" It was out before he could think.

For a moment, he saw the familiar Princess Torina blaze into her face. "Do my old friends believe that drivel? Do I look mad?"

Eric smiled suddenly. He wondered how he could have trusted such a tale.

If she was sane, though, something was very wrong.

He drew her into the darkness of the stable wall, putting a finger to his lips.

"Where have you been, then, Princess?" he asked softly.

"Vesputo killed the king and wants to force a marriage. I've been a prisoner since my father's death. Vesputo says if I tell my mother she'll be killed." The words rushed from her like a flooded stream.

Eric's smile vanished. "V-Vesputo killed King Kareed?"

"Yes, Eric, he did. Please. We must hurry! I just escaped and need a horse."

Eric gaped at her pale, pleading face, her thin hands twisting over each other. Was this, then, the truth he had vaguely sensed? A murderer posing as king? He heard a faint ringing in his ears. His legs and arms floated in a tingling numbness.

He nodded and opened the stable, taking the lantern from where it hung on a hook by the door. Torina followed him in. Lantern light flickered and danced. The animals stirred. Torina went to Amber's stall.

"The king's horse! How will I explain his disappearance?"

She stopped and stood very still for a moment. Under the stillness, she was shivering. She turned to look him in the face.

"I have a long way to go and must travel fast. This is the only horse that can hope to outrun Vesputo. When he finds I'm gone, he'll do everything to hunt me. And if you want your story to be believed, Irene asked for the king's horse. What other horse would he ride?"

"How did you escape? Who guarded you?"

She glanced at her clothes. "The less you understand, the longer you'll live. Oh Eric, come away with me now. That way I won't fear for you." She trembled.

"No, Princess. I asked Nassa to marry me. I can't leave her."

"Please, Eric. You can send for her. If he learns that you helped me . . ." Her eyes spilled over.

"No. Nassa would be at risk then. You must have fooled many guards already to get this far?"

She nodded miserably.

"Vesputo would never hang so many. If he spares any of us, he'll spare us all."

She turned away, back toward the stall, mopping her cheeks with her hands like a child. Eric helped her saddle Amber. She led the golden stallion out into the moonlight and swerved him into the trees.

"I forgot. Are there any stable rags for me to wear? This ridiculous dress . . ."

He darted back into the stable. He came out shaking straw from a bundle, also carrying two thick saddle blankets.

"Here. So you can live to return."

She had mounted the horse. "Which way?" she asked.

"Take the old trail to the river. The only one not guarded," he advised.

She nodded. "And past that? I'm going to Desante."

"Then ride due east. That way, the towns soon dry up. Not many settlements in that part of the foothills, and few garrisons at the border, maybe only one. But it'll be hard going, straight over Missht Pass."

"Thank you. Please, Eric. Come with me."

He gave her a shaky smile. "No. I'm not ready to go, and you must leave now."

They clasped hands.

"Thank you again and again. And if you can find a way to do it without risking your life, please let my mother know."

"I will. Good-bye, Princess."

She kissed her hand to him, kneed Amber, and trotted away.

❖   ❖   ❖

Vesputo stood beside the wooden frame of Torina's bed, holding a cap with a red braid attached. Irene sat on the bed, head in her hands, groggy and weeping. She could feel spikes of hair sticking out wildly from her scalp. Beside her, Toban was shaking his head back and forth. Beron hung behind Toban.

"She wore her dress. She had her hair!" Toban said.

Irene sobbed.

"What did she say to you?" Vesputo's voice clattered, like slivers of ice falling.

Toban thought. "Wait." He turned, waved two fingers, stopped. "That was it. She waved two fingers as Irene does. No words."

Irene wailed, running hands through her hair.

"Quiet!" Vesputo snapped. She smothered her sobs. "Toban, who else knows of this?"

"Only us, in this room."

Vesputo paced, his two index fingers together. After a moment he turned back to Irene, grasping her shoulders.

"Irene, you told me the wedding dress is ready."

She sniffed. "Yes."

"You will wear it. We'll have the wedding as planned. You take the bride's place and wear a veil. The red braid will convince witnesses."

Irene stared, stunned. "A wedding?"

"Yes, my love."

"What about Princess Torina?"

"She'll be found and brought back to be queen in name. But you'll be the true queen. Beron, get me Mavell, the aging priest, the one whose sight is failing. Then meet me at the stables. Toban, give a potion to the queen. Make her too sick to attend the ceremony. She would not be deceived."

The two men left. Vesputo sat beside Irene on the bed. "I assume, my dear, that because you were drugged, you never took the crystal out into the moonlight last night?"

Irene quailed. "N-no, my lord."

"So it will be another cycle before you can dream of seeing the future?"

"N-no, my lord." Her teeth chattered.

"Why no?"

"B-because the crystal was in my dress. I had it with m-me. Torina took my dress."

"Torina has the crystal?"

"Y-yes."

"I see." His eyes appeared very dark.

He got up and went out, leaving her to cry.

Eric paced the night out, his mind stuttering over Torina's words.

As long as she was there beside him, he thought only of how to ease her escape. Once she had gone, he staggered into the truth of what she left behind. And he was afraid. He guessed he was the only one who knew.

Who do I go to? Who will believe me? Who will act on my word? If I tell the wrong man, I'll be killed. If I tell the right man, civil war will tear this land apart.

As dawn broke, an old soldier named Ward relieved Eric's watch. Ward had been in Kareed's service since that king was a baby. Eric was tempted to tell him the events of the night and ask his advice, but thought better of it.

When Eric mentioned that Irene had taken Amber for Vesputo to ride, Ward shook his gray head. Eric went home to his soldier's shack. He lay down, sweating with fear.

❖   ❖   ❖

Far across the plains of Archeld, Amber trotted on. His coat blended with the high golden grasses of late fall.

"With luck, we'll seem to be only a small stubborn wind, blowing east," Torina muttered.

She searched the landscape for a stream. She'd been taught geography. Many narrow waterways edged toward the sea from the eastern mountains.

Beyond the mountains, Desante.

It had been a long, cold night. Torina drew the saddle blankets closer. Never in her life had she known what it meant to be cold or hungry. Always a fire as near as she wanted. Always warm, fleecy capes, the best in Archeld. Food in plenty. Now cloudy skies threatened rain, and even though she knew rain would wash away her tracks enough to hope for escape, she wanted to stay dry. She was too cold, too tired, and too hungry.

They'd followed the old, overgrown trail Eric advised, crossed the moonlit river, and gained the trees on the far banks. There she'd reined in Amber and slid to the ground. With feverish haste, she undressed in the chilly night. She scrabbled in the dirt with her dagger and made a quick grave for Irene's finery. As she tore the braided cap from her head and shook out her short, rough-cut hair, she cried. She found it strange; the tears that had dried into her soul for her murdered father flowed easily at the thought of her long hair, gone.

"I *am* mad, as they say!" She trampled Irene's yellow braid. The rough cloth of the old stable rags rasped her skin.

She looked at the crystal. *Just this once, can you show me my own future?*

In the faint moonlight she looked for some vision, anything at all to help her. But her seer's eye was closed, as she had known it would be. She mounted Amber and rode hard out of the trees, on to the dark plain, following the eastern stars.

Now, all about her, the wide rolling grasses stretched. This was the domain of herds, not people. Beyond, tantalizingly near, the Cheldan Mountains, the border of Archeld and Desante. She guessed the mountains appeared much closer than they were. Guessed, too, that if she didn't cross them before being overtaken, she would lose her life.

The horse was tired. She guided him along seepage that turned into a trickling stream.

"Drink," she told Amber, gliding from his back. "Drink and eat."

Together the young woman and the stallion bent their heads to the soft shining water.

❖ ❖ ❖

Loud pounding on his door made Eric's heart stumble painfully. He prayed he looked like a man wakened from sleep, as he opened to Beron. His boyhood bane glared at him, sullen eyes narrowed.

"What is it?"

"Come with me to the stable. The king wants to talk to you."

"What time is it?" Eric yawned.

"I said come with me."

"Why?"

"A horse is missing from your watch."

Eric forced himself to grin. "I gave out one horse on my watch. Amber. For Vesputo. Are you telling me he stole a horse?"

"Get dressed."

At the stable, Vesputo stood under the cloudy sky, crisp and unruffled. Soldiers said that dust parted for Vesputo. His calm in battle was legendary. Now it seemed horrible to Eric.

"A horse is missing," Vesputo said.

Eric swallowed, trying to find moisture for his dry tongue. He wanted to blurt out everything: the princess, the murder . . .

"Tell us about it," Vesputo commanded.

"Uh, Irene came and said—"

"When was this?"

"Just before the watch changed," Eric lied.

"You're certain?"

"Yes, sir. She said she needed the king's horse. That Vesputo commanded it."

"Irene came to you for my horse, and you gave it to her!"

Eric wanted to shout: not your horse! You are not the king! That stallion is with his rightful owner.

"W-well, there was no reason to question her."

"There is always reason to question when you're the guard on duty. I'd venture to say that questioning is your reason to be there. Why would I send a woman?"

"I wondered on it, sir, but hated to refuse her, you being new to me as king."

"You're certain it was Irene?" Vesputo looked hard at him.

"Blonde hair, sir, and the way she dresses." Eric hoped the fear in his voice would be natural at such a time.

"You acted foolishly. You're relieved of your watch and confined till I give you leave."

"Sorry, sir." Eric caught Beron's malicious grin. "Sir, if I may ask, what happened to the horse?"

"Irene has not returned him."

A gloating Beron, who told him it was his bad luck he would miss the wedding ceremony that afternoon, escorted Eric back to his bed.

"Wedding?"

"Vesputo marries the Princess Torina today," taunted Beron.

Eric clutched the doorjamb. "Excuse me, I need to sleep."

He went inside and heard pebbles crunching as Beron

stomped off. He laid himself stiffly on his bunk, his thoughts jangling like a row of bells.

Had Torina been caught? If she was, where was Amber? Maybe in the excitement of the ceremony he could talk to someone.

Emid! I must speak to Emid. He knows me, loves Torina. He'll know where to begin. But how do I get to him?

Eric crawled to the window, peeking out. He saw a four-man guard from another division take places near his quarters.

❖   ❖   ❖

In the woods beyond the stables, Vesputo knelt, examining the tracks of a large stallion. Beside him, Beron scratched his chin.

"That girl is more clever than I guessed," Vesputo said, swearing. "Can you track Amber?"

"Yes, sir. I doubt she knows any avoidance tricks."

"And if she does?"

"I can track her, sir."

"There's no one else I can send. I need Toban here with me to deal with the queen. This secret is too important to share."

"I understand, sir."

"Then leave at once. Return only if you find her or lose her trail."

"And when I find her?"

"Bring her back, alive. No one must see her but me. Saddle Engan. She's the fastest mare and easy to guide. Torina has a start of a few hours, but she must sleep sometime. Toban prepared a stimulant for you. Use it sparingly." Vesputo handed a small flask to the young captain.

❖ ❖ ❖

Honored guests crowded onto old stone benches in the castle's ancient chapel to see the wedding of their princess.

Emid shouldered his way to the front bench and made deep obeisance to God before taking his seat on the aisle. Servants had gone to a great deal of trouble to fill the chapel with a mood of festivity. Large vases filled with dried flowers stood by the walls. Garlands of bright leaves were hung. But to Emid, the musician's flutes sounded like cheerful whistles at a funeral—out of place.

Mavell, the oldest priest in Archeld, shuffled to the altar, his failing eyes wandering to some inner sanctum. Dark green robes fell around his frail shoulders in deep folds as he raised his hands.

"The queen is too ill to view the wedding. She sends her blessing," he announced in a quavering voice.

Emid frowned. *Too ill! Why not hold off the ceremony till she recovers?*

The trainer was filled with foreboding. He shifted anxiously on the hard seat.

From a side entrance, Vesputo appeared, dressed in traditional bridegroom's green. He looked unusually handsome and strong. Too strong. The man was a rock, unmoved by the waves of lives beating around him. There he was, thrust early into kingship, not turning a hair.

If Landen killed King Kareed as they say, then I'm to blame.

Emid sat rigid, remembering. *That day in the meadow, did I make the wrong decision?*

He saw the shining memory of two royal children, playing at archery and filled with friendship. What had happened to that secret alliance?

Emid sighed. He didn't know. Had never used his knowledge or position to learn more. And now the king was dead.

Did Landen kill Kareed? I don't believe he did. The bright, keen blade of Landen's soul is too sharp and clean for murder.

But if he didn't? Who then?

A chilly current ran over Emid. He shook it off, turning his head with the others, to see Torina walking toward the altar.

Dressed in a pale green bride's gown, face hidden behind an opaque veil, she walked slowly. The thick red hair, hanging beneath a green satin cap in a single braid, was all that identified the once high-spirited girl. Her gloved hands were clenched.

As the soft skirts moved by him, the trainer felt a pressing sense of unease. There was something alien about that faceless female figure. Throughout the brief ceremony, she didn't lift her veil. He gazed at her, straining to catch the whispered syllables that pronounced her Vesputo's wife. He was filled with agonized nostalgia for the unruly princess who seemed to have died along with her father. Sitting straight and stern on the bench, the aging warrior had tears in his eyes.

As the wedding finished, the priest led the gathering in a short prayer. When Emid's head came up, he saw

Vesputo lead his bride out through the side entrance. The door shut behind them.

Emid moved quickly to Mavell, grasping the old priest's arm.

"Mavell."

Clouded eyes looked past him. "Emid?"

"Yes. Mavell, you spoke with the princess?"

"I spoke with the young lady." Gently, Mavell disengaged his arm and turned to the altar. He began chanting one of the long prayers of blessing.

Emid strode from the chapel.

Torina guessed it was close to evening, though low clouds shut out the sun. The air was colder again, gray light changing to duller gray. They were in the foothills. She had ridden all day with no food, taking only a few stops for water and to allow Amber to graze. The stallion trotted more slowly. Torina grappled with the fatigue that begged her to rest. Soon sleep would take her, no matter what she did.

They came to a wide, bubbling stream. As Amber stooped his head, Torina collapsed on the ground. She crawled to the water's edge to drink heaving gulps. Lying on the stream bank, she never wanted to move again. The beautiful stallion lapped the water, then nudged her. She pulled herself up on his back and urged him into the water, across the stream, where trees grew near.

She could go no further. Spreading her blankets under a great willow, she mumbled a prayer. Girl and horse slept deeply in the twilight.

❖ ❖ ❖

Torina woke confused, believing herself in bed, a prisoner of Vesputo. A mist seemed to creep around her. How did fog get into her room?

The horse near her nickered, and she remembered. Her escape, flight, the day on the plains. She was free, and hungry, in the foothills of the Cheldan Mountains. Stiffly, she stood and faced the day.

Mist curled around them, the kind that would soon become fine rain. Torina went to the stream to drink, feeling lightheaded. In the soft mud of the bank were the prints of Amber's hooves, unmistakable. She looked across the quick water and sighed.

"Amber, my friend. You and I must separate."

She drank as much as she could. Amber came up beside her to quench his thirst too. When he finished, she hugged his dripping nose.

"Only you could have carried me so far, so fast. And now, it's time for you to go home."

The horse eyed her and pricked up his ears.

"Yes. Your strength saved me. I can't let it betray me." Her tears ran, as she stroked his huge flanks and rubbed his mane. "Go now, Amber. Go home."

She slapped him gently. He lowered his great head and nuzzled her before splashing across the stream and moving into the grass to graze. She watched him munch for a while, then saw him amble west, taking with him the final tie to her former life.

She took off the sturdy, overlarge shoes and socks Eric had provided, wrapping them in a blanket. She rolled up her trouser legs and forged into the icy stream. Her feet instantly turned a protesting red. From somewhere deep in herself, she summoned the blood of the warrior line of Archeld and waded east through pebbly water. It had to be done. She had not come this far to yield. Next to Vesputo, the cold was nothing.

❖ ❖ ❖

Beron was forced to stop when night fell; the tracks, easy enough to follow in daylight, became impossible in darkness. Dead grass swam around him as he pitched his tent and rolled up in his blankets.

Dawn was well advanced when he rose. A soft rain dripped from gray skies. He ate cheese and bread, then mounted Engan and rode on. By afternoon, he could make out the foothills rising from the misty ground, though he met with no other travelers.

He chuckled when he found signs of Torina drinking beside the stallion. The silly girl knew nothing of how to hide her trail. And she must not have any food with her! It was only a matter of time before he caught up. He paused for lunch.

The grass parted for him, Amber's trail plain as if painted in red. He constantly scanned the dim horizon for any signs of Torina. In two hours, he was rewarded with sight of a persistent runnel in the grass ahead. Soon the runnel produced hoofbeats, and there was Amber, tossing his golden head, neighing to the mare.

Beron frowned. Why had she allowed Amber to escape? Did she fall asleep, slip off his back? Eric said she left at daybreak. She must have ridden hard, without stopping, to come so far.

He tried to catch the stallion's bridle, but the horse would not allow it. Amber was known for being particular. After fruitless attempts, Beron decided to waste no more time. The horse was valuable, very valuable, but would doubtless find his own way home.

As hours passed and the afternoon edged toward evening, Beron was puzzled. Amber's trail was plain. But how had she come so far? Unless Eric lied about the time! Perhaps he knew it was she! That would explain things.

Beron picked up his pace, not wanting to come to the end of the day without finding her. That would give her a chance.

Gray twilight found him at the banks of a stream in the foothills, sodden and bad tempered. Rain was washing away Amber's tracks, but he could still see them by the stream. There they stopped and turned back.

Beron nosed about in the gathering darkness, the brim of his hat dripping with rain. Nothing. Frustrated, he splashed across the water and found a scattering of muddy prints and a depression in the ground. He ran up and down the streambed where the tracks disappeared, cursing. As true night fell, he coaxed a fire to burn and pitched his tent, plotting vengeance on Eric. Amber had traveled too great a distance to have left at the time Eric said. *He lied.*

Torina lay in the crook of a tree hanging over the water. She had made a tortuous trek, wading till her feet were numb and raw, then climbing up an overhanging branch and warming her toes by blowing on them, rubbing them, wrapping them. Then down again into the cold, cold water, pushing on, her lips tight, chin stiff, blankets heavy with rain. Up to some sheltering tree, teeth chattering, blowing, rubbing, wrapping. So the day went, and at last she could stand no more. She climbed into another huge willow. The tree must have stood for centuries. Its twisted branches welcomed the hungry, soaked princess.

She had walked all day and never touched a foot to the banks. She believed her trail was invisible but could not celebrate.

❖ ❖ ❖

Three days later, Beron stood before Vesputo, his clothes a mass of mud, face beaded with sweat. Vesputo's handsome face was grim. "Well, Captain?"

Beron licked his lips. "Sir, her tracks disappeared by a stream bank across the plains, in the first foothills."

"Did you follow the stream?"

"I looked on both banks for a distance of ten miles, and found nothing. No footprints. No hairs of her head."

"Signs of struggle?"

"None, sir. No blood, no bones, no marks of being dragged, not even rearranged ground; but then, it rained."

Vesputo frowned. "Do you believe she's alive?"

"My lord, if I hadn't seen it myself, I would say it was impossible. If a man came to me with the tale I have for you, I'd send him away and curse him."

Vesputo smiled his chilly smile. "Ah, Captain. But I believe you're neither a fool nor a liar. She's simply more clever than we knew."

"Thank you, sir."

"Without help, she must soon starve or freeze. You're certain she traveled alone?"

"Yes, sir. However, I met Amber on the second day of tracking her. And sir, when I followed his tracks they ended in the foothills. Eric must have lied about the time."

❖ ❖ ❖

Vesputo stood on the lookout set atop a high rocky outcropping and took in the wide sweep of valley below. Far away, the formidable outline of the Cheldan Mountains cut the sky. Vesputo had never been across those mountains; his campaigns always waged north or south. King Ardesen, ruler of Desante, had kept an uneasy truce with Kareed. A messenger was sent to him reporting Kareed's death. The man returned with Ardesen's condolences. He spoke of the journey as treacherous.

Could Torina cross the mountains at the edge of winter and live? What would she tell the soldiers guarding the borders? She'd look an odd figure indeed, with cropped red hair, dressed in silk, probably wrapped in stable blankets. Vesputo chewed his lip in agitation. Beron had followed orders too closely, returning when he lost her trail. Now they must trust to cold, damp, and hunger to finish her.

Gravel crunched behind him. Beron led Eric up the path. Eric's hands were tied behind his back, but his step was firm and strong, as though his legs refused disgrace. The clear, dark eyes were circled with fatigue.

Vesputo waited till the other two were next to him.

"Look out across that plain, Eric," he said, "and tell me how a horse taken close to dawn could travel to the foothills and back again by the next day?"

A muscle in Eric's face twitched. "So far?"

"You lied about the time the horse was taken. Why?"

"I—I . . ."

"How long did you know the Princess Torina?"

"All her life."

"She may be on the point of death." Vesputo smiled tightly, watching.

"Y-your wife is ill?"

"My wife is in the best of health." Vesputo made a broad gesture toward the plain. "But Torina, out there alone, without food or warm clothes . . ."

The young man's face paled.

"Yes, she rode due east. Come, Eric, you're too wise a soldier to give away my most valuable horse to a lady at dawn, even if she mentions the name of her king. But a wild-eyed princess in late evening, ah now . . ."

He was surprised to see Eric straighten, the color rushing to his face. "You haven't captured her then! But who did you marry?"

Vesputo ignored the question. "Did she convince you with her babble? Enough to forget that your first duty is to the king you serve?"

Eric took a deep breath, looking out across the valley.

"The king I serve is dead. *You* are not my king. And all your power wasn't enough to stop Torina. I serve *her*."

Vesputo drew his sword. It whistled loudly, stopping Eric's words. Eric twisted, crumpled, fell. Beron's mouth hung open, his eyes glistening. Vesputo guessed his feelings. It was hard, sometimes, to see the death of an old

142

enemy. Hadn't Beron and Eric been rivals since they were boys? Ah, that was much more personal than a stranger picked out in battle.

Vesputo cleaned his sword. "See that he gets an honorable burial," he said. "Died doing his duty."

❖ ❖ ❖

Irene shifted her weight, admiring the exquisite soft lace of her gown. How fine it was! She curled a finger inside her short hair. How long would it take to grow? She smiled at Vesputo, then pouted. "When is Torina coming so I can go out again?"

He gave her a long look. Her scalp prickled.

"Where is the cap with Torina's hair?" he asked.

"In the cupboard. I can't bear looking at it. It reminds me she cut mine off."

"Put it on, my dear." *How cold his voice sounded!*

"Are we going out?"

"Put it on, and I'll tell you."

Irene opened the cupboard. There sat the cap with Torina's braid pinned to it. How Irene wished she dared burn it. Reluctantly, she picked it up between finger and thumb.

"Unbraid it, my love."

Irene loosed the ribbon, and the lustrous richness of another woman's hair spilled into her lap.

"Wear it," Vesputo said.

She put the hated thing on her head, fussing with the fit until it was snug. Vesputo helped her tuck away every strand of blonde, but left the veil up.

"Are we going out?" she asked again.

Strong arms went around her. "Sorry, darling. All I need is a body."

She was melting into him, but her back stiffened at his words. "A body?"

"Sh-sh."

A rending pain tore her as his dagger slid between her ribs. He was letting her go, she was falling onto the bed, her vision filled with the red stain that ruined her dress. Astounded by her bodily agony, she wanted to hurt him back, to see his calm change to fear. From a distance, she heard a roar coming toward her. She must speak before the roar silenced her. She tried to see his face, but it was blurring. Everything glazed over and fell dark.

Chapter 9

Queen Dreea sat in a chair near the wall of her bedroom. Thick, dark curtains were drawn across the windows, making the air dim and gloomy. She stared ahead, trying to find her way through the fog in her mind.

Someone had spoken to her. She knew who it was but couldn't think of his name. A handsome, dark-haired man, very familiar. She rubbed her tired eyes. Her arms felt heavy, as though lead had been sewed into her sleeves.

"Sorry, sir. What did you tell me?"

"My queen, I'm sorry to be the one to give you such news."

"What's the matter with me? Send for a doctor," she said. Her voice sounded far away.

"Certainly, my queen. In time."

"Something is wrong with me . . . Who are you? This room is so dark."

"Madam, I bring you news."

"Where is my daughter? Why does Torina keep me away? I love her."

"Torina is dead. She died yesterday."

"I don't understand you. What did you say?"

The man turned to a shadow behind him and murmured to it. The shadow mumbled back.

She was missing something, something that gave her peace.

"Have you brought my goblet?" It was a terrible effort to speak.

The men were still muttering together. She heard them say "doctor." The shadow shook its head. The dark-haired man stood.

"The funeral is tomorrow. Make her ready for it. She must be there." He faded away.

The shadow moved forward, grabbed her face, looked into her eyes and mouth. Then he too disappeared.

Dreea was alone. She tried to get up and move to the bed. The room spun sickly. She held on to the chair, waiting for the world to right itself. It took a long time. As she stood, her legs trembled. She leaned against the wall. Her hand felt soft drapes. She tugged on them for support. A shaft of brilliant light shot out, stabbing her eyes. A window. Dreea buried her face in the drapes to escape the excruciating light.

"Wait," she said. "Wait for your eyes."

Gradually, her pupils accepted the day. She opened the curtains a little further, leaning on the sill. The exertion made her sweat.

She made her way to the bed, shivering violently. She crawled between the covers, overpowered with anguish.

The shadow came in, carrying a goblet. He leaned over her, prying open her chattering teeth. He was poised to pour it down her throat. But it smelled bitter . . . no, it should not be bitter and dark. It should be sweet and cherry colored. Dreea knocked the goblet from his hand. Sweat soaked her gown.

She tried to sit up. Her body would not obey. He lifted her, gave her a glass. Water—she gulped it, still pouring sweat. She asked for more and he gave her more. Her stomach churned and heaved, expelling its contents. When the fit of sickness passed, he stowed her in a chair propped with pillows. He cleaned the bed.

Dreea felt more exhausted than she had believed possible, but her hazy head was clearing. Something inside told her to conceal this from the man who now lifted her into bed again. Her forehead throbbed. The man paced beside her for a while, then put a hand on her damp forehead. At last, she heard him leave.

What sickness was this? Had she been poisoned? Her dear Kareed was poisoned.

She tried to remember. Thick mist swallowed her recollections. Kareed had been killed. And she hadn't seen her daughter. Torina stayed locked in her room, and Vesputo . . . Vesputo said they must not disturb her.

Why had she listened to him? She was Torina's mother. She knew her child. Torina needed her.

I must go to her.

Dreea sat up, but lacked the strength to stand. Where was Mirandae? The queen called faintly. Why was no one there? The man who tended her, who was he? Where had she seen him before? For he was familiar. He'd been in her room many times, felt her pulse and looked at her tongue. Sometimes given her drinks to help her sleep. Was he a doctor?

"Drinks to help me sleep," she said aloud. An image floated through her mind, a silver goblet on a silver tray. A pretty woman bending over her.

He had left the water pitcher. Arduously, she poured for herself, crying at her weakness. She tried to recall when it had started, how it had started.

❖ ❖ ❖

Torina struggled against a heavy wind, her desperately cold hands wound inside the blanket she clutched around her body. She tried to hear the sounds of her own life, her ragged breathing and shuffling footsteps, but the wind overpowered them. Cracked lips raised to the freezing snow as she prayed ceaselessly for strength to gain the summit. She knew it was close, for nothing grew here, nothing but rocks, snow, and wind.

In this wild desolation, she lost all fear of pursuit and traveled the open pathway, the only one. Here, sharp stones were worn down into a semblance of a trail. The track seemed to tell her this crossing was possible; others had gone before her.

Weariness dragged at her, a cloying imperative companion she longed to send away, one who tried to shout down her inner voice, tie up her spirit; one who promised peace and comfort if only she would stop. The wind seemed to be Vesputo pushing her back. She fought him with all her will, ignoring the demands of fatigue.

There it was: the endless view that proclaimed her triumph. She was at the top. Below, the welcome rim of trees, seemingly close. Not too far away, a garrison post, wedged into the edge of the trees. Beyond that, valleys. She could even see distant cultivated fields and a wide swath of blue sky.

Torina began the descent, grateful that, in Archeld, shoes for stable-hands were made thick and strong, for she knew it was time to leave the path again. If she stayed on the trail, they'd find her. She climbed over boulders and slid on the crunching slag, aiming herself at the tree line, sure that if she could get out of the wind, she'd win those far and beautiful fields.

It was evening. Three more times Dreea's body had sent her through a racking spate of nausea. The same man gave her water and tried to get her to drink the bitter brew. Each time she was sick, he cleaned the bed, saying nothing.

Her body craved something.

When Vesputo appeared with the other man, she knew his name. Her wits were clearing.

She trembled with desire when she saw the goblet resting on its silver tray. Her nerves clamored with raw longing as the man brought it near. It smelled right, not bitter. The man smiled at her.

"Better, my queen?" His tone was deferential, not fooling her.

She doubted he knew she remembered anything. The inner prompting guided her to pretend. "Better, thank you. What was the matter with me?"

"A sickness."

"Thank you for bringing my cordial." Her hands shook with the wish to drink it. "Vesputo, where is Mirandae?"

A small frown appeared on Vesputo's forehead and disappeared like a wrinkle smoothed by a hot iron. "Mirandae has been with her dying mother these last two months, my queen."

"Why don't I remember?" Dreea rubbed her eyes. "So tired. I need to sleep."

"Madam, there is news I must tell you."

"Please, Vesputo. It can wait till morning."

"Madam, do you remember that Torina and I were married several days ago?"

"M-married?" She shook her head stupidly. "No, Vesputo. How could I remember something . . . I knew nothing about?"

"Ah, my queen, your illness is at fault. You were told, of course. Torina particularly wanted you to be there."

"She's better then? She'll see me now?" Dreea's heart fluttered and leaped.

"No, my queen. She is past seeing."

"P-past seeing?"

Vesputo sat in a chair beside the bed and took her hands. "She died yesterday, by her own hand. She never recovered from her grief."

"D-died? Impossible! She would not!"

"I'm afraid it's true."

"It isn't true! I know my daughter. She would never— never leave without saying good-bye." Dreea yanked her hands away from him.

She stared at Vesputo. Looking at his familiar face, she felt as though she saw him for the first time. He was a monster, not a man. He was lying, lying, lying. Torina was not dead.

From a deep, strong cavern in her heart, something told her what to do. She must say nothing to these men. They were the enemy. Dreea made herself stare glassily at them.

"I know this must be a trial for you," Vesputo said.

She didn't answer.

"The funeral is tomorrow afternoon. You will want to be there."

Dreea didn't miss the command concealed in his oily words. She nodded.

"Leave me, please," she told them. "And send me a woman tomorrow, to help me bathe and dress. I need more water. I have a dreadful thirst." Vesputo bowed.

They left. Dreea looked at the goblet, still sitting there, enticing her. She clenched her fists till her nails drew blood. She felt drawn inexorably to the sweet, delicious drink beside her.

"No," she whispered. "No."

Drenched in sweat, she swung her legs to the floor and stood. The room spun. She waited for it to pass. She picked up the goblet.

"Only one drop. Just a sip," she pleaded with herself. "One sip won't do me any harm."

Panting and swaying, she staggered to the hearth. She threw the contents of the goblet into the fire. It steamed and hissed.

"No more," she groaned, stumbling to the bed. She replaced the goblet on its tray.

The shadow man returned with a pitcher of water. She saw his eyes register the empty goblet.

"Will there be anything else, madam?" he asked, as if it were a normal evening.

"No. I need to sleep."

❖ ❖ ❖

The darkness seemed alive, pressing on her. Goblin shapes glided around her bed, hissing at her, gibbering evilly, a reverberating sound that bounced endlessly through her room. The lonely queen feared her reason was undone forever. As a demon form sat on her chest, squeezing her life, she began to wish for death.

A terrible thought occurred to her. What if Torina had also been drugged? What if her daughter was visited by these hellish visions? Would it be enough to impel the girl to stab out her life? Perhaps Vesputo told the truth.

"No," Dreea whispered. The demon grinned and devoured the rest of her breath.

She prayed to God for help, asking for a sign that her daughter lived.

All night, she was mocked and menaced by grotesque forms. It seemed each one seized a piece of her soul and ran about the room with it, cackling in glee. She tried to call back the scavenged parts of herself. But all seemed cut apart, deformed, despairing. And always, the paralyzing doubt followed her. Torina could be dead.

Near dawn, Dreea lay in a pool of sweat, her water pitcher empty, heart hammering a litany of exhausted fear. She was sure death would come soon, that her heart would simply cease to beat. She had given up praying. Her body was turned toward the curtained window.

A pink shaft of light penetrated. The distraught

queen focused on the ray of sun, clinging to it like a frightened child will hold its mother's hand. Someone was walking into the room on that beam of light. Torina. The girl's luminous eyes held her mother. She raised an arm.

"Live," the vision said. "You must live!"

"Yes," Dreea vowed. "Yes. I'll never drink it again."

The apparition faded. Dreea threw off her blankets. She groped for the window. Fluttering hands reached for the wide dawn.

"I'm alive," she told the sun. "And so is Torina."

Later a serving-woman came. Dreea knew her—Amile. A kindly, simple-minded woman. Dreea confided she was hungry, and Amile was glad to bring a lunch. As the queen ate, some of the trembling left her hands. She drank another pitcher of water. Amile helped her bathe and dress. The queen called for a mirror.

The reflection startled her. Her hair was completely white. Purple circled her eyes. Amile braided her hair and wound it around her head, then added the simple coronet Dreea preferred. All the time, the queen sat lost in thought.

She was carried to the cemetery in a litter. The closed coffin, decked with dried flowers, sat near. She was among the first mourners to arrive. Vesputo was there, wearing Kareed's crown. With flawless courtesy, he assisted her to a chair. A few others stood near, Emid among them.

The trainer bowed over her hand. She took his rough, scarred fingers, thinking that he, too, had aged many years in a few months.

"Stay close to me, Emid, please," she said. "It does me good to see you, on this dark day." She looked into his eyes, searching for a sign of willingness to speak her code. He met her gaze. Her frazzled heart smiled as he took a place by her chair.

"Vesputo," she said calmly.

"My queen."

"Vesputo, as I had no chance to say good-bye to my daughter, please, open the coffin before the other mourners get here. Let me see her face."

There was hardly a flicker of alarm on that smooth, handsome face. "Out of the question, madam. The sight is too horrible and you are too frail."

From the corner of her eye, Dreea observed Emid standing rigid, scarcely breathing. Dreea closed her eyes to hide the fierce surge of hope in her heart. Vesputo had answered. She was convinced. It was not her daughter's body in that coffin.

Whose then? And where was Torina?

It seemed to Dreea that in only a few moments, a thousand soldiers surrounded her. They were everywhere, a dark mass of Archeldan green. Did Vesputo have so much power, then? These were all young men, and she didn't remember their faces.

"Ah, my lord, perhaps you know best." She saw him relax. "I must be ruled by you."

He took her hand. "Madam, your wisdom is an inspiration."

"Vesputo." She lowered her voice, but not enough for Emid not to overhear. "I need your protection."

"Protection, madam?"

"Someone has been drugging me."

She had startled him. "Drugging you, madam? In the castle? Surely not."

She leaned in nearer. "I believe it's that woman, Irene. The one who brings my cordial at night."

"How can this be?"

"Believe me, sir. It's the only explanation. My mind has been crowded with grief, but I would never forget my God." She was speaking to Emid, hoping he heard.

"My dear queen, I'll do everything in my power."

"Thank you, Vesputo. I knew I could trust you. Please send for Mirandae to attend me. And ask Emid to recommend a guard. I'll need a doctor too."

"Certainly. You have only to ask." His face was a cold, dangerous mask.

"Now that my family is dead," Dreea told him, "I wish to withdraw from public life. As you know, it's never interested me. I'll weave and visit the poor. The kingdom is safe in your hands. Remember, you can't be too careful. I suggest you hire a taster for yourself."

"I'll consider it." The dangerous edge blunted.

He went to greet important people. She turned to Emid, wanting to hold his steady arm. The trainer gave her the barest nod. She took a great breath and sank back in her cushions, tears of relief welling.

Dreea listened to her daughter's memorial. The crowd of mourners was enormous, most people wracked with grief. Truell, the priest who gave the eulogy, was sometimes too overcome to speak. Poor man. He believed Torina was dead. They all thought she was gone.

Dreea hugged to herself the belief that her daughter lived. But as the service continued, she was consumed with longing for the silver goblet. Sweat started out all over her. By the time the coffin was lowered, her strength had fled. She saw the people lining up to kiss her hand.

"Emid," she said, tugging his sleeve. "I must go . . . take me home."

She saw the shock on his face, felt the welcome power of his arms, heard his great voice summoning help. Boys herded around her; a man with a kind face felt her pulse, patting her back. She was lifted into the litter.

Vesputo was there, ordering every care be given her, urging the people to return home, as the queen was ill.

❖   ❖   ❖

Alone in the king's rooms, Vesputo paced, needing to think.

Toban had given Dreea too much poison; it had nearly killed her. He was told to sedate her enough to miss the wedding. Now, due to her public allegations of being drugged (and Vesputo was sure more than one person had overheard her) it was no longer possible to continue with the charade of slowly diminishing health.

Vesputo swore to himself. A few more months would have accomplished her death, quietly. What was he to do? The people loved their gentle queen. If she died now, rumors would start and questions be asked. Too many questions could lead to civil war, a bad beginning for a new king. Now was the time to consolidate his power, not fight for it.

Did Dreea know her influence? What would have happened if she'd insisted he open the coffin?

"How I'd love to kill her," he told the fire.

This queen never desired power, even when it was given to her. In the great game of life, she was a queen but she didn't know it herself. A queen behaving like a pawn.

He summoned Toban. "You gave too much! I didn't want a public spectacle!"

"Sorry, my lord. Her constitution must be more delicate than I gauged."

"Ah. Will she live? Without your ministrations? For you must never go near her again. Whoever tends her must not trace you to me."

"I agree. Without the drugs, sir, she'll be ill for a while, but should recover. Faben is said to be a fine physician. Have you decided to let her live, then?"

"Don't be crude, Toban. Yes, I have. She's only a woman and does nothing but mouth prayers and weave tapestries. Because of what happened today, if she dies now, it could bring me difficulties. As it is, I must find a way to answer the charge of drugs in the castle."

Vesputo stared at the fire, looking for a solution. At last, he smiled.

"I'll tell everyone we've discovered that Irene was an accomplice of Landen's, that they wanted to kill the whole royal family; that Irene may have given Torina drugs, weakening her mind and causing her to take her own life."

Toban looked at Vesputo with admiration.

"I executed Irene in a grieving rage," Vesputo continued. He cocked an eyebrow. "That will explain her disappearance."

Chapter 10

Sixteen-year-old Lindsa scattered scraps for the chickens. The clucking birds pecked greedily, scurrying about in the chilly air.

Lindsa's eyes wandered to the trees growing up the mountainside. She wondered again why her parents had chosen to build right up against the foothills. True, as they said, they didn't get unwelcome visitors here. But then, they didn't get welcome visitors either.

Lindsa lived for the days when she made the long walk to the village to sell produce and barter supplies. She'd stay all afternoon, laughing and talking. Sometimes she even caught a glimpse of King Ardesen's soldiers and tried out her smile on them. But, here at home, nothing ever happened. Nothing but beans and squash and chickens.

The sinking sun was turning the air colder. Lindsa strewed the last of the feed.

She caught a faint movement in the trees. She squinted through the early dusk. Sometimes animals made their way near, and Lindsa loved animals. She set her basket down and went closer to the woods.

A ragged boy staggered out of the trees. He wore odd

shoes, and trousers that looked foreign. He was wrapped in old blankets. The amber light of sunset lit glazed eyes; his skin was flushed. He seemed to be trying to speak, but only a weak croak came from his cracked lips. He fell in front of Lindsa, crumpling completely.

Lindsa ran for the house, calling her mother. Anna hurried out, kneeling beside the stranger. He lay face down. Anna turned his body, putting her hand on his forehead.

"Mercy! The poor thing's burning up with fever!" Her homey face was full of pity.

"Where did he come from?" Lindsa asked.

Anna was examining the thin figure. "This ain't no boy," she said.

"Not a boy?"

"Help me get her inside. She's near dead, poor love."

Mother and daughter lifted the feather-light stranger and carried her into a bedroom. They removed her damp clothes, proving that indeed she was no boy. They dressed her in one of Lindsa's shifts. Anna bustled about, feeding the fire and making warm broth. Then she gathered the wasted wanderer into her ample lap, spooning broth into the fevered mouth.

"Rest easy now, rest easy," she crooned. "You're safe."

Lindsa took in the girl's straggly, cropped red hair. Under it, her features were delicate but strong, her cheeks thin.

"She doesn't see us, Ma."

"No, poor child. Too far gone with fever."

Anna tucked the stranger into bed, piling quilts around her.

"Will she live?" Lindsa asked anxiously.

"Well, no one knows what God may do. I don't believe she came to us only to die. But we must work to save her. She can do no more for herself, that much is plain. Look how starved she is. That ain't the work of one day. We must feed her the broth every hour all night and keep her warm. The fever's hot, but she's no more heat to spare."

"Where's she from, Ma? Her clothes—why would she be dressed like a boy, with hair like that?"

"You can see it's only just cut. Must have been lovely. She's on the run, and who would she be running from but some man?"

Lindsa took one of the girl's hands. "Do you think so now? How romantic!"

"Humph. Lucky to have found us."

"How long her fingers are." Lindsa chafed them, looking at the girl's burning face.

"This ain't no common girl. This one has spirit." Anna sponged the hot head.

Lindsa picked up the foreign clothes. "Shall I wash them, Ma?"

"May as well."

Lindsa folded the rough trousers. There was a bulge in one of the legs. She put her hand in the pocket and pulled out a small purse of fine velvet.

"Look, Ma!" She held it out.

Anna clicked her tongue. "What did I say? This ain't no ordinary stray cat we have here. Well, open it, maybe it tells who she is."

Lindsa felt inside the velvet. She pulled out a large crystal globe. It sparkled deep in the middle, like a diamond would. Lindsa put it in the strange girl's hand. She held it close and sighed.

"You see, I have the crystal again," she said deliriously. Her accent was as pure as a fine lady.

Lindsa brought out a handful of polished red stones.

"Ma?" She poured them into Anna's palm.

Anna stared at the brilliant jewels, running her thumb over their shining surfaces. "Rubies," she breathed. "Lindsa, each of these could feed us for years." *Hmmm. Rubies, but no horse. Strange doings.* She looked sharply at her daughter. Lindsa sat entranced, staring from the gems to the girl on the bed.

Early on a bitter morning, Captain Hadnell's soldiers were summoned to the central tent of their barracks. As Landen walked across the adjoining field, freezing wind cut into his face. The young men assembled into rows.

"I have news," Hadnell announced. "A new tragedy on our western neighbor, Archeld."

Landen's eyes fixed on the captain, his heart hurtling.

"As you remember, Archeld's King Kareed was murdered over two months ago." The captain's voice rose across the heads of the soldiers. "Kareed had only one child, a daughter, Torina. She was betrothed to Commander Vesputo. After a period of mourning, she married him."

Landen tried to tame his wild breath. Torina married to Vesputo? Was it possible?

"Tragically," his captain went on, "she died by her own hand soon after the wedding, having never recovered her senses after the loss of her father. Vesputo is now king of Archeld without her."

Landen clutched the hilt of his sword as if it could support him. *Died by her own hand? Never recovered her senses!*

Captain Hadnell droned on, but the young man in the second row did not hear him. *Died. Dead? She was dead?* His heart battled with the news, denying, denying.

No, she would never kill herself. She wouldn't marry her father's killer. It's all wrong, a false story, a political lie. Vesputo must have forced her to marry him, then killed her.

But that meant she was dead. *She was dead!* Landen stood shaking in his place, fighting for air. He'd never known with such indelible certainty that he loved Torina. He realized that he'd hoped with eternal, groundless faith that someday their futures would join.

He struggled to believe she must be still alive, imprisoned or even escaped. The girl he knew had the capacity to outdo Vesputo. But then he remembered her wan, lost look at their last meeting. Since then, she'd endured the murder of her father and marriage to a detestable man. If she saw no way out, would it be like her to take her own life?

His arms went rigid. He was seized with the urge to ride to Archeld, find Vesputo, demand the truth. He must know. He must.

"... the chaos of a new king and shocked population has changed our relations with Archeld," Captain Hadnell was saying. "The borders will be heavily guarded and patrolled."

For the first time in Landen's life, he wanted to tear into someone, anyone. He looked straight ahead, sure that if he met a man's eyes he would strike.

Dead. He knew Archeldan customs. A thousand

people must have seen her married; thousands more witnessed her burial. Despicable deceiver though he was, Vesputo could never stage such a thing without her body. She was surely dead.

Landen's breath took forever to draw in and out. He concentrated hard on breathing, watching as if from far off as his body strove to keep upright.

Somehow he managed to stay in formation until the men were dismissed to their duties. From a dazed, freezing distance, he went through the motions of his tasks. When others spoke to him, their words floated in on a slow, lifeless tide. His speech back to them was borne off by the same dull current. He didn't know if his mates noticed and did not care. By evening, his arms and legs felt impossibly heavy. He turned in as early as allowed, lying exhausted on his bunk.

In the night, he woke with tears on his cheeks. He stumbled outside without a coat. As he looked up, it seemed to him the stars ought to fall out of the sky. But there they were, serene and quiet, bright points in the quilt of darkness.

We will never walk together over the fields of earth,
Never hear the birds in the morning.
Oh, I have lived with you and loved you
And now you are gone away,
Gone where I cannot follow
Until I have finished all my days.

He stayed out for a long while until the tears froze on his face.

The next day, he sought out Captain Hadnell to find

what was required to participate in the Desan fights, where soldiers fought criminals to the death.

❖ ❖ ❖

Torina heard soft words. Her lids opened. She knew at once she had lost some time. Where was she? How did she get off the cold mountainside into this warm place?

Two women stood near, talking in low voices. Torina raised one of her hands. It was little more than bone within skin.

"Where am I?" she asked.

The older woman, the one with a face as comforting as the quilts that cozied Torina's body, gave her an eager look.

"Is it you? Are you talking?"

Torina pulled against her pillows, trying to sit up. "Where is this?"

"Lindsa, she knows her mind!" exclaimed the motherly woman. The younger sat down beside the bed.

"This is our farmhouse," the dark-haired girl answered, taking one of Torina's thin hands.

"Is this Desante?"

The women exchanged glances. They smiled and nodded. Torina heaved a relieved sigh.

"I'm Anna Dirkson, and this is my daughter, Lindsa."

Trying to smile, Torina found to her surprise that it was an effort.

"Could you eat something?" Anna asked.

The princess put her hand under the quilt and felt her stomach. Bone. She was all bone! Alarmed, she clasped her hands together. "How long have I been here?"

"Two days," Anna answered.

Torina remembered nothing after entering the trees beyond the summit of the pass.

"But who, and how?"

"We took care of you, my dear."

"I don't remember."

"You were feverish and sick."

"How did I get here?"

"Came walking out of the woods one evening." The woman's speech had an odd, pleasant slur.

"Did anyone follow me?"

"No, dear. No one knows but us and my husband, Tesh, and he'll never say a word."

Torina looked down at her scrawny hands. "Why? Why help me?"

"It was plain you were in trouble. Who else would help, if not us?"

"I feel so weak."

"You'll get well. You have a strong body, as anyone can see. Put yourself through a strain, but you'll be well as ever."

"You saved my life. Thank you."

Lindsa touched Torina's hair. Anna brought a warm slice of bread.

"Try to eat."

The bread was taken obediently, broken in small pieces. Lindsa brought a mug of cider.

"I can never thank you enough."

"No need. We must all help one another. Now, tell us your name and where you come from."

"I can't tell you that. It could put you in danger."

Lindsa's eyes gleamed. "Danger?"

"Terrible danger. You must forget you ever saw me."

"Not likely!"

Torina smiled sadly. "As soon as I'm well, I'll leave."

Anna put an arm around Torina's shoulders. "Where will you go? Can we help you find kin?"

Torina felt tears beginning. "I have no people," she said. Landen's face flowed in front of her. She banished him. "Please believe me. I've done nothing wrong, but I can't go back."

"Back where?"

"No, I must not tell you."

Anna's head wagged back and forth. "My dear, I may look like a simple farmer's wife, and I am. But I've eyes in my head and wasn't born yesterday. My Lindsa may have her faults, same as everyone else. But she ain't no talker when there's secrets to be kept. We've had a look at your clothes and found the little bag of jewels." She paused for breath.

"No need to be afraid of me or my daughter. We looked after you and listened to you when the fever talked."

"I talked?"

"Yes, my dear. You come from Archeld. And, sweet God only knows how, you walked across the Cheldan Mountains alone and lived. And some man wants you back."

"Did I say his name?"

"No, love." Anna looked disappointed. "And you can keep that secret. You can stay here as long as you need."

"I can pay you."

"That I know. We didn't help you to be paid. Now, you're tired. Rest." Anna folded the quilts around her securely. Lindsa said a soft good-night. They took the candle away.

Torina lay and looked at the dancing fire, struggling to think. Her mind felt hazy and worn. Her eyes closed.

❖ ❖ ❖

Rays of morning sun woke Torina. The fire had burned down to coals, the chilly air kept away by quilts. She dragged herself to a sitting position, draping her legs over the edge of the bed. A thick rag rug lay under her feet. She tried her weight and stood, wobbling like a toddler.

The room was comfortably furnished with home-made furniture. She was wearing a rumpled cotton shift. The seams were well stitched.

"Industrious people," she murmured. She staggered to the window. A small, cleared space outside ended in forest. She stared awestruck at its thick, tall trees. She looked down at her feet, valiantly gripping the floor.

"You did it," she told herself.

A comb lay on the dresser. When Anna and Lindsa came in, Torina was combing her short, dirty hair.

The women helped her bathe, the first wish of her heart. Then they took her to the room where they did weaving. When she saw the looms, her heart contracted at the thought of her mother, still in Vesputo's clutches.

Anna set to work. "My dear, we must at least know your name, or what will we call you?"

Torina considered. "Vineda. Call me Vineda."

"Lindsa, tell Vineda what you heard." Anna smiled. "News of Archeld!"

Lindsa leaned forward. "You left your country just as

great changes happened. You must have heard, the king was murdered? That was before you left." Lindsa waited for a nod. "That king had a daughter, who was supposed to marry the commander of his army. While *you* were walking over the Cheldan Mountains, the Princess was being wed. But she killed herself right after. Everyone said she was mad. And now the commander is king. King Vesputo."

"Hush, Lindsa!" Anna ran to her patient. "My dear, we only meant to give you some news of home."

Torina felt the hard frozen spot in her heart harden and freeze still more. *Vesputo! Somehow he tricked my people. Married him! And now dead.*

"Lindsa, get her some water. She must have known the poor lady. Is that it, Vineda? Did you know her?"

Torina closed burning eyes. The room seemed far away. She tossed on the sea of her thoughts. She'd come to Desante with a half-formed idea of seeking out King Ardesen, living under his protection. But now that all the world thought she was dead, and Vesputo was king with an army at his command . . .

If she showed herself to Ardesen, sick, weak, and shorn, how was he to know her? He hadn't seen her since she was a baby. Why would her cause ever be his? She'd either be thrown out as an imposter or turned over to Vesputo. Even if Ardesen let her stay, word would travel. Vesputo had proved he could use poison.

How could I wage war against my old comrades, the soldiers of Archeld?

Had Eric told her mother about the escape? Did Dreea know the death was staged? Could a message be sent? No. Letters might be intercepted.

She wanted nothing more to do with kings and kingdoms. Their violent vyings for power were loathsome. She must stop thinking of herself as a princess and make a life among the common people of Desante. She would leave the entanglements of royalty behind, along with her name.

She came back to the present, feeling as if she'd lived and died in the moments just passed.

"Please, I need to rest again."

Chapter 11

Ardesen, king of Desante, sat stiffly in the tall chair of his council room, flanked by two guards. His gray head was erect, old eyes alert and fierce. Outside winter held the land in her frosty grip. The king was grateful for the warm blaze at his hearth.

Hadnell, one of his army captains, bowed as he was ushered in. Ardesen invited him to sit.

"Do you know why I called you?" the king asked.

"I believe it's about a soldier in my charge, sir?"

"Yes. Bellanes." The king frowned. "He's been fighting in the Desan games, invoking the old rule."

"Yes, sir. He fights till he could easily kill, then spares the lives of the criminals."

"And goes away as poor as he arrived."

"Yes, sir."

"The people are flocking to the games, even in winter. My coffers are filled with a healthy amount of rashoes."

"They adore him, sir. Stand about outside his quarters for a glimpse of him, though they're not allowed in our compound."

"Humph. Hero worship? How does he respond?"

"Seems to have a distaste for it, sir. Goes about his duties as before."

"Tell me, how is he with his duties?"

"Efficient."

Ardesen stifled a grin at the fact that Hadnell had forgotten the "sir." The man looked as if a simple earthen mug he drank from every day had transformed itself into a sacred chalice.

"How many criminals has he defeated and spared?"

"Fourteen, sir."

Ardesen pursed his lips. "Fourteen men. This Bellanes could be rich by now. And the criminals are returned to prison with shortened sentences, as the rule dictates?"

"Yes, sir."

"Can this Bellanes be beaten?"

"An excellent fighter, sir."

Ardesen set the tips of his fingers together. "Why does he do it?"

"He doesn't say, sir."

"Do we know this young man's origins?" the king prodded.

"Comes from Guelhan, sir."

"Ah. Parents?"

"Dead, sir."

"Friends?"

"The other men like him."

"Who taught him to fight?"

Hadnell smiled tightly. "He says a bully taught him, sir."

Ardesen grinned. "What else does he say?"

"Not much, sir. A quiet man."

171

The king extended his feet toward the burning logs. "There's a fight tomorrow between Bellanes and Andris the thief?"

"Yes, sir. Andris is a famous criminal. Stole many horses before he was caught."

"And Andris is a fighter as well?"

"Yes, sir."

"I'll be in the king's box. Thank you, Captain." He waved a hand.

Ardesen enjoyed surprises and ran his kingdom with ingenuity. He looked for inventiveness in the people around him and seldom found it. More often, he got infuriating flattery. Sometimes he found men and women who gave him years of trustworthy service, and he never failed to promote such work. Nevertheless, he often sighed over the lack of more unusual vision.

This Bellanes must be a different sort of man. To fight death battles and forego the gold in favor of mercy was a bold act. Risking his life for nothing, though? That had a desperate stamp.

I wonder what he wants.

King Ardesen was sure Bellanes wanted something.

In the round-walled courtyard, Bellanes stood, wearing leather armor, naked sword in hand. Like a great bowl, the viewing stands rose in tiers above him. A cold, gray sky looked down on cheering spectators in quilted coats. Ardesen, in the king's box, sat at the rim of the courtyard in close view of the arena. His forehead creased in concentration as he studied the fighter.

Bellanes had an exotic face. Thick, curly black hair. His tall, well-built body looked at ease, his grip on the sword almost relaxed. Yet vigilance filled him. For an instant, Bellanes's eyes found those of the king. Ardesen's curiosity was piqued even more; surely, those eyes were too old and sorrowful for such an obviously young man.

Andris the thief appeared, wearing the criminal's loincloth. He was massively proportioned. Half a head taller and several years older than Bellanes by the looks of him. Angry eyes aimed at his opponent as he hurtled into the courtyard.

The criminal lifted his sword above his head and rushed. Bellanes ducked and jumped aside, dodging a blow that would have killed him. Andris whirled quickly and roared as he charged again. Bellanes leaped. A red line stood out on the thief's naked skin. The crowd broke forth in frenzied shouts.

In that mode, the fight continued; the larger man used sheer force while Bellanes relied on agility and skill. The onlookers were wild with excitement, cheering each mad rush and daring dodge. The breath of the fighters came in frosty clouds, their bodies shining with sweat in the chilly air. King Ardesen leaned across the courtyard ledge. Every time Andris swung his weapon, the king felt its whistling power. And still, Bellanes avoided Andris's blows with expert warrior grace.

At last, Bellanes gave a twisting blow as he escaped one more thrust. Andris's sword flew from his hand, clanging against the stones twenty yards away. Bellanes pressed his advantage. Soon his opponent lay on the ground, neck beneath the point of a sword.

Andris closed his eyes. Bellanes spoke.

"Look at the sky," he said, quiet words the king could barely hear.

The criminal's eyes flew open, staring at his death.

"Tell me your name," Bellanes commanded.

From his close seat, Ardesen saw the thief's eyes watering. "Andris," the big man said.

"Andris, you fought well. And because you looked at the sky, I won't kill you. The fight is over."

Bellanes's voice rose to loud, ringing tones. "The fight is over! This man lives!"

He lifted his sword and backed away. Guards came in a rush, leading Andris off. The thief looked over his shoulder at Bellanes. The victor returned his gaze, his strong face shot through with the force of mercy.

King Ardesen sat waiting as Bellanes walked up the steps from the walled courtyard. The young fighter was dripping sweat.

"So this is Bellanes." Ardesen looked him over.

"Sir."

Ardesen noticed that the soldier didn't drop his eyes. This man was looking at him as an equal. Ardesen smiled inwardly, keeping his outward face stern.

"Tell me, did you know before today that Andris the thief was enormously strong?" the king demanded.

"Aye, sir. I'm not a fool."

"Not a fool! Isn't it foolish to risk your life for nothing but sport?"

"He may be strong, sir, but he's had no training beyond hacking with a sword."

"You're saying he was no match for you? I watched the fight, Bellanes. If even one of his strokes had landed, you'd be dead. And he wanted to kill you."

"True, sir."

"You have great confidence in your skill."

"And many opportunities to test it, sir."

"In battles to the death? You didn't kill that criminal, Bellanes. Why?"

The fighter shifted his feet. "He's a man of your country, sir, wearing no armor." The voice had a marked, ringing quality. Ardesen tried to place the accent, sure it wasn't from Guelhan.

"My country!" Ardesen grunted. "And yours?"

"Yes, my country, sir. Though not so much mine as yours."

Ardesen narrowed his eyes. "Indeed?" he said dryly. "You know the reward for dispatching these men. With the number you've defeated, you could be rich. Yet you spare their lives, returning them to prison labor. Why not kill and take your reward?"

"I want a different reward," Bellanes said.

Hah! Now we come to it. "Speak." The king concealed his curiosity behind a forbidding scowl.

"Give me the men I defeat to train as retainers." The audacious request was spoken quietly.

Ardesen snorted. "Impossible! These men are derelicts. Criminals! Thieves and murderers."

"All men can change, sir."

"You ask for a command? Over criminals? Where do you come from, Bellanes?"

"If you give me the command, sir, I and my band will be valuable to you."

Ardesen surmised that Bellanes would not tell him where he really came from, not now, not if they fought side-by-side for twenty years. He described himself as valuable. Ardesen believed him. The king, when given a jewel, was not one to look too closely into where it had been mined.

"If you weren't such a great fighter, I'd call you a dreamer."

"If you never took risks, you'd have no Desan games, sir."

The king bowed his head to hide his thoughts. He sat still long enough for hope to go out of Bellanes. When he looked up, the fighter stood courteously waiting.

"I'm intrigued, Bellanes. Come to me tomorrow morning and we'll discuss your idea."

"A— at what hour?" Bellanes's eyes shone.

"The best hour." Ardesen grinned and swept away. If Bellanes could think for himself, let him show it. If he expected a command over thieves, the king would not make it easy for him.

❖　❖　❖

In a secluded field, Landen stood, wearing standard armor and hefting a sword. A motley group of fifteen unarmed men, Andris among them, ranged in front of him. Blue sky arched over the gathering. Fresh leaves poked out on the branches of surrounding trees.

Landen yelled. "All of you are criminals, and the law says you don't deserve to live!"

Some of the men looked furtively at the trees. No guards were visible.

"Yet you are fighters. I know this because I've met each of you in combat."

The assembled criminals glanced at one another.

"King Ardesen has granted me a command over warriors of my choosing." Landen was riveted by fifteen stares. "I've chosen you."

He watched understanding dawn. "I spared each of your lives once. If any one of you returns to your crimes, I won't spare you again. Any man who does not wish to serve with me can return to prison, now."

No one moved.

"Come forward, one by one. Say your name and tell your crime."

Andris stepped up. He squared his great chest. "Andris. Horse thief."

Landen nodded. "Andris. After today, steal only those horses I ask you to steal."

Andris's heavy features beamed. Another tall, muscled man, the left side of his face distorted by a livid scar, the right side showing almost angelic features, moved next to Andris.

"Bangor," he said in a tenor tone. "I steal anything."

There was scattered laughter. Landen stared at the disfigured face. "Who stole your good looks?"

More laughter. Soon fourteen men stood together in a ragged line. All had been convicted of stealing.

The last man's hard eyes challenged the rest. "I am Sakor. Murder."

"Why did you kill?"

Sakor shrugged. "The man I worked for had me whipped. So I took his son and cut him up."

"The son's age?"

"Perhaps twelve."

Landen handed his sword to Andris, the man nearest him.

"Kill him," he ordered.

Andris leaped. Sakor tried to run, but not fast enough. Andris severed his head in one slice. It rolled to the ground, the body following. Andris shouted his triumph, raising the sword.

The new leader took back his sword and cleaned the blade, concealing sorrowful emotions without comment. Ardesen's first condition was now fulfilled—the murderer's life ended. Landen believed Sakor deserved death, but he wished another justice could have delivered it. Saying a silent prayer to guide Sakor's soul, he apologized for ending his life, thanking him for his part in the emancipation of the rest. *Blood buys respect too often in this world. Andris could have killed me with the sword I loaned. Instead he returned it, and now this group is a band.*

They gathered around him, ready to offer all the passionate loyalty of those who have been given another chance, when they believed their last was gone.

Torina leaned on a hoe in a patch of bare earth behind the Dirkson farmhouse. Close by, in a glade among the trees, Tesh was building her a cabin. She could hear the song of his hammer.

When she gave the family a ruby, Anna's taciturn husband never said where he sold it, only that he traveled a distance to do so. The winter passed in relative luxury for Anna, Lindsa, and Tesh Dirkson, for they were able to buy supplies whenever need came. Torina lived in their spare room, helping weave and sew, learning to bake and cook.

Before long, her weaving earned top prices at the town market. Torina took satisfaction in earning her way.

She dressed only in somber colors, always wearing a plain kerchief to cover her hair. Her smile was rare. The Dirksons passed her off to their acquaintances as a cousin who had waited on a fine lady.

"Would need to be fine, for you don't speak like a common girl," Anna said.

Torina sewed a quilted jacket for herself. When it was done, she took frequent walks alone. She craved solitude.

When spring thawed the ground, Tesh started building her cabin. He was a careful, methodical worker. Soon she would have her own house, with no one to disturb her unless she wished it.

Welcome spring sunshine warmed her as she rested from turning the earth. It was Avril, the month of her birth. She was sixteen. No lustrous gowns or pretty minstrels marked the day; no loving parents at her side, smiling in celebration. Instead, she was planting a vegetable garden.

Setting the hoe down, Torina stretched her arms. She wanted with all her heart to live simply, to gain a normal, workaday existence. Here, basking in the mellow rays of light, it was easy to forget that her sleep often broke into nightmares. She tried to believe that her past could be put away, treating her former life in Archeld as if it belonged to a distant shore from which she had sailed.

She thanked God for Lindsa. The other girl's even, straightforward nature was balm to Torina. The two were fast friends, though Torina went silent when Lindsa broached the past.

But now Lindsa was in love with Anton, a light-hearted soldier.

"Aren't his eyes the most lovely in all the world?" Lindsa said, talking of Anton.

And an image of Landen's eyes flashed across Torina's inner vision: the glowing fires of a sun merging with cool depths of still water.

Now she stooped, filling her hands with dirt, desperately filling her soul with the earth's peace. Lindsa planned to be married by summer. She'd move away to live with her husband and be occupied with a thousand wifely interests.

Torina picked up her hoe and began chopping at the chunks of soil.

Part
Two

Chapter 1

Wind filled the air with dead leaves. Torina swung an empty basket in the crook of her arm and tightened a shawl around her head as she turned into the path of the Dirkson farm. Rounding the house, she came upon Anna in the beanfield, shunting pods into a half-full basket. She bent to help.

"Ah, thank you, Vineda. At this season, I miss Lindsa."

Torina smiled. "You miss her at every season, Anna."

The older woman chuckled. "In a year, I should be used to it. Did you see her in town today?"

"Yes. I stopped and played with the baby so Lindsa could put some pods away."

"Did you? I remember like yesterday when Lindsa was a babe in arms herself."

"She seems very happy."

"Aye. Beautiful child, married the right man. As you should do!" Anna scrabbled among the dry vines. "There 'tis. When I mention marriage, you get that sadness in your face. All men ain't the same, dear. Why not marry? Plenty men asking."

"I have no wish to marry." Torina shook crumbs of dirt from her skirt. "I must see to my weaving." She gave Anna a wan smile.

Her cabin, her refuge, welcomed her. Cozy furnishings cuddled her freezing heart. The tidy floor was covered with a thick rug. Colorful weavings decorated the walls. Torina knelt at the hearth and began a fire. She pulled off her scarf and wound the red braid, grown long again, into a quick crown on top of her head. She sat in the sturdy chair Tesh had made, watching the fire.

Her mind moved haphazardly, like the flames over wood, while her throat clenched with the effort of swallowing tears. Two years since she'd seen her mother, her homeland, her friends in Archeld. Two years cloistered in a village too small to have a name, her fiery spirit banked to a chilly smolder.

She had tried to put away the past, but lately she was haunted more than ever by specters from her old life.

Dipping into her pocket, she shuddered as her hand touched the crystal. She still kept it near her always. The last time she'd looked into it, she almost threw it away again. It had shown her Eric's grave. She agonized over his death, sure that Vesputo had killed him for letting her have Amber. And with his passing, there was no one in Archeld to know that she lived.

Under her bed was a box of writing materials. She sometimes wrote letters to her mother, then laid them away. Snippets of news told her Dreea was alive. Torina yearned to hear that gentle voice again, especially at night when she woke pouring sweat from dreadful dreams. She would never risk her mother's life, so the letters stayed under her mattress.

She stood and paced restlessly. It seemed impossible to live another day in such sad and hidden loneliness. She wondered what the people she had once known would say if they could visit her. What would her mother tell her, or Gramere?

Gramere would want me to find a way past my troubles. And she would understand. My dear, tender mother? She would love me, love me, but she would not understand. My father? He'd fight his way through and stake his chances on victory. Landen? What does it matter? He's gone.

Torina opened her door and looked into the thick trees she had somehow stumbled through during her escape from Vesputo.

Escape! That was what she had to do. She'd escaped Archeld but never left it behind. She must create a future and live again.

The crystal felt cool and dangerous in her hand. Her fingers squeezed it tightly. "Please," she whispered. "Show me something."

It seemed only to reflect her own tired face, made tiny, floating inside tears that dropped on its surface. She waited, passionately beckoning the future.

Light began to swirl in the crystal's depths, brilliant light around a magnificent sword. Torina frowned in puzzlement. The eyes of a warrior looked back at her from the sword's hilt, watchful and sharp, crowned with gold etchings. The blade pointed west. She studied it, lost to its meaning.

The vision changed to the face of a king. She knew he was a king, though his clothes were simple and he was next to an outdoor fire. He seemed about thirty years old, his features strong and intelligent. A bushy head of brown hair lay in unruly waves to his shoulders. She could see a fortress in the distance behind him. He was reading a scroll. When he finished, he handed it to a man beside him, a tall, slim, black-haired fellow.

The king spoke. His voice was deep and powerful through the soft thunder of the crystal.

"One more for our alliance. We will make this coast so strong, none will dare invade. Those plundering Sliviites will find a different land when they come here to pillage again."

"You've done what no one else could do—united the factions to defend one another," said the black-haired man.

Torina caught her breath, peering closely at the kingly face in her seeing stone. She realized who it was.

"Dahmis!" she cried. "The high king."

He kept speaking. "There are still many to persuade. Mlaven to the north, Endak far to the east, Vesputo to the south. What would I give to know what each of those kings will do!"

His brown eyes, full of energy and strength, seemed to look straight into Torina's. A wave of warmth washed into her.

"What would you give, High King?" she said.

The high king! Dahmis, king of Glavenrell, the uniter. The man whose name seemed on everyone's lips. She had seen his face, and she wanted to become part of the future he was making.

The following week, Torina learned from Anton that Dahmis of Glavenrell would be visiting his ally, King Ardesen of Desante. Their meeting would take place in Desan, capital city of Desante. The two kings would discuss the details of the broader alliances Dahmis was forging with other kingdoms.

Torina resolved to travel to Desan and deliver a message to the high king.

Anna and Tesh kept only one horse. Torina had grown used to walking most of the time. Borrowing their farm animal for several days would never do, and Desan was many miles away.

She asked Tesh to hire a horse for her. "A good mare. I'll use the old, beaten saddle."

He brought her a sturdy mare and told her the way. Grateful for the chilly weather, Torina braided her long flaming hair and pinned it into a drab scarf. She put on one of her usual plain dresses, hiding her body in a brown cape.

She rode off into the morning. A light mist covered the ground, and the sky was gray and cool. Excited to begin an adventure she was choosing herself, she skirted the village and headed toward the main road.

By noon, she had gained the wide track leading into the city of Desan. Throngs of people were ahead of her. She quailed at the thought that they had all come to get a glimpse of the high king. How would she make her way among so many? The stream of humanity slowed to a crawl near the city gates. Some travelers were stopped and questioned by the sentries. Her heart beat a tempo of fear as the line moved closer. After two years, would anyone be looking for her? She knew Vesputo's tenacity. Whatever he had made others believe, *he* must know she had a chance of surviving her escape.

At the entrance gate, she gave the guard a tentative smile. He waved her through with a wink. Torina followed the crowds down the main street of Desan.

She wasn't used to the crush of people, but her mare seemed to be. The steady animal responded to her guidance, stepping neatly even when jostled by passers-by. Like a sluggish river, everyone flowed toward the city square, which was backed by King Ardesen's fortress.

In the square, the press of men, women, and children was so dense that Torina pushed to the outskirts, wondering what to do. She tried to listen for individual voices in the hubbub, but the noise was a great blur. She could hardly think.

Turning the mare into an alley, she rode aimlessly till she found a quiet street. She gave the mare her head, sagging despondently in the saddle. How had she ever believed she could meet the high king and hand him a note?

The thirsty mare discovered a public trough. She bent and drank while Torina stretched her legs.

Beside her, a quality stallion nosed in for a place at the water. Torina grinned as he nudged her aside.

"Sorry," said his rider, a man in brown uniform. He swung down from his mount.

Brown. Ardesen's soldiers wear red. This man must serve Glavenrell and the high king.

Torina recognized him with a start. It was the man from her vision who had spoken with King Dahmis. She stared at him.

"I beg your pardon," he was saying. "My horse has better manners when he isn't thirsty. The crowd . . ." He stopped. "Are you all right, miss?"

"Yes. Oh, your horse didn't hurt me in the least. It's, that is—"

"Yes?" He waited with courteous, serious eyes.

"Excuse me, you must think me a simpleton. My mistress asked me to deliver a message to the high king. I had decided it could never be done today, but you—you serve King Dahmis?"

"I do."

"Oh, sir, would it be possible for me to give you my message for him?"

"Certainly." He smiled.

"Will you make certain he reads it while he's here in Desan?"

She seemed to have caught his interest. "I'll do all I can."

Something about this man reassured her. She believed he would deliver her message. She gave him a rolled scroll. He placed it in an inside pocket of his coat.

"May I ask your name, sir?"

"I am Larseld."

She saw he expected her to say her name. She turned away, mounting the mare hastily.

"Thank you, again and again," she told him. "Good-bye."

She clattered off through the alley, dizzy with hope. To meet one of the men close to King Dahmis! It seemed miraculous. Elated, Torina let the mare move without guidance, not caring which direction she went.

When she looked around some time later, she wondered what part of the city she had come to. There were rows of shops, though everyone had shut up to see the great king. She looked idly in the grates and windows. It was apparent from the number of lettered signs that many city dwellers could read.

On a shop wall littered with notices, she felt a sudden chill as she caught the word "bounty." She stopped and read.

Wanted ALIVE, for the murder of KING KAREED of ARCHELD, the man LANDEN. DESCRIPTION: Tall, dark hair, skilled archer and swordsman, good with horses, makes his own bows. PAYMENT OF 20 RASHOES FOR INFORMATION. PAYMENT OF 50 RASHOES FOR CAPTURE. Inquire within.

Torina's heart thudded. They were still hunting him! She sat immobilized in the saddle, her mind filled with memories of Landen. She saw him fall, bound and bruised, the first day they met. Clinging to the face of a cliff; giving her a hand-made bow; meeting her in secret friendship; warning her of Vesputo.

She had tried not to think of him, shutting him from her heart, telling herself he had left too soon, said too little, ought to have done more. Staring at the fluttering notice, she saw things from another point of view. The world was a different place from an exile's perspective. She remembered with searing clarity her cavalier question, "You're willing to live exiled?" and his dry response, "I've lived exiled since I was a boy."

Torina's head drooped. How heartless and senseless her question now seemed. Knowing that her father had killed Landen's father, slaughtered the peace of his country, and destroyed his culture, she had not seen fit to pursue justice for the boy who had befriended her. She'd treated with casual carelessness a precious and rare comrade, even forgotten him for months on end, absorbed in the courtship of a man like Vesputo. Landen had sought her out, taken risks to warn her, told her and no one else of his plans to leave Archeld. And how had she answered him? "You're willing to live exiled?" The question tormented her.

Then, when her father was killed by his own right-hand man, she had blamed Landen for leaving too soon. *Too soon?* He had probably waited too long.

But this notice proved he was alive! Vesputo would never pay for a man already found. Hunted throughout the kingdoms, was Landen living in seclusion, perhaps somewhere in Desante? If so, how might she find him? Forgetting everything else, Torina drew out the crystal and gazed, praying for a vision of her childhood friend.

Nothing. Her seer's eye stared back, serene and clear. No matter how she strained to see, it stayed blank. With quivering lips, she pleaded for something, anything, that might tell her where he lived. The crystal sat in her palm, cool and lifeless.

Another thought seized her. If Vesputo still sought Landen, he might be looking for her too. Of course, he couldn't post bounties on her. She almost laughed at the thought: *Wanted, DEAD, the ghost of Princess Torina Archelda.* But Vesputo had other methods.

She grabbed the reins and listened for the distant roar of a crowd, heading toward it. When she found it, she moved against the tide of people till she reached the city gates. A different soldier waved her out with a yawn.

Chapter 2

D ahmis, king of Glavenrell, high king, was enjoying himself. Dressed as a common soldier, riding a nondescript horse, he traveled a silent
forest path with no escort, smiling to himself. It had been
too long since he last blended anonymously with the
countryside. As he listened to the sound of hooves on
pine needles, he realized how deeply he'd been driven.
Years of ceaseless negotiations with kings whose habits
were hostile and suspicious, persuading them to the
promise of unity.

He was at the end of a trail that promised him a
fortune-teller. The king shook his head, chuckling. He
didn't believe any crone could help him strengthen the
alliances he'd forged. But curiosity had won again.
Larseld, his favorite general, insisted he read a letter. The
man seemed bewitched by this fortune-teller's messenger.

His map said her home was nearby. The king scanned
the trees to right and left, rewarded with the sight of a
well-built cabin. Dahmis swung out of the saddle and
tapped on the door.

A young woman answered. Her hair was tied up, her
dress simple and brown. The face matched Larseld's

description exactly. Vibrant, delicate, arresting features caught the king's attention, especially her eyes, ocean-colored pools of great depth.

"Good afternoon," he said, remembering the character of common soldier. The young woman standing in the doorway stirred him. He wished he could stay and talk with her, walk with her, know her. Small wonder Larseld had acted addled.

"Afternoon," she replied. Her voice had a rich, cadent energy, the accent pure.

"I'm looking for Vineda."

"You've found her."

He peered past her, into an empty room. "*You* are Vineda?"

"Yes."

He dug in his pocket. "I'm the envoy for King Dahmis. He read your message and sends this ring as a token of his confidence in me."

He extended his hand, holding an ornate ring. Vineda stepped inside the cabin. He followed, reaching toward her with the ring. She shut the door, not taking his offering.

"I understand the need for disguise while traveling, King Dahmis," she said. "But did you think to fool me with costumes?"

He threw up his hands. "I thought I'd find a muttering crone. Instead, I find . . ." He stopped, clamping his lips. She was looking at him as if she felt neither fear nor awe of his position. She had just called him King Dahmis. She must know he was the high king.

"Why are you here?" The direct question caught the king off guard.

"I received a message saying you know the future. If that's true, you could be invaluable to me." *And if it isn't true, you're still beautiful.*

"Please." She pointed to a chair. She sat opposite him, taking up a piece of embroidery, for all the world as if they were two equals. It was a pattern of flowers; she began stitching. Dahmis leaned forward.

"Do you see the future?"

"I see, yes. But only what is shown to me. Not everything."

The king felt more and more impressed with this unusual young woman. He almost believed she could do what she said. At least she wasn't making claims to be all-knowing.

"What do you see that concerns the realm?"

Her hand paused in her needlework, eyes probing his face. "If I tell you, will you take action upon it?"

Dahmis cleared his throat. "If it benefits the realm. If it's reasonable."

"Is the truth always reasonable?" Her voice had a flat sadness in it.

The king was taken aback. "I don't suppose so."

"It's the unreasonable things that need to be foretold. Because no one can know what they won't look for. No one can prepare for what they don't think of."

She didn't address him as "sir" or "my lord." It was oddly refreshing coming from her and seemed natural.

Who is she?

"I have no experience of your skill."

"Meaning you don't wish to be tricked into taking an action that could be foolish?"

He nodded. *It's as if she knows my mind.*

"That's only *reasonable*. You don't know me. I could be a liar. So, I'll give you one free prophecy. If you ignore it, it will be the last."

"Fair."

She put down her embroidery. "King Vesputo wants your kingdom and position."

Dahmis leaned back. "Vesputo has exchanged courtesies with me. He's never disputed the borders."

"It's not his way to declare his intentions openly."

Dahmis admitted to himself that Vesputo was said to be an inscrutable man. "And what is his way?"

Her eyes turned inward, voice low. "He strikes at the heart, knowing that once the heart dies, the hands and feet will quickly lose life."

Dahmis's rib cage suddenly felt too small. He tried to look in her eyes, which focused on some unknown point.

"What is it you see? Please tell me."

King Dahmis sat in the private council chamber of Glavenrell's fortress. The walls were thick, the door shut, and he was with the two men he trusted most in the world. Larseld, his best general, and Michal, his oldest friend.

Tension gathered in Dahmis's shoulders and pounded behind his eyes. He had sworn to Vineda not to reveal anything about her beyond her existence. Now he told his friends only that he'd consulted a seer.

Michal, a rugged man with twinkling eyes, occupied a chair across from the king. They had grown up together and enjoyed the firmest of friendships. Larseld, tall, wiry, with serious dark eyes and black hair he kept tied back from his face, sat to the king's left. The three men met together often, not standing on ceremony when they were alone.

"An assassin sent by King Vesputo is supposed to arrive at this fortress by tomorrow evening?" Michal looked incredulous.

Larseld put the tips of his fingers together. "Did she give a description? Could we recognize the man?"

"Oh yes. The description was thorough and detailed."

"If she's right?"

"If."

"Do you believe she tells the truth?" Michal cut in.

"How can I know?"

"But do you believe it?"

Dahmis thought about the young seer with the drab clothes and bewitching eyes. "I don't want to believe," he answered gruffly. "Yet I do."

Larseld stroked his chin. "Then we must arrive at a plan of action. We must treat it as real."

"I can't arrest an envoy of Vesputo's on sight! Vesputo would never let such an insult pass. If this is a hoax, it could create war!"

Michal grinned. "I see your dilemma."

Larseld rubbed his forehead. "We must have guards standing by. If he draws this stiletto she spoke of, they can be ready."

"No, it would need only a prick to kill. Poison."

Larseld frowned. "Then we must devise a different strategy."

"I have it," Michal announced, smiling and spreading his hands. "I impersonate you, Dahmis! Forewarned is forearmed. I'm stronger than you and could block his wrist if he makes so much as a move. You and Larseld can be nearby, with a picked group of soldiers. We find out his intentions, and no one will be put at risk."

Dahmis shook his head. "No. That puts *you* at risk. We could easily carry out the same plan, using the real king, myself."

Michal laughed. "No. If you were killed, these lands would crumble, and all your alliances go for nothing. Besides, I *am* stronger." He winked.

"Stronger than everyone." Dahmis smiled.

Larseld leaned in. "People hear that the high king is a large man with brown hair." He pointed at Michal. "Michal could represent the king to someone who has never seen him. The hair could pass for yours, my lord, and your robes would fit him."

Dahmis set his jaw. "I'll never agree to put you in jeopardy for an office you don't hold, Michal."

"I'm more stubborn than you, King Mule," Michal answered.

"This isn't mock swordplay you talk of!" Dahmis roared.

Their voices were raised far into the night. At last, Dahmis agreed to allow Michal to wear the king's robes and talk with the "envoy"—if the envoy came.

Vesputo had sent no advance messages.

King Dahmis, wearing the togs of a low-ranking soldier, stood in an open field adjoining a wooded area not far from his fortress. Next to him, Michal looked convincingly royal. Michal's powerful frame seemed made for the part. Dahmis smiled at the effect, feet shifting nervously. The sun was low. She had said the time was now.

"If this turns out to be an elaborate ruse—" he began, bending toward Michal.

"Halt! Do not approach your common head so near!" Michal's eyes danced in pretended disgust.

Dahmis laughed. "Scoundrel."

"If this fortune-teller of yours has any other visions, may I be a part of them?"

"Remember, my friend, there's great danger in this charade if it turns real."

"So you say. Look! Larseld, with a stranger who fits the description."

Both men stared as Larseld advanced across the field, escorting a tall, broad-chested man dressed in Archeldan clothes.

"Now, Michal. Be king." Dahmis dropped back.

Larseld led on, a sheen of sweat on his face. He stopped a few feet from Michal.

"King Dahmis, this man is an envoy from King Vesputo," Larseld announced.

Michal stepped forward. "Greetings. This is an unexpected honor."

"Greetings, sir. I bring urgent dispatches from King Vesputo, for your ears alone. Perhaps this evening we can meet privately."

"I regret I received no word of your visit," Michal said. "I am not at liberty to meet with you this evening." He frowned, as though considering, then pointed at the nearby trees. "However, a few moments now, if you're not too tired from your trip?"

The Archeldan's smile gleamed and Dahmis's heart sped. The fellow Vesputo had sent looked dangerous. When Michal volunteered for this duty, did he believe there was any real threat?

Michal and his guest walked toward the wood. They disappeared behind the leaves, trailed by Dahmis and Larseld. All was quiet, except for the soft sounds of the breeze and muffled, calm voices filtering through branches. Dahmis and Larseld stopped and waited.

A shout. They rushed forward. Breaking through thick foliage, they found Michal and the Archeldan struggling for possession of a long stiletto. Vesputo's man held it inches from Michal's throat as Michal pushed it away. The arms of both were taut and shaking.

When the stranger saw them, he jerked away and began to run. Five of Dahmis's soldiers, planted in the wood, sprang out. They tackled the running man midstride. As he went down, they pinned him to the ground, carefully disarming him. King Dahmis signaled them, then hurried to Michal's side.

His friend was breathing hard, pulling the king's robes from his shoulders. "You can have your kingship, and welcome!" Michal thrust the robes into Dahmis's arms, cursing eloquently.

"Did he prick you?" Dahmis asked, sick with anxiety.

"Not a scratch. My lord, whoever gave you news of this is very valuable."

"Yes."

"Your life has been saved."

"And yours, thank God." Dahmis lifted his eyes to the sky. "It isn't done, Michal. I have to decide what action to take."

"Yes, the burdens of the high king." Michal's eyes were regaining their sparkle, but he asked seriously, "Will you ride against Vesputo?"

"No. That would be a terrible waste and could well destroy the balance of what I've built with the alliances. How could they trust a peacemaker who wars on his nearest neighbor?"

"Will you allow it to go without even a warning, or a change in your offers of alliance?"

"No." Dahmis hitched his burly shoulders into the king's robes. "No. A warning must be sent."

❖　❖　❖

The Archeldan stood in the field, closely guarded. His arms were tied, ankles bound. As Dahmis and Michal approached, Larseld handed the stiletto to his king.

"This is poison-tipped, or I'm mistaken." Dahmis pointed the weapon at the prisoner. "A strange gift from a peaceful neighbor."

The man's eyes went from him to Michal. "*You* are the king?"

"I am." Dahmis turned to his general. "Larseld, did you search him?"

"He had full papers on him, backing his claim to be an envoy of Vesputo. His name is Toban Avula."

"Toban." Dahmis examined the stiletto, keeping the tip away from his body. "King Vesputo sent you to kill me?"

Toban looked wary. "No, my king. That imposter attacked me."

Dahmis raised his left hand. "Why did you bring this poisonous weapon into Glavenrell?"

"A man traveling alone never knows when he may need protection. Your roads are not yet safe for a stranger."

"My roads not safe? Why did you try to kill the high king?" Dahmis was stern.

"That was not meant for you, my lord."

Dahmis considered the man in front of him. Hard, crafty eyes in a good-looking face. Vineda had said this man must never be trusted for even a moment. Dahmis believed her. He could almost read in the man's face a long history of corruption and cruelty.

The witnesses to this strange event were a handful of men picked for their discretion. Airing the incident would serve no purpose. Imprisoning Toban could lead to unsavory problems that might be terribly costly to the new alliances. Vesputo was certainly capable of using this to create a wedge for splitting the kingdoms again.

Timing. Unthinkable to send Toban back to Vesputo now. Politically risky to imprison him.

It was a thorny thing Dahmis held. Every way he picked it up, it stung. This one man could be the demise of countless plans. What to do?

"You must think me a fool," the king said.

"No, sir. And I am being detained improperly. I demand the consideration of courtesy."

Dahmis raged inwardly. So they would play on his reputation for justice, using it against him.

"This was not meant for me?" Dahmis raised the stiletto a little higher.

"No, my king."

Dahmis stepped nearer. "No?"

"No, sir."

"Neither is this meant for you," the high king said and, with a quick lunge, he drove the thin point of the stiletto into Toban's shoulder.

"A message needs to be delivered to your king," Dahmis rumbled, withdrawing the blade. "And you are the very one to give it."

Within moments, the man began to writhe, screaming. King and soldiers drew back, watching as he died.

"A man traveling alone never knows when he may need protection," the king muttered.

❖ ❖ ❖

Curled in a chair, Torina tried to drive away the ache in her heart. Her crystal was obstinate about Landen: though she asked daily to be given some sign of him, no vision ever came.

A light knock sounded at her door. The knock was unfamiliar. Torina recognized the differences between Tesh, Anna, and Lindsa, her only regular visitors. She went to the window and peered at her step. A large man wrapped in a goatherd's draggled clothes stood outside. She opened the door to Dahmis, high king. He smiled at her, a friendly light in his eyes.

"Thank you for your vision, Vineda," he said, deep voice gentle.

She reached out to him with quick, unthought gladness. "You caught him?"

He took her hand in a manly grip. "We caught him and sent him back to his king."

"Sent him back?" She dropped his hand.

King Dahmis chuckled. "I see it's true that not everything is shown to you." He gave her a keen glance. "He won't trouble anyone again."

"H— he's dead?"

"He is dead."

"Oh!" Her heart leaped. Toban, her former guard, Vesputo's accomplice, gone!

"Now for more cheerful matters. Come." He tugged at her arm. She followed him outside.

Two magnificent horses, one white, one gray, stood by a tree, their reins looped over a branch. Dahmis unwound the reins of the white horse and put them in Torina's hands.

"For you. With thanks."

For a moment, Torina was a child again, a child in love with a beautiful creature. She put her arms around the silky white mare, blinking back tears. She rubbed her eyes on the soft coat.

"She's much too fine for a village girl," she said.

"Plainly, you weren't raised on a farm. Will you tell me where you come from?"

"No."

"No." The king seemed to be biting back words. "Well."

"I'm sorry."

"Keep the horse. She's yours. The villagers will get used to it. You can tell them you have rich relations. A cousin who fought in the Desan games and won."

Torina twined slender fingers in the mare's mane, shaking her head.

"Please. As a favor to a king."

The mare nuzzled her shoulder. That settled it. "Yes, you beauty," she crooned to the horse, smiling at the king.

Dahmis looked satisfied. "You agree she's yours?"

"Yes. Thank you. I'll call her Justina."

"Justina."

They were quiet together. Torina, stroking the mare, wondered how Amber was doing.

"Vineda, what more can you tell me?"

Her chest tightened. "First, remember you've never seen me. You know nothing of what I look like."

The king put a hand on her arm, turning her to face him fully. He grasped both her hands in his. Reflexively, she pulled away. He shoved his hands in the pockets of the old, patched coat he wore.

"Don't ever fear me," he told her.

Vesputo stood in the courtyard, flanked by Beron, staring down at the training exercises Emid was holding. His mind was far away, in Glavenrell. Where was Toban? He should have reported back by this time.

A commotion behind made him turn. He heard voices calling and the sound of horses being reined in. Several of his soldiers gathered around a contingent of men dressed in the brown uniforms of the high king. A soldier stepped forward, bowing.

"My lord."

Vesputo inclined his head the minimum that courtesy dictated. The day was warm and mild, but he felt as if a cold wind blew on him. His hands were icy as Dahmis's captain gave him a scroll.

"The high king sends you this message, with his regrets."

The high king sends? Is Dahmis alive?

The captain nodded to his men. Four brown-clad soldiers lifted a casket from a horse-drawn cart and carried it to Vesputo. They set it down on the stones of the courtyard. The captain bowed again and made the sign of peaceful farewell.

"Wait," Vesputo said. "Will you take some refreshment, rest here for the night?"

He was answered with a bow. "No, my lord. Our thanks, but the high king requires us to return quickly."

The man mounted his horse with rapid ease, the contingent following his lead. In another few moments, Vesputo looked after their dust on the road.

Slowly he untied the strings on the scroll and read.

It is with regret that I inform you of the untimely death of one of your envoys who had the misfortune to be set upon by bandits while in my dominions. There are still pockets of lawlessness within my kingdom. My condolences for your loss. Dahmis, high king.

Vesputo ordered Beron to open the casket. Toban's bloated face confronted him in death.

"Bury him with honor," he said. His voice cracked, but that was all right. Let the men believe he would grieve for them if they died. "I'll attend the funeral. Beron, come with me."

He swept from the courtyard, striding so fast that

Beron had trouble keeping up. He made his way to the king's private room. There he flung the message on the floor and ground it under his heel.

"Only one person could have warned the high king," he growled.

Beron stared, baffled.

"Dahmis is not a suspicious man," Vesputo continued, the muscles in his neck taut with suppressed anger.

"Who?" Beron's heavy eyebrows furrowed.

"She's alive." Vesputo almost shouted. "And somehow, she has Dahmis's ear. She must be living in his court with that cursed stone."

"Princess Torina?" Beron gasped.

"Never say her name out loud. Yes!" Vesputo folded his arms, mastering himself. "You will find her," he said, "and the crystal she keeps." His voice was as cold as the wind he had felt in the courtyard.

Chapter 3

D ead, draggled leaves were wet under Justina's hooves as Torina cantered into the small meadow by her cabin. A misty rain dampened her face. As usual, her head was completely covered. The horse had become her dearest companion. She often rode out, away from inhabited land, seeking hidden, wild places where huge trees grew. As she leaned against their ancient trunks, she could sometimes remember the singing of her soul. More often, she felt only the dissonant tide of bitter regret, seeing what might have been, if she had been wiser sooner. The seasons were turning on another year, leaving her still exiled.

When she visited Lindsa, her friend's happiness soothed her troubled heart. The child, Antonia, loved Torina with dazzling persistence; she toddled to her and held up chubby arms. Sometimes they went for slow rides through the village together. Torina knew the villagers wondered about her. In her mind's eye, she could see the picture she made: beautiful horse, dull scarf, brown dress, unsmiling face. Yet the people accepted her, perhaps because she'd been among them for nearly three years.

Young men still asked to court her, though her answer was always the same. No.

And the high king? Dahmis had little time to devote to solitary trips to Desante. When he asked her to tell her visions to other trustworthy men, she refused. One evening in late spring, they had devised a coded system for messages. She wrote to him weekly now, hiding the carefully worded letters in a hollow tree deep in the forest. From there, Dahmis's men picked them up. The soldiers never saw her, nor she them.

She saved King Dahmis quite a bit of struggle with her insight, as he told her in his coded, unsigned replies. The alliances multiplied as more kings were won over to the value of mutual assistance and open trade. Mlaven and Endak, haughty rulers of northern lands, had recently joined, pledging to give the required allegiance to the high king.

Dahmis paid her handsomely. Torina was rich, but her riches sat forgotten in a basket behind her bellows. Gold did nothing to thaw the loneliness in her heart. She hadn't seen Dahmis since their meeting before summer, and now autumn was in the air once more. She slid from Justina's back dispiritedly.

"Come, my beauty, I'll rub you down," she said, leading the mare toward the stable Tesh had built.

King Dahmis, dressed again as a soldier, stepped in front of her.

"Oh!" Torina cried.

The king looked well. He wore his growing power like a well-tailored mantle.

"Sorry I startled you." He grinned at her.

She was overwhelmed with happiness to see him.

"I need to speak with you," he said. "Are you alone?"

"Always." It was out before she thought.

The king put a finger under her chin and lifted her face. "You're lonely."

She turned away so he wouldn't see the treacherous tears starting. Justina edged closer. The king stepped back.

"Attend to your horse. I can wait."

Torina rubbed Justina until her face was clear.

"Shall we go in?" she asked Dahmis.

She offered food and water. He said no, sitting in the chair he'd taken the afternoon of their first meeting. She laid a quick fire.

"Vineda, this visit takes me away from urgent demands."

She reached for her crystal. "What do you need to know?"

"No crisis of state. It's that I have reports of men inquiring about a seer."

Torina sat up taller, breathing fast. "And?"

"The description is very particular. A young woman with red hair."

Torina's fingers flew to her kerchief, checking to be sure every hair was hidden. Dahmis got up with sudden speed. He yanked the scarf from her head in one swift jerk. Her hair tumbled down in thick waves, as the king stared. Torina scowled at him, her hands winding up the telltale red.

"Who are you?" he cried. "You're so beautiful."

"Who is looking for me?"

He shook his head. "I haven't been able to find out. If you could bring yourself to trust me, my task would be easier. Tell me at least the kingdom he comes from."

She considered. "I trust you enough to tell you I never see visions of my own future, so I don't know."

He raised his eyebrows. "You can't help yourself with your gift?"

She twisted her hands, regretting she had told him. "No."

"But can you guess? Someone from your past? Where do you come from?"

"No. I won't tell you."

"Vineda, I trust you with my life. Can't you trust me with yours?" His honest face was a trace impatient.

She wanted to pour everything out to him, lay down the burden of secrecy. And why not? Fate had led her to a position of trust with the most powerful man in the kingdoms. He would believe her.

But then, what about her beloved homeland? She had learned that Vesputo's army was still as formidable as during her father's time. She knew almost nothing of the political events shaping Archeld. What if her claim would lead to a devastating civil war? In the minds of her people, she was long dead.

"Yes, with my life I trust you. But if you knew . . ."

"It might lead me to war?" he asked. At the look on his face, she shrank further from the thought of conquering Vesputo with Dahmis's help. No one else must die for her. No one.

She nodded reluctantly.

"I see," said the king.

They were silent together, Torina braiding her hair, Dahmis watching. Then, to her astonishment, the king knelt in front of her chair, eyes on a level with hers. She felt the force of his presence.

"Vineda. Move to my fortress. There you'll be safe."

She flung up her hands, letting her rebellious hair escape. "There I'll be killed! It's what they will expect."

"Who will expect? You can't ignore the danger!" Dahmis enclosed her fluttering hands.

She shook him off. "I won't live a prisoner in a king's fortress."

A sudden torrent of rain beat on the roof. The fire flared and sputtered as drops fell into it.

"Let me protect you," the king urged. "If you won't move to my fortress, allow me to guard you."

"If you send soldiers here, you'll only draw attention to me. And I won't go with you," she answered.

"I am high king. You know this. Do you feel no awe?"

She met his gaze. "I feel awe. But not of kings."

"Vineda, on my knees, I ask you. Let me help you."

"I never wanted you to kneel to me. If you want to help me, find the man who is looking for me, before he finds me and goes back to . . ."

"Back to?"

"Back to where he came from," she snapped.

Dahmis chuckled. The chuckle grew to a laugh. He got off his knees and bowed to her.

"Forgive me. Keep your solitude. I'll keep hunting these rumors."

"Thank you." She smiled.

"If you change your mind, one word will bring all the help you ask for." Dahmis put his hand in his pocket and drew out a glasslike black stone suspended from a red cord. It was carved with his crest.

"This will gain you passage through any checkpoint and open all doors to me. There are only five of these in the kingdoms. Please take it and wear it. All guards are instructed to respect this, no matter who bears it."

She took it, aware of the honor she was given. "Thank you, my king."

He bowed a little awkwardly. Torina watched him ride away in the rain. She went inside and listened to the wild beating of her heart.

In the castle of Archeld, Vesputo met with Beron, just returned from several months of travel.

Beron rumpled his thick eyebrows. "My lord, I loosened tongues in every way I know," he said. "No one had heard of a crystal that could tell the future. I tracked down a few red-haired lassies living around the fortress of Glavenrell. She was not among them."

"If she lives, we must eventually find her," Vesputo declared. "You searched the neighboring kingdoms?"

"Yes, my lord. I rode as far north as Mlaven's lands and all the way east to Desante."

"How did you find Desante? What did you learn of the band of Bellanes?"

"Not much, sir. Bellanes is almost as elusive as the princess, though his fame is spreading."

"I wonder who this Bellanes is," Vesputo said, stretching his legs to the fire.

"He leads a band of criminals, sir, that much I learned. King Ardesen let him begin it as a lark, and liked it so well that now Bellanes is entrusted with the most secret missions."

"Indeed? What was Bellanes's crime?"

"They say all the men are thieves, sir. Bellanes too. Ardesen has them steal things for him. Weapons, treasure, secrets. They say Bellanes can get in anywhere, find anything, and bring it back before it's missed."

"Hmm." Vesputo's eyes narrowed to slits.

"King Ardesen allows Bellanes to come and go at will," Beron continued.

"I wonder if this Bellanes could find and steal a fortune-teller for us? Or a fortune-teller's stone?"

Beron stared. "Of course. He can steal anything."

"How would I get a message to this man?" Vesputo tapped his fingers together. "I could do it through King Ardesen."

"Yes, my lord."

"If she's alive, she's hidden somewhere, and hidden well. You left spies?"

"Yes, and promises of fortunes made if we get word. I passed out the seals that will bring letters direct to you."

"Thank you, Captain. You've done well."

Beron swelled with pride.

King Dahmis watched the archery practice of his troops. All reports agreed the Sliviites were massing for an attack. The only thing unknown was where they would strike first. Vineda confirmed what his spies reported: hordes of Sliviite soldiers and mercenaries training together, and Sliviite wealth being poured into building new ships. Sliviia already boasted the finest navy in the world, but the new ships were staggeringly large: each one big enough to hold seven hundred men! Initially Dahmis was inclined to believe his spies exaggerated: the sheer mass of a boat that big would surely sink it. However, he received more and more confirmation, and he worried over the news. Sliviites had harried the coastlines for decades, making themselves hated and feared as pirates. But this. This indicated a full-scale invasion.

Nearly all the northern kingdoms had joined Dahmis now, and he believed those who held out would soon seek the protection of his alliance. Everyone knew the Sliviites were massing for war, and no kingdom wanted to try to fend them off alone. Even Vesputo had been sending conciliatory messages, sounding out Dahmis's intentions.

Dahmis sighed. Should he let bygones be bygones and allow Vesputo a place in the alliance? After all, the might of Archeld's army was nothing to treat lightly.

With enough soldiers and good fortifications, there were many ways to defend against an invader who hit from the sea. The question was, where would the Sliviites land? Which bay would receive the onslaught? Try as he might, Dahmis had been unable to get spies placed to find out. Until he knew, his forces and those of his allies would remain ineffectually scattered.

Vineda had looked, again and again, for a vision to help him. All she saw was a terrifying array of huge ships. She couldn't determine where they would sail to. She thought the Sliviites must still be undecided.

The king wished he had time to travel alone into Desante. Perhaps he and Vineda together could figure out the right questions to ask.

Autumn was beginning to flirt with winter, bringing lingering frosts. Dahmis believed he had until spring to prepare. Traditionally, the Sliviites waited until the thaw before sailing out to plunder.

At his elbow, Larseld handed him a message scroll. It carried no seal. Dahmis was surprised to receive it unopened.

"What's this?" He turned it over casually.

"Look closely, my lord."

Dahmis examined the small, neatly bound scroll. His eyes widened. It was carefully tied in a series of knots. The binding was a code he'd nearly forgotten. His post had been alerted to watch for it, but no one knew its meaning besides himself.

Thank God for vigilant men!

He was receiving a direct message from Dreea, King Kareed's widow.

The code was one she had initiated. She'd sent him a present of a lovely piece of weaving. There had been little fanfare attached to it; it was delivered, along with a few other courteous offerings from Vesputo, by a small coterie of soldiers. Remembering Vesputo's poisoned stiletto, Dahmis had the gifts thoroughly searched. All had been found to be innocent. However, one of the soldiers in the coterie had arranged, through Larseld, for a brief meeting alone with the high king. There, Dahmis had been shown the knots—Queen Dreea's method for reaching him secretly.

Now this. Dahmis headed up King's Hill—a small, high rise of ground near his training fields. The high king used it when he wanted to be alone. From its promontories, he could see anyone coming a long way off.

At the top, he leaned against a pile of boulders and read.

My dear King Dahmis. I write to you because everything I hear tells me you are a good and honorable man. You should know that the Sword of Bellandra was not destroyed and remains in Archeld. It should not stay in Vesputo's hands. I can do nothing except let you know where it is, which my husband told me before his death.

There was no signature, but Dahmis shuddered at her bravery. If the message had been intercepted, everything would point to Dreea.

"The Sword of Bellandra," he breathed, hands shaking as he drew out a neat map of Archeld castle's floor plan. "So, it really was stolen when Kareed conquered Bellandra." Kareed had quelled all rumors of the Sword, saying it had been destroyed.

Dahmis rolled the scroll tight and put it in his pocket. He turned his face to the sky, talking out loud.

"How I am to take Bellandra's Sword from Vesputo is hard to see."

When the grim-faced king returned to the archery field, he and Larseld stood apart, conferring. An hour later, a royal messenger was riding hard in the direction of Desante.

Chapter 4

King Ardesen waited for Bellanes. He looked forward to the meeting as he would fine entertainment. Bellanes was everything he had hoped: ingenious, unpredictable, effective.

The young man came forward with his trademark quick grace. Ardesen studied him as he bowed and took a chair opposite the king. The restive, exotic face with its ice-fire eyes greeted him with a brief smile.

"You sent for me, sir."

The king handed a scroll to his guest. Bellanes's eyes darted across it. Ardesen saw a tensing of shoulders, movement as if the young man wanted to crumple it in his fist.

"No, sir." Bellanes handed it back.

"No?" The king squinted in pretended disbelief.

"No. That letter is from King Vesputo."

"He wants to meet you. Invites you to his kingdom for a task he believes only you can do. Promises to pay you richly."

"No, sir."

"Yes, that is what it says."

"I know what it says, sir," Bellanes told him. Ardesen felt singed by the burning in the fighter's eyes.

"Well? Aren't you tempted to find out what King Vesputo wants?"

Bellanes shrugged. "No, sir, not in the least tempted."

"What shall I tell Vesputo?"

"Whatever you like, sir."

Ardesen glared ferociously to hide his amusement as he considered Vesputo's discomfiture. "You surprise me."

"Will that be all, sir?"

"No. I have another letter for you."

With great satisfaction, Ardesen reached into his robes for a second scroll. Bellanes scanned it. This time was different. The young man seemed filled with surging force.

"I can be gone within the hour."

"So, serving the high king is not a matter of indifference to you?"

"No, sir. Do you know what he wants me to do?"

"No."

"I'll start off today." Bellanes bounded from his chair. "Thank you, sir."

He bowed and was gone. Ardesen thumped his fist on his knee in solitary enjoyment, then pounded his forehead because he had not asked *why* Bellanes did not care to meet Vesputo.

"He would never have told me, even if I had asked," the king declared.

Dahmis's breath smoked in the air as he looked out from his favorite spot. He could see Larseld walking up King's

Hill followed by a tall man dressed in a quilted jacket. The stranger moved easily along the steep incline.

"Here is Bellanes, sir," Larseld said.

Dahmis reached out a hand. Bellanes shook it firmly.

"Thank you, Larseld." Dahmis smiled at his general. Larseld nodded and began descending the hill.

"We meet at last, Bellanes. Your attendants are being treated to a supper, I hope?" Dahmis asked.

"I came alone, sir." Dahmis tried to place the clear, ringing accent. Though he'd traveled widely, he couldn't pinpoint it. It nagged around his mind like something remembered from a dream.

Dahmis chuckled. "Perhaps some of the rumors about you are true." Bellanes's dark hair lifted in the breeze. "Yes," the king continued. "There are many reports of you."

"As there are of you, sir."

"It's said you're the most valuable warrior in the kingdoms, yet you shun killing." He lifted his eyebrows. Bellanes stayed impassive.

Dahmis sat on a rocky ledge, looking out at his fortress. "They say you would be true to any cause you fight with, but swear allegiance to no king. That you ride at the head of a band of criminals, fanatically loyal to you alone."

Bellanes gave a faint nod.

"It's even said that this force you lead cannot be defeated," Dahmis went on. "This shows you a leader of men. Yet you keep to yourself. They say you're proud, but allow no servants. A lover of women, with no wife or home." He saw a muscle twitch in the man's cheek.

"Everyone has heard of you, but no one knows you." The king paused. "Do you deny these things?"

Bellanes folded his arms and smiled. "You didn't bring me here to learn my story, sir," he said. "If you did, you'll do better listening to the tale-bearers you've heard already. Their yarns are more entertaining than the truth."

Dahmis laughed. "It's also claimed you can do anything, and no secrets ever cross your lips."

Bellanes grinned. "And what do they say of you, High King? That you can do the impossible, uniting kingdoms sworn to enmity. And that you know far more than anyone can fathom."

"Ah. And that is true. So Bellanes, will you serve with me?"

The young man bowed. "What fortress must I get inside, sir?"

"Vesputo."

Bellanes squinted, as if the sun had suddenly grown too bright. His fists clenched. "Vesputo. Why him?"

"He has something I want, and he won't give it to me voluntarily."

"Do you always hire a thief at such times?"

"No, indeed."

Dahmis considered the reserved warrior in front of him. The man was struggling to hold in some overwhelming passion. The king thought of Vineda. When he had trusted the unknown fortune-teller, it had saved his life. Should he trust this stranger with the half-crazed eyes? More than his own life rode on this choice. If the Sword could be put to dark uses, all the kingdoms might fall. And if this man turned traitor, Dahmis might as well whistle to the wind.

Dahmis sighed. "This item must not be left with Vesputo."

"Then it's yours, sir?"

"Do you only steal for the rightful owner?" Dahmis asked. "The truth is, it's neither mine nor Vesputo's. It belongs to someone else, who is away."

"What is it, and where?"

"A pyramid box, containing treasure. A vault beneath the castle of Archeld. I have a map. It shows a passage to a hidden door leading out of the castle."

Bellanes looked startled. "Hidden door, sir? But how did you find out about it?"

"I cannot tell you."

"I'll memorize the map," Bellanes said. "Carrying papers is unwise."

"Then you'll go?"

"Am I to know what's in the box, sir?"

"No. You must agree not to open it."

"Very well. Name the time and place when you and I will meet again. I'll have the treasure for you, sir."

The men shook hands again. Dahmis picked a meeting spot and a date three weeks away.

"Welcome, Bellanes," the king said, elated to find a worthy new ally. "How will you get into the castle? They say Vesputo keeps a constant guard, thick as a battalion."

Bellanes smiled grimly. "I don't yet know. But I will."

All during the ride back to Desante, Landen wrestled with himself, taking up and throwing down mental plans for how to steal the pyramid box for the high king. He felt he couldn't bear seeing Archeld again, perhaps passing Torina's grave. Yet this task was the chance and challenge of a lifetime. To refuse it would mean the death of his dearest living ambition: to work with King Dahmis for the greater peace.

He entered the camp of his band unobserved, circumventing the lookouts. When he strolled into the firelight, most of the men were sitting together, talking loudly. Andris was making arrows.

"Ha!" Landen cried. "I leave, and the lot of you don't even pretend to work, except this lout," pointing to Andris.

Chagrined, they welcomed him, clapping him on the back, berating him for sneaking up on them.

"For a pack of thieves, you're easy to surprise."

"Where do we go next, Bellanes?" Bangor asked, his scarred face full of expectation.

"Not we. I," Landen answered. "And you, Andris."

"Not us!" The other men clamored like children, begging to take part.

"I can take only one of you, and Andris was fool enough to be working when I spied. So he comes." Landen's tone was final. They stopped questioning to listen.

"Andris and I will be gone several weeks. Bangor will captain you."

He looked around, quick eyes seeking objections. There were none. The men called Bangor the "Angel-Devil" for his face, and respected him for his shrewd imagination.

"Good," their leader continued. "And if we don't return, I urge you to keep together."

The firelight seemed abruptly cold, as if the night

crouched low over their circle. All the faces were somber and intent. Landen knew they understood he wouldn't say such a thing unless he meant it.

"Andris, the decision of whether to ride with me is yours."

Andris put down his tools and raised his fists. "These go with you," he blustered. "The rest of me must follow."

Landen looked across the fire at the big man. "Thank God for that. We leave at dawn."

He spent a few more hours talking with the band and gave Bangor a letter for King Ardesen.

In the pink new morning, Landen and Andris rode away. Five miles out, Landen stopped in a bare glade.

"Andris, I don't want to do this, but it must be done."

His huge companion smiled. "Eh, it's too late you are, for killing me."

Landen grinned. "That wasn't in the plans, though it will be if you tell anyone what I'm about to say."

Andris grew serious. "Is it so?"

"Andris, no one else must know. Not even the band."

"I swear. Even before I hear it."

Landen took a sharp knife from his saddlebag. He turned his back and began to scrape off his dark beard.

Andris laughed. "Are you admitting you're ugly beneath the beard? Is that the great secret?" he howled.

When Landen faced him, clean-shaven, Andris gasped. "Dear God, man, you're . . . lovely." He raised his right hand. "But I swear to tell no one." He broke into unrestrained sniggers.

Looking at his friend's face, Landen whooped with laughter. When they stopped, they wiped tears from their cheeks.

223

"Now for the real secret."

"Ah."

"I'm not who you think I am. I was raised a prince in Bellandra, captured by my father's killer, King Kareed of Archeld, who let me learn to fight. King Kareed met a bad death. I didn't kill him, but his murder is linked to my name. I am Landen, and there's a bounty on my head."

Andris stood stock-still, mouth half open. When he recovered, he put a hand on Landen's shoulder.

"Landen. You? Eh, Bellanes, that is, Landen—"

"Still Bellanes to you. To everyone now."

"The Prince of Bellandra! But why do you tell me this, man?"

"Because it will help us get into Vesputo's vault."

Beron loafed in the courtyard, scowling. Winter was coming, and he hated the short days and cold. It had been a dull week. No news of anything, except a message from King Ardesen telling Vesputo that Bellanes and his band were so taken up with important business that Bellanes would be unable to visit Archeld. This answer to his invitation had put Vesputo in an evil mood.

Beron, his back to the road, looked out at the bare landscape, chafing over the lack of excitement. His fists itched to punch someone.

Behind him, there were shouts. Beron turned in annoyance. These new guards were so green they looked like they'd just been weaned. Strutting around with their "Halt!" and "Who goes?" Beron forgot he'd thought himself quite the man at their age.

A giant man in Desantian clothes and leather armor stood on the steps to the courtyard, holding a rope. The rope was passed around the neck of a ragged man beside him.

"Ho, sentries and halt yourselves!" the big man bellowed. "Bring out the king!"

Beron thrust himself in front of the guards. "The king is too busy to mingle with the scum today," he growled.

The soldiers laughed.

"Does he pay on a bounty or not?" the stranger yelled.

"Bounty? Ha!" Beron sneered. "What bounty? The only bounty King Vesputo has posted is . . ."

The hulking Desantian yanked on the rope he held. The shabby captive shuffled forward in boots full of holes. His hands were tied. His burly warden jerked the hood off his head. Beron gawked as Landen's face looked back at him. Landen. Oh yes. A three-day growth of beard and filthy skin could not possibly disguise those features.

"Landen." He glowered at the prisoner. Landen looked back at him as if Beron were no more than a bug flying across his path.

"Well?" demanded the bounty hunter. "My bounty?"

Warm with elation, Beron slapped the fellow on the shoulder. This news would lift Vesputo's spirits.

"My friend, your bounty shall be paid with interest!" He reached for Landen's halter.

The huge man put up a fist. "Nay! I captured him. I deliver him."

Beron shrugged. "Whatever suits you. You there, soldier! Tell the king."

❖ ❖ ❖

Vesputo strode to the bounty hunter, face alight with dark charm.

"You are the hero who captured this murderer?"

"I am, sir."

"Welcome! Tell me your name, good fellow."

"Corbin. Of Desante."

"Desante. I suspected as much, but he eluded us all this time." Vesputo looked Landen over with satisfaction. "While I celebrate, Landen, you will have a very hard bed."

Landen said nothing.

"We will feast this evening, Corbin. Join us?"

Corbin seemed delighted. "Eh," he asked, in his outlandish way, "will there be wine?"

Vesputo smiled hospitably. "A man in your line of work should never go thirsty. All the bottles you wish, and we'll discuss other bounties that perhaps, with your talents, you can bring in." Vesputo's nod to Beron was friendly. "Take him to the lower west cell," he ordered.

Beron reached again for the prisoner's rope, but Corbin wrapped it more securely around his wrist, speaking to Vesputo. "Sir, I always watch my bounties safely locked away."

The king chuckled. "As you wish, Corbin. Captain, show him to the cell."

Corbin dragged on the halter, and Landen moved to follow.

❖ ❖ ❖

In the elite banquet room of Archeld's castle, Andris sat across from King Vesputo. To his left was Captain Beron, who seemed to scowl even when happy with wine. There were several other men, all getting drunk. Two maids scurried in and out, cleaning the remains of a feast and pouring wine. Andris held up a large goblet to be filled. Wine sloshed as he brought it to his lips.

King Vesputo had already put away four goblets. Beron and his companions were roaring, but the king hardly turned a hair.

Andris remembered Bellanes's instructions. His leader had been sure the "bounty hunter" would take part in a feast once he delivered the bounty.

"Andris, you must drink as little as possible without calling attention to yourself. Spit in your napkin, spill like an oaf. But don't let Vesputo outdrink you. Everything depends on it."

"Bellanes, I could drink any man under the table."

"Not Vesputo. Andris, swear to me you'll keep sharp. I need your wits. You must seem to be drunk, but stay sober."

"But you know I love wine!"

"Yes. And I know you love me enough to give up a few glasses to stay keen for this battle."

"Battle? You say no one will die. What battle? I'd do better with a battle."

"This will be your greatest battle, Andris. Promise!"

Andris had promised.

During the banquet, when the king looked up, Andris lifted his glass to drink; as Vesputo's eyes bent to his plate, Andris squirted the wine into his napkin. Soon the cloth was soaking. He kicked the drenched square under the table and stole another from his neighbor to the left, who never noticed. Even so, there were times when he had to swallow, for Vesputo was sharp eyed. The Archeldan maids never stinted on portions, and the goblets were as big as bowls. Andris was beginning to feel more than tipsy. The other men at the table toasted each other in loud voices.

Now that the food was cleared away, Andris found Vesputo's eyes fixed on him.

"Tell me, my friend," the king asked. "How did you catch this murderer?"

Andris took a healthy swallow of wine. How delicious it was! And how he hated to hear Bellanes talked of that way. Murderer? Bellanes had never killed anyone. Went out of his way to avoid it. Some of the band had goaded him about it; one, Eban, going so far as to taunt Bellanes with "weakness."

"Was it my weakness that allowed you to live, Eban? Let me tell you about weakness! Killing the strong to prove your strength is foolish weakness. Killing fools is easy weakness. Killing the weak is evil weakness. Accomplishing your ends without killing, mastering your mind when you want to kill— that is strength!"

The entire band had been reminded that Bellanes had spared their lives. Eban apologized.

The prince of Bellandra. No wonder he's never killed.

Andris came back to the present and Vesputo's cold face.

"Eh, sir, it was part luck. I chanced to be near when he let it slip to someone he thought he could trust." Andris deliberately slurred his words, finding it easy, too easy. *Eh, Bellanes. I feel the wine. This man seems made of stone.*

"Were you looking for him?" Vesputo asked.

"Yessh, sir. Fifty rashoes ain't nothing to laugh at. I was hunting him."

The king poured a long gulp down his throat. As he set down the empty goblet, his eyes were glassy. *He is flesh after all.*

"I had to knock the bastard out cold." Andris said.

"Ah. He will be very cold indeed by the end of tomorrow," the king answered, tripping on his tongue just a little.

Andris's heart quivered with anxiety. So the prisoner was to be killed tomorrow. He raised his goblet in a toast.

"To bounties!"

He drained the goblet and slammed it down. Vesputo called for more wine. A maid ran to pour for them.

"To you, Corbin. In the morning, I will have more bounties to tell you of. How are you at hunting women?"

The king tipped his head back, guzzling the wine like water. Beron staggered to his feet, then fell heavily to the floor.

Andris laughed boisterously. "None better! To women!" he cried, and took a swig of wine, tasting it all the way down.

Vesputo emptied his goblet again. A maid was instantly beside him, pouring.

"To captive women!" the king toasted.

Andris drank, and Vesputo watched him.

"To wine!" the big man roared. He clinked goblets with Vesputo, spilling on the table.

The king gulped more. Andris looked around. The rest of the men were settling into stupors. Finally Vesputo slid down in his chair and slumped to the floor. Andris let his head sag to the tabletop, pretending to snore.

He heard maids laughing to one another as they blew

out the candles. Then they slipped away, talking of having a feast themselves before they came back.

❖ ❖ ❖

In the pitch darkness of his cell, Landen pushed against a wall to steady himself. This was no common jail. It was an underground vault, silent as a grave. He could neither hear nor see anything.

The blackness and absolute quiet pressed on him. The past was so close he felt he could touch it with the hands that braced him against the prison wall. Walking into the familiar courtyard had unstrung his nerves. He remembered the way Vesputo had thrown him in front of the princess, the day he first arrived. He recalled her radiant sympathy as she helped him to his feet. Her childish voice. *"I can do whatever I want with him? I set him free."*

Torina. He kept loving her. Loved her even though she was gone. Dead. It had taken terrible effort not to attack Vesputo in the courtyard. He knew Andris would have helped him if he changed plans. Landen still trembled with the need to choke Vesputo, shake the truth from him.

Come back to the present moment, he ordered himself, taking his palms from the stone, slapping his shoulders and face.

Even in darkness and sorrow, the moment is vast. The old teachings came echoing back.

Why was he here? For Dahmis, high king. Why take such risks for him? Because he was a man of peace.

230

What is there left of my life, but the legacy of Bellandra? My father lived for peace and died by the sword. Did he live and die for nothing? Where is justice?

"No, no," he told himself. "That way leads to madness. Do not ask where justice is. Ask where Andris is. Where is Andris? How long have I been in this tomb?"

He felt along the wall to the locked bars and clung to them, believing he heard stumbling footsteps. Yes. Someone was coming.

Landen hovered, as a man groped his way down the passage. Heavy breathing came nearer.

"Is that you at last, you drunken sot?" he hissed.

"Shh, Bellanes. Yes, it's me," said Andris's voice, slightly slurred. "Sorry. It took a long time to drink him down."

"The guard?"

"Will have a headache tomorrow."

"Candle?"

"Here." Andris grunted. A match was struck. The candle was thrust through the bars. "Hold the light so I can find which of these blasted keys fits."

Andris held up a wide band of keys. Landen smiled with relief.

"The king's keys! Did you get his ring too?"

"Easy enough, once he passed out."

The bars creaked as they opened. Landen embraced his deliverer.

"You deserve death by hanging. Did you have to drag so hard on that rope? You nearly separated my neck from my shoulders!"

"I was trying to save you worse, Bellanes. That Captain Beron hates you. You told me—"

"I know what I told you." Landen grinned. "Thank you. Now, the box we are to steal is almost beside us, if the map in my head is right."

❖ ❖ ❖

Emid had taken to walking at night after the barracks were shadowed and still. He drew strength from the silvered sky and earth that way, as he had once drawn strength from his devotion to duty. He no longer knew why he trained young men to be soldiers; the thought of King Vesputo filled him with revulsion. Emid didn't forget the strange, red-haired figure in the chapel, the woman who could not be Torina. He'd pondered and pondered over where the true princess might be. He haunted the edges of Vesputo's councils, looking for clues, finding none. When he could, he told stories of Princess Torina to the boys in his charge, keeping her legend alive. Not the poor, demented weakling Vesputo had crafted. The vibrant, imperious firebrand he knew.

And Queen Dreea? He rarely saw her. Whenever he did, he met her sad eyes and believed she shared with him the same secret hope, that her daughter was not buried in the grave that bore her name. They never spoke of it. After Dreea recovered from her illness, she floated through the castle, pale and quiet, weaving, sewing, helping run the household. Emid noticed she preferred his arm to any other on state occasions when her presence was required.

A few weeks ago, when Vesputo was away, the queen had asked to observe Emid's daily training exercises. She sat on a bench with Mirandae, wrapped in warm shawls, watching the youngsters. She found reason to send Mirandae into the house. Then she smiled at the boys, asking Emid's supporting arm so she could get back to her weaving. As they walked together, she slipped a scroll into his sleeve.

"I'm giving you a death sentence for myself and you if anyone finds this," she told him, facing forward with a serene expression. "I trust you, Emid, to get it to the high king. If you wish to read it, please do so. Study the knots on the binding; you must duplicate them exactly when you tie it again. They contain my personal code to King Dahmis."

"My dear queen, you honor me. You can trust me with anything as long as I'm alive. Tell me what the letter says. I'm not practiced with ribbons."

"It gives the location of the Sword of Bellandra and urges him to take it from Vesputo."

Then she had talked of the weather, while Emid's head buzzed, his thoughts absorbed with the mythical Sword of Bellandra. Dreea knew where it was! She needed his help to protect it from Vesputo.

The scroll had been sent by underground messenger.

On this night, Emid passed the guards with a quiet wave as usual, tramping around the grounds. He wished, as he had a thousand times, that he was a man with a political ear. He simply did not understand the tangled subterfuge of Vesputo's reign.

If I knew for certain Torina was alive, I would proclaim it to anyone who would listen. But I know nothing. I cannot rally the people around a ghost. Even if she lives, she might never return.

There was no snow, but the air smelled like a storm might come soon. Moonlight glowed on the tree-surrounded walls of the south side of the castle, where the doors had been bolted for winter.

As Emid paced on, he blinked at one of the walls. It seemed to be moving. He glanced around. No guards in sight. The trainer melted into thick shadows.

The wall moved again. A hidden door chinked and opened. Emid saw a hooded head appear and swivel around, checking the territory. The man, whoever he was, beckoned over his shoulder and emerged, carrying a large, pyramid-shaped box. Stealing out behind him, a huge fellow pressed the door closed. The moon shone on a seamless wall again.

Emid stood rooted as the two men hurried forward at a crouch. They quickly gained the trees. Emid's mouth opened to call the guards, but he didn't yell. There was something about the hooded man's agile step that was eerily familiar.

The men huddled not ten feet from where he was. He could hear them breathing.

"Get some horses, using his ring," the hooded man spoke very low. "Gray stallions. This country is full of them. Meet me in the woods behind the stable."

"Which way?" the big man asked.

His partner told him, punctuating the whispers with gestures. "And remember."

"I know. No killing." The larger man hustled toward the stables.

Alone in the trees with the thief, Emid regulated his breathing so as not to give himself away. He feared this familiar stranger would sense his presence. *Who was it? What was in the box?*

The man knelt beside it. He looked back toward the castle and put his two hands over his heart as though grieving. His fingers came up, brushing the hood back from his face. The moon illuminated his features.

Landen! It was Landen! Whatever could he be doing here? Only that evening, there were announcements of his capture.

The trainer looked hard at the profile chiseled in moonlight. The face was dirty and stubbled, older.

Did he kill King Kareed? Studying Landen, Emid did not believe those sad, determined young features belonged to a killer. And what had the other man said? *No killing.* Would a murderer have such a standing order?

Emid wanted to rush forward, ask Landen a hundred questions. Where had he gone? What had he seen? Who was the grieving gesture for? Princess Torina, maybe— who else would Landen mourn?

But still he hung back.

Landen shouldered his burden and left with a tracker's invisible steps.

The trainer came back to life. He started forward. His foot jingled into something. Bending to the ground, he picked up a great ring of keys.

The king's keys! How did Landen get Vesputo's keys?

Thoroughly puzzled, Emid turned the keys in his hand. Walking on with measured pace, he shoved the keys into his cape, following his course as if there had been no interruption, exchanging nods with guards along the way. He timed his steps so that when he reached the rear stairs of the courtyard, the guards had their backs turned. Then he laid the king's keys in a shadowed part of the balustrade, where they would be sure to be found in daylight.

In the morning, when Vesputo asked him what he had seen, Emid knew what his answer would be. The moon shining on bare winter ground.

❖ ❖ ❖

Just after dawn, on the rocky coast of Archeld, Landen and Andris guided two gray stallions. The thirsty horses stopped at a streambed. The riders dismounted.

"How you found your way through to the sea in the dark and led us this far, I can't know," Andris said.

"I told you, I know this land." Landen looked out at the ocean. "We'll be riding all day, my friend. Thieves don't live long if they get caught." He grinned. "They should be holding their heads about now."

"Aye," Andris sniggered. "The party is about to wake up." He thrust his hand in front of Landen's face. On his finger, Vesputo's ring flashed. "Two horses, my man, and quickly," Andris ordered, parodying his actions from the night before. "Easiest horse-stealing I ever did!"

"Vesputo will die of shame."

"Which is the proper death for such a man." Andris winked.

Snowflakes began swirling down out of the dim sky. Landen caught one on his tongue. "Andris, we're saved."

"Saved? This will make for slow, cold riding, Bellanes."

"For our pursuers too. It will cover our tracks." Landen swung into the saddle. "We'll ride northeast."

"Ain't that out of our way?"

"Some. They might track us to this point. Beyond

that, they can whistle for our direction. Come, man! Vesputo won't take this defeat kindly. He'll have every soldier he can spare combing the countryside for Landen, vile murderer."

By nightfall, the travelers were so cold and weary they had trouble setting up their tent. By scrounging a few sticks of dry wood from the soaking grass and bushes of the plains, they made a pitiful little blaze. They agreed to take turns feeding it. Andris took the first watch, sitting beside the faltering fire.

Sometime during the night, Landen woke shivering. It took a few moments to realize where he was. The tent was totally dark. Poking his head out, he found Andris wrapped head to toe in blankets, snoring next to the snow-covered remains of the fire. Landen wriggled out of the tent. Thick snow covered the ground and fell steadily around him. The air had the hushed, odd luminescence of night snow. The temperature had dropped. Crouching beside Andris, he brushed snow from the big man's blankets and tried to wake him. It was useless. Landen gave up, covering the sleeper with another of his own blankets.

He searched for dry tinder. He lifted rocks, inspecting the ground underneath. Wind had driven the snow under and through everything. Hugging and slapping himself, teeth chattering, he tried to see which among the ghostly humps of the snowy plains might conceal something dry. The cold thickened around him.

He stumbled and fell headlong. He pulled himself up, rubbing his shin. Whatever tripped him had a hard edge. He bent to examine the snow. His gloved hands felt the outlines of the steel box they had stolen for the high king.

His palms tingled painfully where they rested on the box. There seemed to be heat emanating from it. Landen sat down next to the pyramid, leaning against it. No doubt about it, the treasure gave off warmth. He felt strangely comforted. Prodding himself to get up, to rouse Andris, he continued to be still.

There in the night on the frozen plains of northern Archeld, the softest fire stole across his life, burning away sorrow, anguish, and regret. His heart felt light and free as it had in childhood. Dreamlike, he was lifted higher and higher on soothing flames, transported to another world, where love thrummed in the atmosphere like music. Floating in a timeless, humming ecstasy, Landen drifted into sleep.

❖ ❖ ❖

Sunlight dazzled Landen's eyes. Andris's face, red with cold, was over him.

"Whatever are you doing against that hard, cold box?" The big man's voice was hoarse.

"Not cold," Landen insisted, then realized it *was* cold. He touched the box, testing its contours with his fingers. Cold. He shook his head. "I dreamed so well."

"You're a strange one, Bellanes. I never saw a man look better after a night of freezing. Get up, man. I want to see if your legs will hold you."

The bright day reflected Landen's mood: renewed and strong. He grinned at his companion, getting to his feet easily. He knelt beside the box, swishing snow away from its planes so as to inspect the locks.

"Andris, this time I wish I hadn't given my word."

"You want to see the treasure?"

"Aye." He patted the pyramid. "Well, my friend, let's load up and ride. When we get to the forest, we can try for a fire."

Chapter 5

"**B**ellanes!" The high king pumped his hand. "I confess I'm surprised to see you here. I expected to get a message instead, saying you were delayed or telling me to take the treasure to hell. And here you are, telling me you have the pyramid box. What you've done is next to impossible!"

Andris and Bellanes had carried the steel box across the plains of Archeld into the forests of Glavenrell. There, Bellanes insisted on stopping at a collapsing, deserted shack, the appointed meeting place for his rendezvous with the high king. Andris had wondered, right up to the moment King Dahmis and General Larseld rode up disguised as farmers, if such a spot could be the one they wanted. But so it was. The flash of gold when the farmer took off his gloves convinced Andris that the king was real. And the high king's horse, under shabby trappings, was among the finest Andris had ever seen. General Larseld drove a rickety farmer's cart packed with straw and drawn by two more horses. King Dahmis led a magnificent brown stallion behind the one he rode.

The big man stood silent, overcome by awe to be in the presence of the high king dressed in a patched coat.

The men were meeting outside, for the half-fallen shack offered little protection. It had stopped snowing, though drifts surrounded them.

Bellanes laughed, a carefree sound Andris had never heard. "I'd say what *you* have done is impossible. The coalition of kings, the peaceful trade . . ."

Dahmis smiled. "Good to see you."

Bowing, Bellanes handed the signet ring of Archeld to the high king.

"Vesputo's ring."

"How did you do it?" King Dahmis demanded, taking the ring.

Again, Bellanes gave a free laugh. "No, my lord, I never agreed to reveal my secrets. It's enough that I deliver the treasure, unopened."

Andris was amazed to see the high king bow respectfully to the man who had just told him no.

Bellanes turned to a heap of snow beside them, digging out the pyramid box. King Dahmis bent to it, putting his hands on it.

"This is the box." He shook his head in admiration. "Name your reward, Bellanes."

Andris watched as his leader shifted feet. "We agreed on a fee."

"Yes. That was when I didn't believe you could do what you've done."

Bellanes stared at his boots.

"Come, man," General Larseld spoke up. "You've done a priceless service. You have the right to ask for a reward."

"The reward I wish for is priceless too."

"Name it."

Bellanes swallowed. Andris could see water filming his eyes. "Your friendship," he said hoarsely.

The king put a hand on Bellanes's shoulder. "I'm high king over thousands. People seek me out for favors, for protection, for aid in resolving strife. I count my friends on two hands. Each of them is more precious than all the kingdoms." He paused. "It would be an honor to call you friend."

Andris saw his leader's glistening smile, General Larseld nodding approval, the high king beaming. As he watched Bellanes moving with ease among these great men, Andris felt himself to be witnessing events of mighty consequence.

The pyramid box was packed inside a crate with straw and laid in the farmer's cart. The high king agreed to arrange that Vesputo's gray stallions be hidden for, of course, they would be missed and looked for.

"Now for your fee," King Dahmis said, handing the reins of the two brown stallions to Bellanes. "No other man in the kingdoms, Bellanes, has ever made me part with such fine horses."

When Andris understood that he was to have his own wonderful horse, he brimmed over with gratitude, thankful for the day he had lost in the Desan games.

❖ ❖ ❖

King Dahmis sat silent, staring into a roaring blaze. Beside him, Larseld and Michal played chess.

"Ha!" Michal said, gloating. "I have you now, General."

"Indeed?" Larseld countered. "I'm always at your service, of course, Michal. But this time, it's I who have you. Checkmate."

Michal gaped at the board, protesting that Larseld had an unfair advantage because he was a general. "One more move and you would have been mine!"

Dahmis chuckled. "That's why Larseld controls my troops, Michal. Because his last move comes before the enemy's."

Michal glared. "Keep out of this, Dahmis. Go back to being morose. The fire is fit company for you."

"Can't a man think in peace, without his friends calling him morose?"

"Thinking! Is that what you call it? What are you thinking of?"

"I can guess," Larseld answered.

"The general speaks! He knows the thoughts of his opponents and friends! Thus he catches them when they least expect it."

"Larseld doesn't know my thoughts," Dahmis growled.

"He's thinking about the Sword of Bellandra," Larseld said.

Startled, Dahmis turned in his chair. "Impressive, General."

"He's wondering whether to use it to defend Glavenrell against the Sliviites."

Dahmis sighed. "Almost, Larseld. You're nearly there, but you have the wrong track."

Michal laughed. "A flaw in the general's expert stratagem?"

"I'm only sorry, because I know the Sword of Bellandra is not for me."

"It's supposed to be a powerful weapon," Larseld said.

"It may be all that myth has told of it," Dahmis answered. "However, that doesn't make it mine. If I brought it out to use in battle, I'd be taking the first step to corruption."

"Who does it belong to, if not to you?" Michal asked.

"The prince of Bellandra, wherever he may be."

"But he's wanted for the murder of King Kareed," Larseld put in.

"Wanted by Vesputo, who's now conveniently king," Michal said.

"Ever since Vesputo sent a man to overthrow me with poison, I've wondered if the prince of Bellandra might be innocent," Dahmis said. "The prince fled Archeld. No one ever heard that he died."

"And if he did?" Larseld asked.

"It wouldn't make the Sword belong to me. I know this with my soul. No, my friends, the Sword stays locked away in that pyramid box, shut inside an ugly crate."

Chapter 6

In the middle of a howling winter storm, Torina's cabin was snug and warm. The young woman cooked a simple evening meal and ate absently. She was healthy and strong from riding so much. Healthy, not happy. Letters in a hollow tree couldn't sustain her need for companionship; looking into the crystal gave her glimpses of all the kingdoms, but not a single sight of Landen.

She listened to the wind moan. Gazing at snapping flames, she was reminded of her former self. *Once I was as luminous and full of motion as fire. Now I live cold as winter all year long, more alone than a hermit nun.*

She stared at her writing paper. One word, Dahmis had said. One word, and he would send for her, let her live under his protection.

Torina loved going where she wished, without escorts, guards, or permission. To mount Justina when the mood took her, ride as far and as lost as she wanted, come home when it suited her; all this she treasured.

What good is my independence without freedom to show my head? She gripped the arms of her chair. She had made up her mind. She would send the "one word" and go to live in

Glavenrell. The next time she saw Dahmis, she'd petition his help in finding Landen. Between them, they could discover if he lived and where.

She wrote the letter immediately.

Dear Cousin,

How is your village? Though well, I am feeling the weather and wish I might join you in a warmer house.

Vineda.

She rolled the message, tying cords with practiced fingers. She grabbed her worn jacket and opened the door. A gale-force wind greeted her, driving needles of snow into her face. Torina laughed and shut the door again. Of course, she would need to wait for the storm to pass.

She hung her coat, glowing and happy. Tomorrow she and Justina would find their way through the drifts to the hollow tree. Even if it took a few weeks to move to Glavenrell, it would happen. Life! She felt ready to dance. Full of energy, she decided to make the most of the confining weather. She would consult her crystal for the high king, perhaps add an important postscript to her letter.

She unbraided her long, burnished hair, luxuriating in the feeling of having it hang free. She put another log on the fire.

Bringing out her seer's eye, she let herself be drawn into its depths. First she asked again for a vision of Landen. The obstinate globe showed her a circle of men sitting around a fire. She had the sense that it was a group of criminals. One of the men had a monstrous scar on the side of his face. Was Landen in the company of such men? She peered anxiously, but he didn't seem to be among them. The image faded.

Never mind. Soon the high king would be searching for him.

She kept looking in the crystal. This time, she saw Vesputo and Dahmis standing together. The high king shook Vesputo's hand. His voice rumbled in Torina's mind like an ocean storm. *"We are now allies."* And the hated voice of her former betrothed: *"Count on me to honor the terms of the alliance."*

She stared in disbelief, but the horrifying sight persisted, the two kings in smiling agreement.

"It can't be. No, no, no," she chanted, wanting to throw the crystal into the fire and watch it heat until it cracked. "No, no, please," she moaned, as the high king and her father's murderer toasted each other with glad faces.

Torina jumped up, tossing the crystal away as if it would burn her. Grabbing the scroll she'd written earlier, she unwound its cords, crumpled the message into a ball, and slung it at the fire. As the flames took hold, she sank back in her chair, rigid with anger and loss. While winter raged outside her cabin, she felt as if all the ice of the world was packed around her heart.

Dahmis watched his soldiers train, forehead wrinkled with worry. Spies daily brought him reports of Sliviite might: thousands of mercenaries sharpening their blades behind the Sliviite banner; droves of Sliviite slaves learning to man the enormous navy ships; swaggering Sliviite soldiers drilling from dawn till dusk.

Still no definite word of where they would make their onslaught. More troubling, Vineda had sent no messages in three weeks. That was not like her. What if the men hunting her had been successful? What if she had been abducted or killed?

Dahmis didn't like to admit to himself how much the lovely seer occupied his thoughts. Now, when his mind should be on his troops, his allies, strategies for war, he spent time he couldn't spare wondering about Vineda. Tempted to send a trusted spy to find out if she still lived in the Desantian forest, he was annoyed with himself for having promised her he wouldn't tell anyone where or who she was.

As if he knew who she was. Did anyone know? Why was she so secretive? With her gifts, she would be welcome, sought after, celebrated, in any court she chose. Instead, she lived hidden away, as though she'd committed some heinous crime and feared discovery.

I would have thought she was too young to be willing to give up all the splendors her beauty would earn. But even that beauty she hides under ugly clothes and disguising scarves. Is public adoration so loathsome to her? He remembered her angry words: "*I cannot live a prisoner in a king's fortress.*" What young woman could believe that life in the high king's fortress, surrounded by awed attendants, would be imprisonment? And what about that other statement, spoken with such bald, scornful sadness: "*I feel awe, but not of kings.*"

Dahmis shook his head in exasperation and called for Larseld. When his general was at his side, the king explained that he would be gone for several days.

"My lord, the council of kings?"

"I'll return in time for the council."

"I thought we would prepare."

"We will. Just not in the same room. This errand is necessary, though inconvenient to everything."

"Pardon me, sir. Can no one else do this . . . errand?"

"No, Larseld, no one else. Come, we'll talk with Michal and settle all pressing business before I leave in the morning."

Dahmis, dressed as a messenger, took a swift horse and rode in the direction of Desante. This disguise best excused the fact that he was mounted on one of the best animals in the kingdom. As he galloped down the main roads, no one seeing him questioned his speed; urgent messages were growing commonplace among the allied kings.

As he neared Vineda's cabin, the king's fatigue was acute. He half expected to find the place deserted. The thoughts that had driven him on the long ride clamored in his head. *Is she safe?*

He dismounted in her clearing beside a dark, silent cabin. Peering inside, he saw embers in the hearth; checking the stable, he found Justina munching straw. Dahmis decided to wait for Vineda. If she didn't come back soon, he would ask at the farmhouse for news of her.

Weary as he was, the king rubbed down his horse and gave him food.

As he left the stable, Vineda walked into the meadow. It was now full night, though a bright moon lit the snow to a pale likeness of day. Her usual scarf wrapped her head, and a threadbare jacket covered her body. Wonderfully relieved to see her, Dahmis wondered again why she would conceal so much beauty.

"Vineda," he said, all his tiredness forgotten. He touched her shoulder affectionately, then stepped back, nonplussed by the lack of welcome in her face.

"Vineda? What is it?"

Her eyes looked opaque in the moonlight. "You have allied yourself with Vesputo," she said, as if he'd done something unforgivable.

Dahmis gritted his teeth. "So I have. It was necessary. Vineda, there are times when this sight of yours is a curse. I wanted to tell you myself."

"He will betray the alliance."

"His soldiers fight well. His coastal borders are vulnerable to Sliviite attack!"

With set face, she began walking to her cabin. "He *will* betray you," she said over her shoulder.

Dahmis pursued her. "Have you seen this? If you have, why no message?"

She whirled to face him. "I don't need a vision where Vesputo is concerned!"

"So, you have *not* seen it." He stared at her face, whitened by moonlight. Again he reached for her. She shrank from him.

"Vesputo knows his interests, Vineda," he said, trying to talk reasonably. "The Sliviites are a far greater threat to him than anything he's ever faced. And a greater threat to me than one king with a lust for power. Only a complete alliance can stave off the Sliviite forces. All reports agree they're massing for the greatest invasion we've ever endured. It's only what you know yourself."

The lovely young woman balled her fists. "Why are you here?"

"Two reasons. Foremost, I came to see if anything had happened to you. Second, if I ever needed your help, I do now."

"You will not get it."

"Please, Vineda. The alliance is important. Vesputo commands a sizable army. As soon as the ice melts, everyone in the kingdoms is in danger, including him."

"Have you forgotten? He plotted against your life."

"The high king cannot afford to hold grudges. I need Vesputo. His position is central. To overthrow him would exhaust my forces when they are needed most. The alliance is the only good choice!" His voice rose, blowing clouds in the frosty air.

"Then may it profit you," she answered.

"Will you help me?"

She lifted her chin, lips trembling. She turned her back.

"Vineda. Please. Help us!"

She went inside and closed the door. The high king stood alone, lifting his eyes to the starry sky. He wanted to beat down her door, force her to serve him. He wondered where and when she had learned to hate Vesputo with such passion. She must be ignorant of kings if she could not overlook the chessboard moves they often made against one another. Vesputo wasn't the only one who'd tried to take Dahmis's place. Early in his kingship, Dahmis had been challenged in every possible way: some overt, many covert.

Now, Vesputo had provided the missing piece for Dahmis. His spies had been able to discover where the Sliviite invasion would land. He'd allowed Dahmis to interview several men and one woman, all of whom had made the dangerous journey to Sliviia. Each had intercepted the same intelligence: the Sliviites would sail to Bellan Bay, one of the largest bays on the whole coast.

Dahmis realized how much he'd grown to rely on Vineda's skill. He didn't like moving ahead without it. He'd ridden so hard to be next to her. Now, in front of him, her cabin was dark. She might as well be across the ocean.

"God help us," he prayed. Moonlight fell around him, not answering.

❖ ❖ ❖

Vesputo arrived early for the joint council of kings. He wanted a chance to observe all the rulers as they walked in. The room chosen for this historic meeting was spacious and well furnished. Every smooth surface was polished till it shone, the thick Glaven rugs brushed soft. After greeting Dahmis with deference, Vesputo stood to the back, face set in regal reserve. He controlled his fear that Torina had warned the high king. He would need to watch carefully and gauge his actions accordingly.

Ardesen, king of Desante, swept in, frowning, treating Dahmis to a curt bow, his gray head taller than the high king's. Fierce Mlaven, ruler of Emmendae, the harsh land north of Glavenrell, embraced Dahmis.

"So, my friend," Vesputo heard Mlaven say. "What does your fortune-teller advise?"

A muscle jumped in the high king's cheek. "She has ceased to help me," he replied softly.

"No prophecies! That is hard news. You must find out her price, my lord."

"She doesn't respond to those inducements," Dahmis answered.

Vesputo clenched his jaw with the effort not to break into victorious laughter. Torina had broken with the high king! Now the fool would have only his own starry-eyed visions to guide him.

Once the council was under way, Dahmis encouraged Vesputo to tell the others what his spies had learned: that the main thrust of the Sliviite attack would be Archeld, in what was formerly Bellandra.

"Bellan Bay is more accessible than anywhere south of Emmendae," he said. "The waters will be warm within a week. From there, they can pillage Archeld and make their way in force to Glavenrell."

"It's what I'd do if I had their navy," boomed King Mlaven.

"What are our assembled numbers?" Ardesen of Desante asked.

"Fifty thousand troops among us," Dahmis answered. "We estimate the Sliviite invading force at thirty thousand strong, including mercenaries."

"How shall we distribute our soldiers?" asked Endak, quiet king of Davia.

"We cannot leave any country without protection, of course," Dahmis asserted.

"If everyone agrees the brunt of the attack will fall at Bellan Bay, I advise we concentrate our forces there, and devise a way to send messages quickly so that if any surprises occur, we can cover with reinforcements," Vesputo put forth.

❖ ❖ ❖

After the council was over, the kings returned to their homelands. All had agreed to send their most seasoned soldiers, under a trusted general, to the coast of Archeld. Larseld would coordinate the other generals for concerted defense. Troops would be on the march within a week. Dahmis was elated with the progress of their cooperation. History was made: the collected kings had conferred together with only minor hostility, each submitting to the good of the alliance. It was a victory the high king rejoiced in. It seemed to him the stars must be singing with happiness. The only sad note came when he thought of Vineda.

A message was sent with Ardesen to ask Bellanes and his band to visit Glavenrell. In a few days, Dahmis got word that the men were camped outside Glaven City. Bellanes, still shunning his spreading fame, thought it too risky to meet the king in public. He sent word of where to find his camp. Dahmis rode out with Larseld to see him.

They arrived in the evening and were halted by a man with a livid scar on his face.

"Give the password."

"Peace awaits."

The man led them to a campfire circle where Bellanes met them with a smile.

"My lord." He swept the circle with his hand. "This is my band. Men! The high king, and General Larseld."

Dahmis was amused at the sudden galvanism among them. Plainly, Bellanes had not prepared them. They stood as one. The guard who had asked for a password seemed stunned. "I— I, my lord!"

"Bangor, the high king understands the need for passwords," Bellanes told the flustered man. "My lord, your time is short, I know. What is it you need?"

Dahmis addressed the entire band. "The council of kings met and decided the Sliviite attack will be focused on Archeld, at the coast near what used to be Bellandra. All the allied members are pledged to send troops there and agreed to work under Larseld's direction. Larseld leaves in the morning. I want you to go with him. Your skills may be invaluable there. King Vesputo particularly requested your participation."

Bellanes frowned. "Vesputo is now part of your alliance?" His voice was hard.

"Yes, he has joined us."

"So late?" Bellanes folded strong arms.

Dahmis sighed. "He may be motivated by self-interest, since he believes his shores vulnerable. His spies report Bellan Bay as the first Sliviite target."

Bellanes stood taut as a ready bowstring. "My lord, forgive me for what I have to say."

"Please, speak freely."

"My band and I won't go to Bellan Bay to defend Vesputo. I beg you not to weaken your forces in Glavenrell. The Sliviites fight intelligently, and though Bellan Bay may be a likely access point, they must know Glavenrell and Emmendae have bays as well. What if they realize that by invading Glavenrell and smashing the high king, they would meet only disorganized resistance afterward?"

Dahmis stepped closer to the fire. "You believe the Sliviites will aim at Glavenrell first?"

"You are the central power among the kingdoms. They can't be ignorant of that."

"What about the information from Vesputo's spies? If we can blunt the first attack with the alliance, we stand a far better chance collectively."

"Have other sources confirmed it? Have your own spies told you this?" Bellanes probed.

"No, though all agree the Sliviites are prepared for war and are even now launching their ships."

"If they land on your shores, and you've sent away your best troops, how will you fight?" Bellanes's clear voice beat at him.

"I can't forsake the alliance now. I've pledged my word. It would go against everything I've worked for."

"Then, my lord, my band and I will stay in Glavenrell, where we can help you if needed."

Looking around at the attentive faces, Dahmis felt that this group of men was in absolute unity with their leader.

The high king bowed his head. "Thank you, Bellanes. Keep me informed of where you make camp."

Chapter 7

Torina dug in her garden, wrestling stubborn chunks of soil. Cool air met her hot cheeks and wafted around her covered head. She was tired of the cumbersome kerchief and felt wretchedly warm. Sweating in the weak sunshine of early spring, she beat the resisting ground as if it could yield relief for her pent-up spirits.

She hadn't looked at the crystal in weeks. When her heart reproached her for forsaking the alliance, she revived the image of Dahmis and Vesputo toasting each other.

Today the crystal called her. Her arm tingled and throbbed. Torina threw down her shovel and slammed into her cabin. Wrapped in cloth on a shelf, her seer's eye seemed to stare through the fabric into her mind. Dripping sweat, Torina reached for it, her hand pulsing and humming. But before touching the stone, she drew back, clenching her fists.

"No, no, no!" She ran out of the cabin.

She rushed to saddle Justina. The horse seemed to catch her mood, running hard through the meadows. Torina tried to lose herself in the flowing movement, not caring where they went.

It was late afternoon by the time she approached the village again. Exhausted, she noticed how much the temperature had dropped and how thin her dress was against the cold. When she realized Justina was making her way toward Lindsa's house, she brought up short.

Two local farmers plodded toward her, men she knew slightly. She pulled Justina aside to let them pass. As they drew abreast, they stopped, staring. Torina sat waiting for them to move on, caught in a vague sense of foreboding.

"Vineda?" one asked.

The sun was lowering, but there was still enough light to be able to tell who she was. Torina looked into the man's lined face. "What is it?"

"It is you, Vineda?" he persisted.

"Yes."

"Why, lass, you're beautiful. Don't believe I've ever seen you with your hair down."

Raising her hand, Torina felt damp strands. No kerchief. When did she lose it? It must have been during the ride. Now they had seen her and, if anyone asked about a red-haired woman, they could answer. No use asking them to say nothing. This was news.

"Thank you," she faltered, guiding Justina off the road. "I must be going." She plunged through the shadows, not looking back.

For years, she had hidden her head. Now, in a moment of carelessness, all that secrecy was undone. *It doesn't matter! After so long, Vesputo, along with everyone else, believes I'm dead.*

An ominous cloud followed her. She glanced nervously around as drops began pelting her bare head.

Swift, harsh lightning cut the air. Torina's dress was soon drenched, while Justina bent to the whipping wind.

When they reached home, there was no solace in being there. As Torina rubbed Justina in the dark stable, everything she saw, all she did, seemed to belong to someone dead.

"We'll go away," she told her horse. "We can't stay here, between worlds. We'll go to Desan and live."

Pushing out of the stall, she staggered to her cabin, hounded by the wailing storm. Inside she stooped to light a fire, while rain and wind rattled the whole place. When she sank into her chair, her skin burned with fever.

❖ ❖ ❖

Vesputo was resolved to unleash the Sword of Bellandra at last. Thanks to his careful efforts, the best of the allied forces from Dahmis's coalition of kings were gathering in one spot, within his domains. Now would be the perfect time to strike, to master them all.

Kareed never used the Sword. He disdained Bellandra's magic enough to brave it head on, but feared to tangle with the curse.

Kareed's warning, that the Sword would bring doom to anyone who used it for conquest, had struck Vesputo forcefully when he first heard it, the day they locked the Sword away in the vault. But that one glimpse of the magnificent weapon had been enough to stoke his ambition for almost a decade. History and legend agreed that the warrior who wielded the Sword became invincible. The thought of the Sword's curse was losing sway. The beautiful thing had lain untouched all this time. It must not have any power unless held by human hands.

Kareed lacked the courage to take up the Sword and use it. I have the strength. Destiny has delivered this weapon to me.

Vesputo believed the only reason the pacifist fool, King Veldon, had been conquered was because he never lifted the Sword to defend Bellandra, trusting in its reputation alone to ward off enemies. The Sword was last raised in battle during the time of Veldon's great-great-grandfather, Landen the First. Ironic that his distant grandson and namesake had been dispossessed before coming of age.

Landen. Every time Vesputo thought of him, it rankled more. The man had been locked in the deepest recesses of the castle and escaped. The bounty hunter disappeared along with him, and Vesputo still wondered what role the mysterious Corbin played. Was he in league with Landen? It was the only sound explanation. But why would Landen allow himself to be imprisoned, only to vanish? Aside from Vesputo's ring, nothing had been taken except a pair of gray stallions—surely not enough to risk freedom and life for.

Did Landen come out of hiding just to laugh in my face? In his place, I would have killed.

Yes, the time had come. Vesputo's destiny had arrived. He would take up the Sword and take his rightful place in history.

Filled with suppressed excitement, Vesputo dismissed his guards and descended the stairs to the secret vault alone. His torch flickered on dim walls. With rising anticipation, he entered the vault.

Thrusting the torch ahead, his first thought was that the pyramid box had been moved: it wasn't in his line of sight. Hands turning to ice, Vesputo searched the four walls. All he saw were scattered shadows of covered boxes too small to hold the Sword. Fighting panic and rage, he examined the musty room, casting about with the smoking light. Nothing.

It had to be there. Setting the torch in a sconce on the wall, he uncovered each box in the dank space. There were few, and he was soon done. The Sword of Bellandra was gone. All that was left to him was dust. Sitting on a moldy wooden case, he beat his fist into his palm.

How? Vesputo wasn't superstitious; he had always felt master of his fate. It never occurred to him to explain this disappearance as a conspiracy of magic. No, this was the work of a human being.

Who?

He sat fingering his ring of keys, counting them over till he touched the one to this vault.

Only the king has this key.

Suddenly he was gripping the engraved metal so hard it cut him. Blood dripped on the floor and he never noticed.

He remembered how he had gotten back his missing keys. A group of frightened young soldiers had approached him in a body, each too afraid to get near him alone. They swore the king's keys were found on the courtyard steps the morning of Landen's disappearance.

Landen. The keys. He locked his cell again when he left, so people would think Bellandran magic spirited him away, but I know he had the keys. That would explain his coming. That would account for him putting himself in my power. To gain the Sword of Bellandra.

Vesputo grasped the torch again, holding it close to the floor. His own footprints were clear, trampling the dirt. Everywhere else, the floor had been swept, showing no trace of trespassers.

They were here. I know it. Landen and Corbin. But if he took it, why hasn't he used it? And how did he know where to find it? The greatest secret in my kingdom. I've told no one, no one at all. Kareed must have revealed the place to someone else.

Who?

Was it Torina again? Had she hooked up with Landen? Seen the Sword in that stone of hers and told him where it was?

However it happened, the Sword was gone, and with it Vesputo's cherished plans to master the allied armies immediately. Without the legendary weapon, only a fool would try an attack now: he'd be outnumbered and outfought. And Vesputo had never been a fool: no, he would simply have to bide his time a while longer.

The angry king arranged his face for public scrutiny and left the vault. He would never tell what he knew about the Sword of Bellandra. Let it remain as it had been, a mystery enhancing his power.

If Landen has it, I'll find a way to take it back.

Above ground, Vesputo strode through the halls, wishing he could find some object to vent his fury on.

Beron came running to meet him, waving letters. "My lord!"

Vesputo longed to kick the man as he would an annoying hound. "What is it?"

Beron looked right and left. "Private, sir."

They went to the council room. Beron handed him two messages. Vesputo read them, then sat back in his chair, arms crossed behind his head, feet up. He let Beron wait a few minutes, till he could sense the man's overbearing agitation.

"She is found."

"The pr—"

"Yes. Just across the mountains in Desante. Both messages agree. A quiet, sheltered country village." Vesputo spoke with clipped satisfaction.

"Why did no one tell us before, sir?" Beron's eyebrows met in a single line.

"She always kept her hair hidden, until now. Who but Torina would do that? She must believe she's out of danger."

Vesputo closed his eyes and let this news spread like balm over the wound of the Sword's loss.

"Shall I ride for Desante, sir?" Beron was like an attack dog straining at the leash.

Vesputo smiled. "Not yet, Captain. You're needed here now until the war is finished. I want that crystal, and I want that woman, but I want them in my own time and way."

Beron's forehead furrowed with the effort to understand. "How's that, sir?"

"The allied kings know Dahmis consults a seer. Through him, she's helped many of them. Now that she's refusing to work with the high king, it will be easy to spread rumors that she's turned against him. Then, when allied lives are lost at Sliviite hands, the fortune-teller can be blamed. We'll sow the story among the common soldiers that Dahmis's seer has given information to the Sliviites. You can help me in this, Captain."

Torina would serve Vesputo without ever knowing it. The only hitch in his plans to collaborate with the Sliviite lords involved the possibility of suspicion landing on him. No one must guess it was Vesputo who told the Sliviites which bay would be least protected. Torina's abilities with the crystal made her a believable target for the rage that would follow the allied defeat. *I want her to be anathema, respected by no one.*

He held out the messages. "See to it the spies are paid what was promised."

❖   ❖   ❖

King Dahmis looked at Michal in a nearby chair, then past him through the open door.

"Come, Dahmis. Brooding and pacing won't give the messengers wings."

"I need Vineda," Dahmis answered. "There are too many bays to guard!"

"Why doesn't she help you?" his friend asked.

"She broke with me when I signed an alliance with Vesputo. It seems she hates that king."

"I'm not fond of him myself." Michal smiled wryly.

Loud, clattering footsteps approached. The king hurried forward, met by a breathless guard.

"My lord, a messenger!" The guard ushered in a mud-spattered man in brown uniform.

Dahmis guided the soldier to a chair and made him sit. "Something to drink?"

"No, sir." The man clutched his chest, catching his breath. Mud from his clothes smeared the king's furniture.

"Drink!" Dahmis handed the spent soldier a glass. The man seized it and gulped.

"Now. The message? Who sent you?"

"A navy lookout's message reached Captain Medron. He sent me."

"Medron? He is posted at—"

"Castle Bay, sir."

"Castle Bay?" Dahmis's knees weakened. "Tell me."

"The lookout spotted the Sliviite fleet. Unless the wind changes, they'll land in hordes by morning of the day after tomorrow."

"The Sliviites are headed for Castle Bay?" Dahmis forced himself to understand the soldier's meaning.

"Yes, sir. It must be the main attack. There are so many of them!"

"That bay is small and remote." Dahmis reviewed the disposition of his troops. Many at Bellan Bay in Archeld. Others guarding the coasts of northern Glavenrell and Emmendae, where large bays were numerous. Castle Bay was about a day's ride from Glaven City. It was sparsely populated and little used, being too small to accommodate ships of any size.

"Aye. Small. They'll be invading with longboats— won't be able to bring in the big vessels."

"How many ships?"

"The lookout counted forty, sir."

"Forty ships! I've been told they can each hold seven hundred men."

"Big," the man nodded.

"Almost thirty thousand men! Even if they leave a crew aboard each, we can never hope to match their numbers." Dahmis estimated that no matter how fast soldiers marched, less than a thousand men could gather at Castle

Bay in a day and a half. He himself had argued with his generals that the rocky peninsula of Glavenrell was the least likely place for an invasion to arrive. The Sliviite vessels would seek large bays, to maximize their cannon power and give them access to land. Or so he'd believed, and so he'd persuaded his generals.

"Captain Medron's men?" the king pressed.

"Camped just south of the bay, waiting your orders, sir."

"How many?"

"One hundred, sir."

Dahmis turned to Michal. "How can the enemy have chosen Castle Bay? Our forces are weakest there and farthest from reinforcements. It's as if they knew."

His mind roved. Not many had the general positions of all the troops. The kings. The generals. Unthinkable that any of them, with so much to lose, would relay information to the Sliviites. Fields burned in Glavenrell or Desante would mean widespread famine. If anything united them all, it was collective resolve to beat the Sliviites.

"Sir," the soldier threw in. "It's said your fortune-teller turned against you and became informer to the Sliviites."

Dahmis wheeled on him. "Impossible."

"I only repeat what I heard," the man fumbled.

Images of Vineda spiraled and sparked through the king's mind. He bent a stern look on the soldier. "Do not repeat it again," he ordered. "Now tell me, do you know how long it will take for the lookout's news to reach the other troops?"

"Nothing will be spared to give them messages, my lord, but all are far away from your peninsula."

The king moved to the door. "Michal, we ride to Castle Bay. Thank you for bringing the news, soldier.

When you're rested, follow. We'll need every available man."

As Dahmis and his friend hurried through the immaculate halls of Glavenrell's fortress, the king shouted orders, calling for messages to be sent to every corner of the kingdoms, for his remaining guard to ready themselves instantly for a march, for Bellanes to be given the news.

"Though God knows we'll need more than the Band of Bellanes to stem this tide," he said.

When the high king rode into Medron's camp, it was early evening and the air was chilly. He ordered the troops to get some rest. Sitting by the fire next to Michal, he listened as Medron told them all he knew. The captain confirmed the Sliviite fleet on the horizon.

Head in hands, the king wondered how the few hundred men he had mustered could hold back thousands. He gazed so deeply into his thoughts he was startled when Bellanes and Andris stepped into the firelight.

"Bellanes. Good to see you, my friend. And you, Andris."

Bellanes's lean face looked as if he'd wrestled for days with a terrible foe. He seemed years older and full of sadness.

"As you see, Bellanes, your prediction was true. You know the battle we face. How can we surround an army that launches from the sea? The wind has dropped, and I believe they'll land by morning, before more troops can journey here. I fear this night will tell our futures."

"The only way is to strike where you aren't expected," Bellanes said.

"We're expected to be very much as we are—a small force far from reinforcements, arrayed against the biggest gathering of pirates ever seen." The king's voice was hollow with worry.

"You must destroy their ships, which hold great numbers of fighters." Bellanes spoke heavily.

"My navy is south. It would take days to reach us and is no match for the Sliviite ships."

"Castle Bay is famous for making pitch?" Bellanes seemed not to hear him.

Dahmis turned in bewilderment to Medron. The captain nodded. "The people produce pitch that lights hearths from here to Archeld."

"How many men can I have?" Bellanes asked the king.

"Perhaps a thousand by morning."

"I need thirty-four to combine with my band. Steady, brave men. Strong swimmers."

"When do you need them?"

"Now."

Castle Bay fishermen and coal-tar workers were roused and sent scurrying to bring coracles and buckets of oozing pitch. Carpenters donated braces and augers. Women collected paraffin-soaked rags.

During all this bustle, Landen stood alone on a beach by the southern rim of Castle Bay, staring out at the dark waving water.

Father, you taught me that taking a life is an unforgivable offense. I have lived as a warrior, because your peace was sacrificed in a war you couldn't fight. But until tonight, I've never killed a man myself. Now I plot against the lives of thousands, and my plan is so dangerous it will surely end in death for many of my friends.

Landen didn't hear the high king approaching. When Dahmis touched his shoulder, he turned despondently.

"My friend," the king said. "You don't need to go yourself. If you're killed, there's no replacement."

"There's no replacement for any of these men," Landen answered. "And I have no family."

Dahmis was quiet a moment, and Landen wanted to lean against him. "Bellanes," the deep tones were softened. "It's still rumored that you've never killed."

Landen's chest felt as if it would burst. "The rumor is true."

"Then let these soldiers undertake your strategy."

"I can't stand by while others take my orders to risk their lives."

The king put an arm around the young man and steered him to walk along the narrow beach. "You never told me who your parents were."

"They're dead," Landen mumbled.

Dahmis's compassionate face soaked up moonlight. "But once they lived. Who are you?"

The question seemed taken up by the restless ocean, sent back to Landen in swells of water, rolling toward him from some unknown source beyond the horizon. *Who are you? Who are you?*

"I am what you see before you," Landen choked out.

The king sighed. "Bellanes, those men on board the Sliviite ships—you didn't make them train for pirates. You never taught them to maim and kill."

Landen waited for the king to keep speaking. It seemed his life hung there in the path of the moon.

"We find ourselves at a juncture in history, wishing for peace, headed for war," Dahmis went on. "If we allow this invasion, our culture will be destroyed. Even if we escape with our lives, many innocent, unarmed people will be hurt or will die."

Landen drooped. *Oh, my king. I know this better even than you.*

"There are slaves on that ship, my lord."

"And that is a great sadness. Killing the innocent too."

"It's unbearable!"

"Yes," Dahmis answered. "It is. All war is. There's no escaping it."

They stood on the sand together, near the lapping waves. Landen saw the moon's train of silver on the sea.

I was a slave once, Dahmis. Until a child set me free.

Dahmis raised his eyes to the sky. Clouds were moving in. "My friend, though we wish with all the might that is in us, we cannot wish away this war. The time to act is now."

As Landen looked at the grim face of the high king, he understood that Dahmis longed for peace as much as he did himself.

❖ ❖ ❖

When night was thickest, Landen and his crew were assembled with their supplies. The small group of soldiers and members of his band huddled in a boathouse near an old, sunken pier of Castle Bay. Torches lit faces determined and wakeful despite the hour. The high king stood quietly against a wall, his presence lending grandeur.

Landen began by asking each man to verify that he could swim well, then outlined the plan.

"You've volunteered for dangerous duty. The risks are high and the chances good that some of you won't live through this task. Unless we work with perfect precision and absolute silence, our lives are over." He looked around.

"We begin together, all in the large boat. It will carry forty coracles, our supplies, and us. We'll row in a half-circle south of and then past the fleet. The Sliviite ships are anchored in two lines about five miles out.

"Then you'll each act alone, taking a coracle, brace, auger, bucket of pitch, flint, tinder, and waxed cloth." He swallowed. "Each man takes one Sliviite ship, approaching under the hull on the side away from shore. If the clouds keep up, the moon will be covered. We'll carry no lights. Silence and darkness are our only chance to slip by the Sliviite lookouts."

Avid, resolved faces listened.

"As soon as you reach your ship, bore two holes with your brace and auger, low to the water. Paint as much of the side of the ship as you can reach with pitch, then fill the holes with the cloth wicks.

"Right now, men are gathering wood for a bonfire on the beach. In about two hours, the bonfire will be lit. You'll be on the west side of your ship, facing the ocean, probably unable to see the fire's light. Listen for the sounds on deck above you, telling you the Sliviites have seen it. Then, strike your flint and set a spark to the wick."

271

There was a collective exhale.

"Now comes the real danger. Although the bonfire will provide distraction for a moment, unless they're careless, they'll spot the fire on the other ships even if they miss the fire on their own. Once they alert one another, they'll look for us with their arrows."

Wide eyes watched him. "As soon as you know your fire has caught, leave your coracle and swim to shore."

Uneasy silence greeted him. "It's quite a distance but not impossible. The large boat will return to the dock as soon as we leave it. I thought of swimming back to our boat, but that way, if we were sighted, we would all be one target."

Landen tried to give his voice the ring of confidence. "Local fishermen say there's often a riptide out to sea from the bay in the wee hours. However, to the south it ceases. We'll swim south until the tide no longer pulls. Each of you will have a log float to rest on. Remember to bring it with you. Swim with all your might across the tide, never against it. Once you've escaped the rip, drift south. There's a beach of sorts a half-mile down from here."

He could see the men measuring themselves against the tide, darkness, and danger. He plunged on.

"The water will be cold. Your skin will adjust. Take off your boots when you first get into the coracles. Peel off heavy clothes before you light the fire. Then dive and swim for dear life."

He waited.

"Uh, Bellanes," Andris put in.

"Andris, you won't be with us. We all know you're helpless in the water."

Tight laughter flared up.

"Will you be going, then, sir?" one of Dahmis's soldiers asked.

Landen clenched a fist. "I will."

There were muted sighs of relief around him.

"I only meant to ask if the ships would catch fire," Andris said, sounding peeved. "Will they sink?"

Sweat started on Landen's forehead. "Aye. The pitch will burn hot and hard, and the timbers will catch. As the top burns, the keel will sink lower and be flooded from the holes we make."

"So," Andris said. "The Sliviites will drown."

Landen looked around at the men. "If the vessels burn quickly and sink fast, yes, they'll drown. If they have their wits about them, they'll take to their longboats and head for shore. For all we know, they may be planning to invade us in the boats tonight."

So much depends on timing we know nothing about. If they're on their way toward us as we row out to them, what then?

"I believe if we get there in time to start the ships burning, the Sliviites will try to save their vessels," he said. "Without ships, they have no way to return to their own lands. It's also likely some of them can swim as well or better than us. But if they swim encumbered by weapons, they'll have hard going. And they may not know about the tide, which can weaken the strongest swimmer and slow the most powerful oarsman."

"Sir," Bangor asked, his sweet tenor voice contrasting with the scarred mask of his face, "the Sliviites who get in the boats and make it to shore—what about them?"

Bangor was one of six in the band, including Landen, able to swim.

"Since we'll swim south at first, instead of toward shore, we'll likely miss them in the water."

"But Castle Bay?" Bangor persisted.

"Castle Bay is at risk of attack," Landen answered.

"So if the Sliviites jump in the boats because of us—"

"We may provoke the invasion sooner," Landen finished for him. "But if we don't act tonight, we lose surprise and our forces will be slaughtered."

"How do we defend the beach, swimming south?" Bangor asked.

Landen looked at the Angel-Devil with affection. "We don't."

The high king stepped forward. "You'll do your part with the ships. My soldiers and I stand ready to guard the beach. When you reach shore, drag yourselves to the south camp and get warm. For you, the fighting will be over."

"Once in the water," Landen told them, "look out for yourselves. Remember, never swim into the riptide, even if you think it will save a comrade. If you do, you'll exhaust your body and won't be able to make it to shore."

He folded his hands, wondering how many of his friends would come back. He told them they could stay on land if they liked, now that they knew what was in store. No one backed out, so he drew a map of the fleet and began assigning ships. Then he went over the plan again.

As the men moved to leave, the high king addressed them. "What makes this possible is your courage. Before you go, please accept my honor and thanks. The future of many kingdoms lies with you."

Chapter 8

Clouds covered the moon as Landen's crew set out, their oars gliding through black water. The men rowed in stoic silence, watching the boat captain's arm rise and fall in place of a drum, coordinating their strokes.

Before long, they could see the Sliviite vessels, opaque outlines against the dark sky, looming up from the shining darkness of the ocean. Darkness over darkness.

The massive ships, anchored in two long rows, crammed the horizon. Landen lifted his eyes, trying to fill his heart with the great sky, the vastness of eternity. As they neared the fleet, the night reached out to them, carrying Sliviite voices. Landen froze. The Sliviites must be getting ready to invade. With two hours until dawn, only their lookouts should be awake.

He wished there were some way to lasso time, to make the minutes obey his will so he and his friends could reach the great ships before they were too late. Pushing the sea under his oars was the only outlet for his urgency.

Now they were past the ships, rowing frantically. When they reached a point west of the fleet, they stowed their oars, the men shaking with the effort of silence. All eyes were on Landen as he signaled in the gloom. He watched as one by one they slipped into the water in their coracles and paddled away.

Then it was his turn. His coracle was lowered and he dropped into it. The light craft, made of hide and green branches sewn together with leather thongs, bobbed on the swells of the ocean's surface. Landen saluted the boat captain and floated off. The pull of the tide was intense as he guided the coracle toward his designated ship. The closest ship, since he was last to start. He had to fight hard against the water with his paddle, trying to keep quiet.

He felt naked and exposed, sitting in the tiny makeshift circle of the coracle, approaching the bulk of the Sliviite warship. It seemed the soldiers on her deck must be able to hear his heart, and if they looked down, would they be able to see him? Would he look like a spot of ink moving in the waves? Or like what he was, a young man bent on destruction?

Do no one harm. The tenet of his childhood came echoing back. Landen turned his thoughts to the other men in the water with him. He imagined them crouched on their knees like he was, the smell of pitch mixed with brine heavy in their noses, pushing against the tide toward the ships.

His heartbeat was the drum commanding his progress. When he slid into the shadow of the ship's hull, the coracle moved rapidly. Though he tried to slow down, it bounced against the ship's side. Landen searched for something that would hold him against the great vessel, but there was nothing to grab but smooth wood. He wondered about the other men as he realized he'd have to get into the water and use the brace and auger there.

He pulled off his boots while the coracle swirled and bumped. He drew out a bootlace, tying one end to his wrist and the other to the frame of the coracle. A moment later, he was in the cold sea, intent on fixing the brace against the hull, boring with the auger, praying no one heard him, that no one chanced to be on the other side in the hold. He twirled his auger with all his might while the tethered coracle tugged at him.

The timbers were thick, solid oak, and resisted his strength. At last, they yielded a hole and Landen started on another. When he had two holes, he passed the lace from his boot through them, tying the coracle. He heaved his dripping body into the tiny craft, almost capsizing it. Dipping a thick brush into the bucket of pitch, he painted with a frenzy, in and around, above and through the cavities he'd created. When the pitch was gone, he stuffed paraffin rags into the holes.

He sat and waited, shivering, trying to smother the sounds of his frazzled breathing. The soft thudding of the coracle against the ship seemed to make a furious thunder, beckoning the Sliviites to find him.

How were the others? Did they find a way to use the brace and auger and keep their coracles close by? Would they all have time?

Landen stripped off his wet clothes, dropping them into the bottom of the coracle. He listened to the night, straining to understand the voices from the ship. Some sounded near, as though soldiers stood directly above him on deck. He huddled, every nerve crying for the release of action. The beach fire was supposed to draw the Sliviite lookouts with its glow. Was it lit? Should he start his wick?

277

Suddenly the air was filled with shouting. He heard running footsteps on deck. The Sliviite outcry echoed from ship to ship.

Landen struck his flint and tinder and watched the spark catch on the paraffin. The little flame ate away at the wick, then burst into crackling life when it reached the pitch.

Just before he dove, he saw answering flickers from other ships. Taking a huge gulp of air, he plunged deep into the waves, swimming south. As soon as he got a little away from the ship, he felt the grip of the tide, sucking him out to sea as if he were no more than a leaf traveling a rapid watercourse. With an effort, he kept his head and swam across the rip, not against it. He had forgotten his flotation log; it lay in the bottom of his coracle, shrouded in his sodden shirt. Impossible to go back for it now.

When he surfaced, the tide had sent him fifty yards west of the Sliviite ships. He tread water for a moment while the surging current moved him farther away. He could see the blaze he'd ignited, burning with ravenous heat, eating away at the ship. In its light, dazed foreign faces stared over the deck. Shouts blasted the air and fire roared.

The tide was carrying him so fast he would soon be too far for their arrows. He thought of the men who had torched the eastern line of ships. The tide would move them into the path of the western row. Landen searched the orange sea, bright in reflection of the foundering ships. A head surfaced near the ship closest to him. He pounded the water, trying futilely to stop the gaining tide. The man went under again, reappearing twenty yards from the ship. Arrows hurtled through the night as the man dove again.

Landen tried to reach his comrade, forgetting his own advice about fighting the current. There was a splutter in the water only a few feet away, and Bangor's one good eye stared at him.

"What you doing, man?" the Angel-Devil shouted. "You told us never to fight the tide!"

Landen gazed at the flickering, strangely lit ocean. The inferno silhouetted men on deck like black figurines on a stage. He could see Sliviites struggling to lower boats from the stern. Archers shot at the ocean. As the blaze lapped higher, a few soldiers leaped pell-mell into the water. The next ship in the row was listing badly, her side consumed by towering flames.

He felt an iron grip on his shoulder. Bangor shook him.

"Come, Bellanes! Swim, man!"

"But the others!"

"Leave be! They took their chance, same as you and me. Come, this tide's murderous." Bangor shook him again. "Where's your log?"

"Forgot it."

"We share mine. Swim, man! If we don't get across the tide, we'll be meeting the sun coming up in the broad ocean."

Landen tore his gaze from the ghastly scene and began to swim. Side by side in the cold sea, the two men pushed south with all their power.

❖ ❖ ❖

A bleary-eyed Andris waited along a stony beach south of Castle Bay, scanning the ocean in the faint light of predawn. The high king had assigned him to prepare camp for Bellanes and his crew; every other man available was needed to guard the bay. The tide was beginning to come in, so the big man started a fire well up on the gravelly sand.

The swimmers drifted in on rising breakers, clasping their flotation logs with numb hands, so exhausted they had to crawl through the shallows, helped by the faithful Andris. They couldn't respond to his eager questions. Many were unable to make their way past the tideline to his fire, falling asleep by the water's edge. Andris dragged them to the warming blaze and went to search for others.

The sun was up, a dazzling dance in the waves, and still no sign of Bellanes. Or Bangor, for that matter. Seven other men were missing as well, soldiers from Dahmis's troops. Andris walked up and down the shore.

He couldn't bear the waiting. A fishing boat was moored to the tangled roots of an ancient log. He tugged it into the water and jumped in.

Buffeted by large waves, it seemed he made no headway. At last, he got beyond the breakers and squinted hard. Nothing.

He rowed farther out till the beach was a distant line, his head wagging ceaselessly, seeking his friends. Still nothing but the blinding glint of sun on water. Tears rolled into Andris's beard. He kept rowing, only because he had no heart to go back to shore. It seemed the ocean was an enormous bowl of endless water, met by an inverted bowl of endless sky, and himself a lost speck consumed by the blue.

It was then he spotted a dark dot on the horizon. His heart pumped with renewed vigor. He strained to row harder. Slowly, how slowly the time went, and the ocean seemed reluctant to give up any distance between Andris's boat and what he pursued.

At last, he was close enough to see. Two men. One seemed lifeless; the other hung on a short log, holding his companion's head out of the sea.

Bangor. Bangor passed Andris the dead weight of Bellanes and helped haul him into the boat. Then he heaved himself in, lying in the bottom while Andris pleaded with Bellanes to waken.

He pressed the unconscious man's lungs, rocking the boat, till water squirted from Bellanes's mouth. The young man coughed and began shivering violently. When his eyes opened, he smiled.

"Andris, am I dead? Because *you* look like an angel."

When he tried to sit up, Andris pushed him down. Bellanes closed his eyes. Beside him, Bangor sprawled asleep. Andris summoned the strength to row again, lips moving in wordless gratitude.

Elation over saving his friends brought a burst of energy, but outraged muscles soon rebelled. The oars grew too heavy to move. Andris slumped on the bench, tired eyes groping for sleep.

Fierce rain woke Andris. He jerked upright. His body felt as if it had been beaten. He stretched wooden arms and tried to ease cramped shoulders. Angry dark clouds held the sky hostage, but a glimmer of sun in the west told him it was afternoon. The tide had done its work, and he could see the beach perhaps a mile off. His companions were stirring; Bangor thrust out his arms as if to shoo away the pelting rain, while Bellanes sat up and looked out across the choppy water.

"Thank you for coming after us, Andris," Bellanes said. He pulled himself to the bench opposite Andris, letting rain wash over his naked chest.

"Aye," Andris said. "Had to."

Bangor groaned as he scrunched to a sitting position. "Good man, Andris."

"So," Andris asked, grabbing the oars. "What happened out there?"

"Eh, mate," Bangor grunted. "Some ships caught fire. Don't know more than that. We was trying to save our lives and swimming blind."

Andris glanced at Bellanes. His leader's face was pale through the rain, eyes dim.

"Andris." Bellanes's voice was stark. "Andris, turn around slowly."

The big man shipped his oars and swiveled. "What?"

"There, along the gunwale." Bellanes pointed.

Andris caught a glimpse of human hands holding on to the rim of the boat. They let go and there was a splash.

Bellanes leaned over the side. "Wait!" he called. "Show yourself."

The man swam. Bellanes lifted the oars on his end, rowing along with Andris. They soon overtook the swimmer. The stranger was clearly too tired even to dive away from them. Andris picked up a fishnet and threw it over him, yanking it tight, pulling him against the side of the boat.

"Speak, and tell us who you are," Bellanes said.

No answer. Andris and Bellanes pulled him into the boat like a great fish. Once he was over the side, Bellanes opened the net. The motionless man's skin was puckered and bluish. On his chest was a patterned scar, cut in the shape of a star.

"Not one of the crew," Bellanes said.

"Sliviite!" Andris roared. He raised his oar, intending to bring it crashing down on the stranger's head.

"Stop!" Bellanes commanded.

Andris checked himself in midair. The man fixed his eyes on Bellanes and put out his hand, palm up. On his wrist was a mark.

"Sliviite slave or conscript," Bangor breathed.

"Strong, brave man," Bellanes answered.

"What shall I do with him?" Andris glowered.

"Teach him," Bellanes murmured, gripping the man's hand and giving him a reassuring look.

"Teach him what?"

"How to be a free man and a brother. Andris, meet the newest member of our band."

"You can't mean it!"

"I can. This man has spirit and strength more than any of us. The kind of man we need." Bellanes chafed the man's swollen fingers.

"You've gone daft in the ocean! Bellanes, the band has no need of another man!"

But Bellanes was smiling as if all the weights on his soul had lifted. His eyes were lit with unreasonable happiness. "Andris, there's always a need for good men."

"Look!" Bangor grinned.

Lying swathed in folds of fishnet, drenched with rain, the Sliviite snored. Andris glared, while Bellanes chuckled.

"He must have kept himself awake in the ocean, fought through the tide, then caught hold of our boat while we slept. He could have capsized us, Andris, but only held on. He's not a man of war; he's just trying to save his life."

Andris shook his head. "Well, if you must, you must."

Bellanes bent to the oars. "I must. Let's take us home."

When they reached the beach, the rain had lightened. The tired trio found a burned-out fire surrounded by dazed men hunched under sodden blankets. When roused, they gave no news. Perhaps a battle raged on the beaches of Castle Bay. Maybe Dahmis was killed. No messages. Nothing.

Seven men from the attack crew were missing.

Bangor fell to the ground in dead sleep, while Andris and Bellanes tethered the boat with the last of their ebbing strength. Bellanes insisted on covering the Sliviite with a blanket before collapsing himself.

❖ ❖ ❖

Landen woke to a clear sky softened by the hint of approaching dawn. He sat up. Something had wakened him.

The beach was strewn with men who looked thrown to the ground, sleeping next to a heap of ashes. They ought to have posted a sentry. He listened, unfurling his body from the rough sand. Warily he moved toward a pile of huge black rocks that lined their camp.

Soft, crunching footsteps. He ran at a crouch toward the sound. A shadowy figure emerged from the boulders. The high king. Landen embraced him.

"Bellanes. Thank God you're safe."

"And you, my king. What happened at Castle Bay?"

"First tell me how it went with the crew."

"Seven soldiers never made the beach," Landen told him sadly. The king bowed his head. "All the rest came back."

Dahmis put a hand on his shoulder. "The work done by you and those brave men made it possible for us to defeat the Sliviites. Your fires destroyed many of their vessels. We met what was left of their forces on the shore. Some arrived in longboats, and they were desperate fighters. Others came in nearly drowned, too tired to give battle. It's over, Bellanes. Our world lives on, because of you."

Landen breathed deeply, looking at the glinting surf. The same ocean he had watched the night before, when so much was unknown and dangerous, beat against the rocks now. They'd been granted victory and life. It could have gone the other way. War was cruel, and courageous men had perished. But Landen savored the sweetness of his breath moving in and out in rhythm with the waves. It was good to be alive: to feel the harsh grains beneath his feet and hear birdcalls heralding the dawn.

He stood talking with the high king until the sun rose.

Chapter 9

As Vesputo and his followers converged with the other kings and their soldiers, they were met by worn-out men and women displaying the euphoria of victory. Most soldiers were sent home at once, relieved by the containment of the Sliviite menace; home to their families, home to help tend the fields and towns of their beloved countries. They would carry with them the story of how the great invasion had been staunched; how the band of Bellanes, together with soldiers of the high king's army, overcame a fearsome array of navy ships; how a small, determined group of fighters, led by King Dahmis, met the surviving invaders on the beaches of Castle Bay and put an end to their piracy.

That evening, the kings met in council in the biggest house in Castle Bay. Though they shouted to hail Bellanes as a hero, he disappeared without so much as a bow in their direction. It was a disappointment to Vesputo, to miss the famous thief again. Anger fueled his eloquence as he argued that Dahmis's seer must be at the bottom of the attack on Castle Bay. "How else would the Sliviites have redirected their fleet to the most unprotected outpost of Glavenrell?" he demanded. "She's the only one with both the knowledge and motivation to give such information to our enemies."

Soon, the other kings took up the call to have her hunted down. Dahmis grew more and more serious as the seer was denounced, defending her steadfastly. But his reasonable words couldn't sway the haughty monarchs.

"You admit she no longer helps you!" Mlaven roared. "That means she knows too much. If not with you, she's against you. With all she knows and can see, she's dangerous!"

"Think of the losses we might have sustained," Vesputo urged.

Dahmis stood, strong face hard as oak. "Very well," his deep voice rang. "Find her if you can. But her foresight may defeat you all."

"Where is she?" called out Mlaven.

"I'm sworn not to reveal that," Dahmis answered.

"Of course, then, you must not," Vesputo jumped into the babel of dissenting voices. When the assembled kings stopped, staring at him, he pressed on. "None of us would wish the high king to break a vow."

Dahmis bowed stiffly to him.

"There can be no objection to making another promise, my king," Vesputo continued. "Assure this company that you will not warn her. Then each of us can do our utmost to find her. Tracking her will be a fitting exercise for our soldiers. I myself have been able to determine she lives somewhere in Desante."

Vesputo saw he carried the moment, as the collected kings raised glasses, toasting him. He knew enough of battle to understand that these men, who had been poised for war and denied a share in the fighting, were itching for action.

The high king set down his glass. "Allies," his voice reverberated around the room. "I'm sorry we've used this occasion, the celebration of peace and our liberation from Sliviite piracy, to condemn one who has assisted many of us. Let us turn our thoughts to rejoicing. Our unity at this historic time is worthy of festivity. I invite you all to a feast tomorrow evening to commemorate it." He paused and they cheered him. "For tonight," he went on, "you must excuse me, for I am in need of rest."

Anyone with half an eye could believe the great king was almost dead on his feet with fatigue. Rumor said he'd not slept for days.

Chiming in with the rest of the kings, Vesputo saluted as the high king turned away with a majesty remindful of Kareed in his prime.

❖ ❖ ❖

Vesputo lost no time speaking to Beron. "All the kings are agreed. The seer must die."

"The prin—"

"Yes. Everyone will seek her. To heighten the chase, I have whispered her description and hints of her location to the other kings. But we know just where she is, so you can be first to reach her."

"Do you want her captured, my lord, and taken to you in Archeld?"

Vesputo stroked his chin. "I've decided it would be too troublesome to keep her under guard. No. All I need is the crystal. Another woman can be trained to use it. Irene told me how its secret can be unlocked."

"Kill her then, sir?"

"Kill her. Before you do, take care to find out where she keeps the crystal. I want that stone."

"Of course, my lord. How do I—"

"No poison." Vesputo jerked a finger across Beron's throat. "Take the shortest route to Desan."

"Yes, my lord. I'll leave now."

"Good. And wear a mask."

❖ ❖ ❖

As Dahmis emerged from the council house, eager towns-people crowded around him, offering comfortable beds and anything else they had. Grateful for their goodwill, but filled with intolerable urgency, Dahmis caught Larseld's eye. His general had arrived that afternoon.

Within minutes, Larseld maneuvered matters so that Dahmis was escorted away. Polite assurances were delivered to the adoring populace: the high king thanked them all for their kindness; the high king had a bed waiting for him.

Dahmis and Larseld galloped south toward camp, leaving good-natured guards to soothe the people and keep them off-limits. The gibbous moon gave enough light to guide the two men. Sleep kept washing over Dahmis like waves at high tide. He forced the tide back.

When town was out of sight, the king reined in. "We aren't going to camp," he panted. "We ride to Bellanes. I need to speak with him alone."

"Is he still nearby?"

"About five miles." Dahmis told where, then asked Larseld to lead his horse. The general wound the king's reins together with his own.

❖ ❖ ❖

Dahmis struggled out of dead sleep. Gentle hands, very strong, were lifting him off his horse. He opened his eyes to starry skies, wondering where he was, trying to recall the insistent worry that pounded at the edges of his mind.

"Awake, sir?" He knew the voice. Soft and ringing. Bellanes. Why was Bellanes beside him in the night? Then he remembered.

"Yes, I'm awake."

"Larseld said there's something important?"

Dahmis cleared his throat. "Again I turn to you."

"Tell me." Bellanes sat across from him on the ground.

Dahmis rubbed the back of his neck. "It concerns a woman." At Bellanes's expression, he raised a hand. "No, it's not what you think. This woman has been of service to me for some time and, through me, helped some of the other kings as well." Dahmis's heart ached as he called Vineda to mind: defiant intelligence, lovely eyes, shining hair he'd seen only once. "Have any rumors reached you, Bellanes, about a certain fortune-teller who has turned against me?" Dahmis squeezed his eyes to focus them, looking at the quiet face in front of him.

Bellanes shook his head. "No, sir. A fortune-teller? Turned against you?"

"It seems she has a hatred for King Vesputo. After he joined the alliance, she stopped helping me. Now it's said she gave information to the Sliviites."

Bellanes frowned. "Information? What sort?"

The high king looked up at the distant stars, feeling a

cool wind in his hair. "She can see things that happen, even when she isn't there. She sees it in her crystal. She can even see the future."

Bellanes's face in the moonlight went white as a beach shell. "A seer?" He put his hands to the ground as if he needed the earth to hold him up. "I once knew someone . . ."

Dahmis peered hard at the young man. "You know this woman?"

"No," Bellanes said hoarsely. "The one I knew has been dead for years."

"I don't understand."

"Your seer's name?"

"Vineda."

"Forgive me. The mention of a seer—of course there are others. Where does she come from?"

"Desante."

"What is it you need?" Bellanes returned to the subject.

Dahmis tried to shake off the burden of weariness. "The kings want her killed. They say she knows too much."

"And you?"

"I have . . . agreed."

The young man's shadowed eyes burned with revulsion. "You ask me here to be your assassin? To kill a woman?"

"No, my friend. I only gave the appearance of agreement. It was necessary to save her life. Though I suggested to the kings that her sight would prevent capture, it won't. She doesn't see her own future."

"Sir. Forgive me. I— what is it you want me to do?"

"Give her safe escort into exile. Before you agree, Bellanes, you must know: she won't come with you willingly. She's very proud and disdains help. Also, each king will try to outdo the others in this, sending the most skilled assassins. Somehow Vesputo has learned at least part of her location. I fear he may know exactly where she is."

Bellanes smiled darkly. "How much time do I have?"

"The council met last evening."

"Then I'll be on my way. Dawn will come soon."

"Bellanes, whatever you need or wish for, name it."

"There is something, sir. Where is she and what does she look like?"

Dahmis chuckled. He drew a map in the dirt. Bellanes committed it to memory.

"As for her looks, they're very distinctive. She keeps most of herself hidden in drab dresses and ugly kerchiefs."

Bellanes grinned. "How am I to know her from any other old woman in Desante?"

"Ah, my friend. She isn't old. Young, with lovely features and eyes the color of the ocean. To be certain, pull off her kerchief. If the hair beneath is flaming red, you have the right one."

The high king stopped, amazed to see the young man shaking from head to foot, his face bone-white again, breath coming in gusty pants.

"What is it?" Dahmis cried.

Bellanes leaped to his feet. He jumped on his horse.

"Bellanes! Where are you going?"

"Desante, my king," the voice rasped. "I will find her, or . . ."

Dahmis didn't catch those final words. He heard only the sound of retreating hoof beats.

Torina looked around at her neatly swept cabin. On the chairs, a few tightly packed bundles rested—everything she would take with her to Desan. Most of the high king's gold was stashed in the storage cellar of the Dirkson farm. She had burned the letters to her mother one by one, rereading each one before consigning them to fire. The crystal, still wrapped, nestled in her pocket. Beneath her faded dress hung the red cord holding Dahmis's emblem: it would be useful if anyone tried to delay her.

Beside her, Lindsa and Anna smiled, while Antonia played in the soft evening air just outside the open door.

"I planned to be long gone by now," Torina said.

"You couldn't have left any sooner, with that sickness," Anna soothed.

Torina wrapped her arms around her middle. Anxiety hovered near, as it had ever since the day she'd resisted the crystal, shown her hair, fallen sick. She knew in her heart that something was wrong; knew she'd made a mistake, strayed from the path.

"Eat something," Anna urged.

A prickly feeling crawled up Torina's spine. She felt as if she were forgetting something important that was right in front of her.

Sounds outside signaled a rider approaching. Then Antonia began to cry.

Lindsa ran to lift her child. Torina's heart lurched like a lame horse as a tall, masked man burst in on them. The slits of his eyes fastened on her as he lunged, catching hold of her arms. Frightened shrieks erupted from Anna and Lindsa as a great fist slammed into Torina's head.

She saw bright silver stars drifting around her and fell with them into blackness.

Chapter 10

Torina woke lying on the ground, covered with a rough blanket. Pine needles under her told her it was high country. A cold breeze brushed her aching head. Dark trees greeted her, and a swath of stars was visible. Moonlight filtered in, silhouetting the black shape of a tethered horse.

Torina propped herself on an elbow. A few feet away, the masked man leaned against a tree trunk, his chest rising and falling with the rhythm of sleep.

He hadn't bothered to tie her! She crawled forward, feeling for roots or stones, moving slowly, while her body screamed at her to run. Her hand touched something. A leather pouch. She stopped.

Run away! her body cried.

But she had to know. Who had kidnapped her? She slid her hand inside the pouch. She drew out a little bag and explored it with quivering fingers. Some large, heavy coins. In the corner, a ring! Perhaps a signet ring. If so, she could learn the identity of the sleeping man.

She pulled the ring out, examining it in the dim moonlight. A simple band set with a round stone.

I know this ring! It once belonged to me.

A miniature crystal, set in gold. The last time she'd seen it was the day her father was killed.

Torina was on her feet, dizzy and crying, moving toward the sleeping man. Instantly awake, he leaped to her side as she swayed and tottered. His arms circled her, holding her up. Great sobs wrung her body, years of pent-up tears washing over her cheeks. He took off his mask. The shadowed face, dearly familiar, was revealed.

"Landen," she whispered.

"Hello, Princess." His quiet voice shook.

"You." She took his face in both her hands, stroking his features, not knowing what she did, barely aware that he was doing the same with her, his hands warm and dry on her saltwater skin.

Her hands fell. "But— I don't understand."

His hands dropped to her shoulders. "Sorry about the blow. It was necessary."

"Why?"

"Now the other assassins will think I got there first."

She looked around. It was night. Was she in a dream?

"Other assassins? Are you one of them?"

"No. But we want them to think I am."

"Wait." She pulled back, to see his face. "I'm to be killed?"

"Yes, Torina, you're marked for death."

"Death? Who sent you?"

"The high king."

In a daze, she shook her head. "Dahmis sent you to kill me?"

"No. To give you safe escort out of danger."

"The high king knows our history?" Her mind reeled.

There was moisture in his eyes. "No. Torina, I thought you were dead."

She blinked sadly. "And I knew nothing of you."

He leaned closer. "Nothing?"

"My crystal never showed me your face, all this time. I looked, Landen. I looked every day for—" Her throat closed over the memory of that long, futile search.

"Princess, if I . . . Torina, my . . ." He swallowed. "Come, we must keep moving."

He boosted her into the saddle and swung on in front of her. "Hang on."

She wrapped her arms around him tightly. As they rode higher through the night, she lay her head against his back. Tears of peace dampened his shirt.

Landen marveled to look down and see Torina's slender fingers interlocked at his waist. They rode into a sheltered, high valley just as dawn broke. It was situated so that it was invisible unless one stumbled upon it or knew where it was.

Fatigue was working on him. Awake for days and nights except for his nap in the forest, he cherished the thought of sleep. The poor, tired horse must feel the same. Landen drew rein with profound relief, helping Torina down.

He'd built himself a rustic hut here in the evergreens, for a refuge in Desante. Now it looked like a palace.

He led the horse to a nearby spring and rubbed his coat. Torina followed, helping care for the stallion. Watching

Torina's quick, knowing movements, Landen wanted to weep with gratitude for her safety. Her life.

Torina bent to the spring and took a long drink. Landen knelt beside her, reviving himself with water. *She cried over me last night. What does she feel today?*

"Come inside?" he said, and she trailed after him.

Makeshift chairs and a bed were the only furnishings. Landen sat on the bed, taking off his boots.

"Thank you," Torina said.

He reached a hand to her. "Sit by me?"

She moved beside him.

"Let me look at you." He tugged at her scarf. "Dahmis told me to pull this off in order to know you. As soon as he said that, I knew it was you, that you weren't dead."

He wondered what the years had done to his face as he traced the effects on hers. Eyes the same blue-lit green, but where mischievous joy once danced, now he saw sadness, deep as the ocean. Her cheeks were thinner. There was something else too: the arrogant pride of a princess seemed to be extinct. Yet the indefinable, untamed quality of her spirit remained. Yes, it was Torina.

Large tears fell from her eyes.

"What is it?"

"It's that I'm so ashamed. Can you ever forgive me?"

"Forgive you, Princess?"

"Landen, you know I was a fool. I can hardly bring myself to remember how foolish I was. Thoughtless, superior, spoiled!"

He took her hands and kissed them. "Please, Torina. If you're crying for my forgiveness, you don't have to cry."

"Landen, you have the wisest heart in the world. When you lost everything, you made a new beginning. I buried myself so far I may as well have been dead."

"From what the high king tells me, that's not so." He gathered her into his arms. Holding her felt wonderfully right. Landen's body and soul relaxed immeasurably. Sleep took him so fast, he didn't have time to think about the tense look of guilt that crept into her face when he mentioned the high king.

Chapter 11

Beron rode up to Archeld's castle spattered with mud. He received with disdain the eager help of soldiers on duty. Of course they treated him with respect; he was important to King Vesputo.

People made way for him to go straight to Vesputo. The king rose, giving him a steady hand in welcome. As soon as they were alone, Beron blurted his news.

"She is certainly dead, my lord."

"By your hand?"

"No, sir. When I arrived at her cabin, she was gone. The people there told me a masked man had knocked her senseless and ridden off with her only an hour before."

"Ridden off with her! Did you search where she lived? Did you find the crystal?"

"I searched, sir. Turned it inside out. She was set for a move. I went through everything. There wasn't much there. The crystal was gone."

Vesputo pounded his desk, swearing. "Did you track the rider?"

"I—no, sir. I spent the time searching her cabin. By then, night had fallen. No one seemed to know which way he'd gone. The farm peasants were scared witless and wanted to know what she'd done and who she was."

"You didn't tell them!"

"No, sir. Torina's been dead for years. Now she's buried."

"You traveled as fast as possible?"

"Yes, sir. I hardly rested."

"Odd that someone would get there before you. I thought King Dahmis was the only one who knew where she was."

"Perhaps others have hunted her as we have, sir, with more to go on from the high king."

"Perhaps. I wonder who has that stone? Not King Dahmis. The fool would never break his word. He pledged not to warn her."

Vesputo paced, his handsome face controlled and shut. Beron wanted to rub the exhaustion out of his eyes, but thought better of it.

"Now that she's dead, my lord—"

"If she's really dead, Dahmis has been his own undoing. He was extremely fortunate to fend off the Sliviite attack, but he won't be so lucky this time. He has no one to warn him now."

Torina scooped water into her hands. The day was clear and fresh as a new flower. Her soul seemed washed by the purity of her surroundings. Stately pines towered above, reaching for an azure sky. Wildflowers carpeted the ground. She wanted to embrace the world. What ecstatic relief to be herself again, a young woman called Torina, who let out her hair.

Staying with Landen these last few days, she felt transported from a land of bitter hardship to a place of innocence and renewal. They walked, talked, and breathed a companionship as fragrant as the pines. Often it seemed they were back at the secret meeting spots of childhood. The easy closeness of former days held them, giving a ground to stand on as they caught up to the present.

He told her of his doings as Bellanes and how he had traveled to Archeld for King Dahmis, believing her dead. She related her daring escape and the years spent half-mad with restless loneliness. They discovered that out of five of the high king's obsidian emblems, they had two between them.

She drank in his presence, like the sparkling water of their spring, unwilling to be sad that they'd both spent so much time in Desante, ignorant of each other. How lovely to turn and see him near, not to have to plead with her seer's eye to show him to her. She gloried in watching him move, hearing him speak, seeing the way his dark hair curled.

Every now and then, she felt the edges of the world gathering around them and knew this time would have to end. At night, she was often wakeful, listening to his cherished breathing and feeling pursued by the dark fate her heart told her she deserved. *Gramere warned me always to benefit others. Did she know I was stupid and heartless enough to let my anger stand between me and my conscience?*

Landen seemed too good for her. He would never

allow bitterness to corrupt his actions. She wanted to pour out love to him, kiss him, ask him what he felt for her. She felt unworthy of him.

Since that first morning when she'd apologized, he'd seldom touched her. When he did, it was with affection—stroking her hair or squeezing her shoulder. Affection yes, but love?

Torina sighed. She heard Landen behind her and turned.

"Landen?"

"Princess?"

"How odd it is to hear 'princess' again. I'm not a princess anymore, you know."

"Always, to me."

"Landen, you say not even Dahmis knows where we are?"

"True."

"You haven't told me why I was to be killed."

He sat beside her, clasping his knees. "It was said you informed the Sliviites of the location of the allied troops, so they'd be able to invade us successfully."

"What? It was said—"

"There was a surprise attack on Castle Bay, in Glavenrell. Most of the troops were posted elsewhere, many of them in Bellan Bay."

She shivered. "The high king sent troops to Vesputo?"

"Yes."

"What then?"

"We were able to stop the invasion," he said.

"We?" His head was lowered. "Landen, look at me. Landen, who is this 'we?'" She bent to his face and saw the deep shadows in his eyes, the burden of what he'd witnessed. "I never gave information to the Sliviites."

"I know, Torina."

"But what I did— Oh! What I did *not* do." Her eyes stung as if a desert wind blew into them. "I knew it was wrong. Landen, I was so angry over the alliance with Vesputo that when Dahmis asked for my help with the Sliviites, I refused. I've never looked in the crystal since that day. I was furious with the crystal, too, for it wouldn't show me anything of you. To think I could have prevented you from being in a battle! I can never make it up to you." She shrank into herself.

"Torina. It wasn't your fault. It was war."

"War should be fought by men of war!"

"Yes, it should. But most often, that isn't how it happens."

She beat her fist against her forehead. Landen restrained her arm. "Torina. You're not to blame for the war. It was won with as little loss of life as there could possibly be for such a large-scale attack."

"How?"

He ignored her question. "When the high king ordered me to Archeld, I defied him, too."

"Did you? But you never turned your back."

"You could still help him. Perhaps his greatest danger is yet to come." He picked up two stones and knocked them together.

"Of course!"

She fumbled in her pocket, finding the lump of cloth that wrapped her stone. The crystal glinted sharply in the sun. Torina let her eyes go soft, asking for a vision.

She saw Vesputo in her father's study, his handsome face calm. Next to him, Beron. Vesputo murmured orders and plans.

"Dahmis!" she gasped. "Oh, we must warn him!"

"What is it?"

The sight in the crystal faded and changed, speeding up. She saw Beron's triumphant grin. "It's Beron. He's become Vesputo's right-hand man. He's killing the high king!"

Landen's face clouded. "When? Is there time?"

"Then," she rushed on, "with the high king gone, chaos falls. In the aftermath, Vesputo means to topple the other kings. He wants to do it by using"—she looked up at Landen, stunned—"the Sword of Bellandra!"

"The Sword! But Kareed destroyed it."

"No, the Sword is hidden somewhere, not destroyed."

"Surely Vesputo would not dare."

"Could it be done? Could Vesputo make the Sword do evil?"

Landen suddenly seemed as remote as if he were half a world away, face impenetrable. "There was supposed to be a curse on anyone who used it for conquest. What if that meant in the wrong hands it could do great harm? I have to find it before he tries."

Goosebumps rose on her skin. He must hate her for what her father had done. "Landen, I swear I never knew!"

"You say the Sword is hidden? Where is it?"

Eagerly she returned to the crystal. She stared and stared. All she saw was a vague, muted outline.

"I'm sorry, Landen. It's concealed somehow. I can't see where it is."

305

His hands clenched. "Tell me how Beron plans to kill the high king. I'll ride to warn Dahmis, then go to Archeld for the Sword."

"It may already be too late. He's on his way. Take me with you!"

"No, Torina. I must ride hard. There's only one horse, and the country is full of assassins seeking you."

Blood beat loudly in her ears.

"I'm sorry, Princess." His eyes softened. He scooted close and wrapped his arms around her, rubbing his face in her hair. "Dear Torina. I can't face the idea of sacrificing you to this danger. You must stay alive." He caressed her cheek.

"Hear me," he went on. "Even if you feel only friendship, Torina, I've loved you since the day you helped me to my feet. I tried so hard to stop. Then I thought you were dead, and my life hurt every day."

"Y— you love me? After all my stupidity?"

"Could you ever doubt it?"

She felt an utter, endless belonging. How had she doubted? She no longer knew.

"And you. Never doubt, Landen. I love you. I believe it was always so, except for a while I lost my senses."

Landen's face shone with gladness. He pulled her closer and their lips met, leaving sorrowful uncertainty far behind.

Chapter 12

It took Landen three days to get to Glavenrell's fortress. He arrived in the middle of the night. Covered with dust, he dismounted his horse in one leap and ran for the entrance. Guards crossed spears in front of him. He held up the obsidian emblem and the way opened.

He'd never been inside the fortress. Its towering dimensions bewildered him. Carrying the black crest dangling from its red cord, he persuaded the night guards to wake the high king.

Deep in the maze of corridors, behind a studded door, Dahmis greeted him and nodded the guards away. Landen sank into soft cushions, peering at Dahmis through a fog of fatigue.

"You look as if you haven't slept since we last talked, my friend," Dahmis said. "Did you find Vineda?"

"Yes, she's safe."

Dahmis let out a great sigh. "Thank you. I must ask— is she the one you used to know?"

"She is. Did you believe she betrayed you?"

"No. Her character wouldn't allow something so despicable."

"You're right. She's sorry, now, that she didn't help you."

"Ah. Tell me, my friend, do you by chance know where she comes from? May I ask where you knew her before?"

Landen wondered how much to confide in this strong king. Should he speak for Torina? Now would be the perfect time to tell Dahmis the full truth.

No, it would be wrong without her consent. She didn't want force applied to Archeld for her sake, didn't want the high king to strong-arm her birthright.

Landen rubbed his eyes, his weariness turning to raw pain. "My king, I can't tell you that. But she wants to help you now," he said.

Landen would not stay for all the high king's hospitable offers.

"Please, Bellanes. If you hid Vineda yourself, I'm sure she's hidden well. And what sort of protector is a man dead from lack of rest?"

"No, my king. I must go."

He accepted a fresh horse, unwilling to tire his good stallion any further. Though fatigue clawed at his senses, slowing him, he believed that even if he lay down he wouldn't sleep. Bellandra's Sword, dismissed from his mind for so many years, now burned inside him with unquenchable heat. Torina had said it wasn't destroyed after all, that Vesputo sought to use it to bring the kingdoms under his rule.

Landen couldn't allow that. He must find where

Vesputo had hidden the Sword. He could almost feel it in his hand: a mighty, glorious weapon, powerful enough to finish Vesputo.

He rode off into gray light on a black mare. The sky seeped sad rain, turning his road muddy. He rode in a delirium of haste toward Archeld, never stopping except to exchange horses.

He left the road before the border checkpoint, entering Archeld by way of boggy fields. When he was well past the border, he still kept off the main thoroughfares, galloping through scattered hamlets. The rain stopped. Soon mud covered him and coated the legs of his tiring horse. He would have to change mounts again.

Landen found a village big enough to boast an inn. He inquired about a fresh horse. The innkeeper eyed him suspiciously. Landen forgot what a strange appearance he must present, spattered in muck. He forgot to smile and flash gold at the man.

"It may be I have a horse for you," the innkeeper said. "Wait here."

Landen leaned against the hitching post.

When the doors to the inn opened, soldiers bounded out. Soldiers in green. The village wasn't only big enough for an inn: it housed one of Vesputo's patrols.

Landen was so tired from lack of sleep that he simply ran from them, leaping on his poor, exhausted horse. The horse did its best to obey his heels, running hard. The patrol overtook them easily.

In desperation, Landen showed the high king's emblem.

"If you allow me to go, you'll be spared the high king's wrath."

It convinced the soldiers he was someone of importance, someone who should be seen by their king. They trussed him up.

❖ ❖ ❖

Torina spent two idyllic days alone in the hidden high valley. She thought of nothing that might bring sorrow or worry, reflecting instead on the beauty of nature and her reunion with Landen. Love hummed in her heart, making her dance. The meager food supplies at the hut tasted finer than any delicacy she'd eaten when living as a princess.

Sitting beside the spring, taking luxuriant breaths, it seemed the world was hardly big enough to hold her gratitude. She was almost ready to thank Vesputo for betraying her and driving her into the suffering of exile.

Each morning and evening, she looked in the crystal, relieved to find it blank and quiet. She believed Dahmis would be spared the death Vesputo planned; Landen would recover the Sword of Bellandra and Vesputo's time of power would end. She told herself nothing more was needed from her. She'd won a second chance from fortune; now she could let others take the actions necessary.

So it was a shock on the third day when she gazed at the crystal. She rubbed it against her skirt, trying to wipe away the image, gasping in horror as it held steadfast.

Landen. Bruised and bound, standing before Vesputo in the castle of Archeld.

Torina's hand closed over the crystal. She jumped to her feet.

"God help me!"

She dashed into the hut, searching in panic for her scarf. When she found it, her trembling fingers would hardly allow her to tie up her hair.

Racing out into the evergreens, she headed down the foothills.

Beron was getting close to Glavenrell's fortress; its outlines were visible on the horizon. The day was pleasant as he jogged along at a steady pace, filled with anticipation. Vesputo had entrusted *him* with the paramount mission of assassinating the high king! The rewards would be enormous.

Beron remembered the day Vesputo enlisted him and thought of all that had happened since. Vesputo's rise to kingship; the riches he granted those who served him. What might he give in return for this undertaking? Beron's imagination soared.

A weak voice nagged inside him, telling him Archeld was not at war with Glavenrell, had in fact pledged allegiance to the high king. He remembered Emid's lessons: to kill an ally was a terrible deed. He could still get out of it, ride north into Emmendae and disappear. No. Vesputo would seek him through all the kingdoms, just as he did Princess Torina. *Besides, Vesputo is my king. He's a good king. Archeld is better off now than ever. Kings have always tried to extend their lands. It's their right.*

Beron rode up to the gates of Glavenrell's fortress, sure of the welcome given emissaries of the allied kings. He reined in at the checkpoint, dismounted, and stretched his legs.

"Urgent message for King Dahmis's ears alone," he told the captain of the guard. The man signaled for a groom, and Beron's horse was led away to be tended. Waiting for his papers to be checked, Beron yawned.

The captain looked his seals over, said something to the soldiers standing nearby, and waved Beron through the gate.

Two soldiers escorted him inside the fortress. Beron tried not to look awestruck, but Glavenrell's grand archways and marble corridors impressed him. At sight of all the watchful uniformed men patrolling, fear began in the small of his back, crawling inexorably toward his throat. Vesputo had promised that the tiny vials of poison he carried in his sleeves would be slow acting, giving him plenty of time to meet with King Dahmis and leave the fortress. Now he wondered if he'd ever come out alive.

He was conducted into a room and invited to wait in a rich chair. Wine was brought for him. He gulped it, nervously waiting. If there had only been a second goblet, he might have mixed the poison instantly. As it was, he sat for what seemed an age. He poured more wine, unable to keep himself from drinking more than he should.

When King Dahmis entered, General Larseld was with him. Beron rose, bowing formally.

"I'm honored to meet with you, my king."

"Your king? I thought you served Vesputo." Dahmis's words had a discourteous edge.

"Certainly. But you are high king. He acknowledges that."

"Does he indeed?"

"Of course, my lord. And the message I have for you is only for your ears."

Making no move to dismiss General Larseld, the high king took a chair facing Beron.

"But perhaps I already know your message." The king's voice sounded ironic.

Beron shook his head slowly, feeling fogged, his fear mounting. Was this the way honored envoys were treated? The memory of Toban's face, hideously distorted in death, came to his mind.

"I doubt that, sir," he said, smiling. His words seemed to hit the floor with a dusty sound.

"Do you? The sentence for treason is death," Dahmis answered.

Beron flinched. "Treason? What are you talking of, my king?"

"Turn out your sleeves. And don't think to run. There are a hundred men within yards of me, each itching to test their weapons on you."

Beron slid down in his chair. How could Dahmis have known? The Princess Torina was dead. Or was she? Had someone else learned to use her stone? Who had told Dahmis? Who had undone his life?

As General Larseld stripped his shirt from him, shaking out the vials of poison, Beron wished his mouth would work so he could ask King Dahmis about Torina. But his tongue wouldn't form words.

He watched as the poison was stirred into his wine. There was plenty there to kill several men his size.

General Larseld extended the goblet. "Drink it," he said.

Beron wavered. Should he dash the wine into the high king's face? Strike down Larseld?

"Those men outside are quite ready to force this down your throat," King Dahmis said. "Or, you could drink it yourself and keep what dignity remains to you."

Slow acting. Perhaps it will be quicker, since they've given it all to me.

Dully, Beron's hand closed around the goblet. Without protest, he swallowed the wine.

❖ ❖ ❖

Torina found a road. She wondered which direction to take, for it led north and south and she wanted to go west.

A horse was coming down the bend: a fine, well-groomed animal, stepping along at a leisurely amble. Riding him was a dapper young man, bow and arrows slung across his back. He ignored Torina until she stepped in front of his horse and held up her hand. He looked at her pointedly; she could feel him taking in her threadbare clothes, hot dusty face, and drab scarf.

"Hello," she said. "Do you know the way to Archeld?" She stroked the horse's mane, calming her frenzied nerves.

The young man pointed back the way he had come. Torina steeled herself to his disdain. "My name is Vineda. Yours?"

"Samed," he answered, as if he was used to his name being password to anything he wanted.

"Will you let me borrow him?" she asked, caressing the horse's nose. "Please. It's important."

Samed sniffed. "You must be joking."

"Please. At least, take me part of the distance I must go."

Samed sneered in disbelief.

"A fine bow, I see," Torina persisted. "Are you a fair shot?"

"Better than fair."

"I can outshoot you."

"Ha!"

"I can."

The young man abruptly dismounted. He unslung his bow. "Show me."

"No, no. First we place our bets. I bet you the horse and bow that I can outshoot you."

"High stakes, ma'am. What do you have to put up?"

What did she have? Dahmis's emblem, which was probably priceless, but Samed wouldn't know or believe its value, and besides she could never sell it. Putting her hand in her pocket, her fingers closed over the crystal. She brought it out and held it up. Sunlight flashed in its depths. She felt a sharp pain at the thought of giving it up. But it was all she had and surely valuable enough.

Samed took a step toward her and stared at her body as if he were looking over goods he might buy. "No, ma'am. I have all the jewels I want. No." He came closer. "Drop your stakes or bet yourself," he said, leering.

Herself! Torina put the crystal away, heart thumping. He seemed very sure of himself. What if he was a great archer? She'd hardly set finger to bowstring in years.

"High stakes," she quavered. "Please, reconsider. Take me to town out of the goodness of your heart."

The young man smiled disagreeably.

Her face grew hotter. "Since you have no heart, you deserve to lose your horse," she flared. "Very well, I bet myself against your horse and bow."

Chapter 13

At a remote outpost garrison near the three corners of Desante, Glavenrell, and Archeld, sentries played a game of cards. Equan, one of the new soldiers serving King Dahmis, held the best hand he'd been dealt in days. Scanning his cards, he did his best to keep the excitement from his face. This time he'd win.

One of his companions stood up.

"Not so fast," Equan said.

"Look there," the man said, pointing at the rocky trail they were posted to watch.

A horse was coming on at a furious pace, much too fast for the terrain. Equan put his cards face down.

The rider brought up short with expert handling and slid to the ground in one fluid motion. Equan stared. It was obviously a woman, though where she'd learned to ride like that he couldn't guess. Her face, under a grimy kerchief, looked wild. Strangest of all, a bow was slung across her shoulder.

"Where is this?" she asked breathlessly.

"Whoa, miss," Equan's captain replied. "You're at the three-corner border. Archeld, Desante, Glavenrell."

317

"You're wearing brown," she panted. "You must serve the high king."

"Yes, miss."

"Good. Then you can take a message to him for me."

The senior sentry smiled. "A message to the high king. From you?"

Her hands shook as she pulled a red cord from around her neck. The captain touched it and handed it back, his face changing to bewildered respect.

"Certainly, miss. Tell me what you need."

"First some water. Then writing materials, a fresh horse, and men's clothes."

"You shall have them."

❖ ❖ ❖

Andris sat on a stump, cleaning his immaculate knife, preparing to sharpen what was already well honed. The high king had let him know Bellanes was on a private rescue. It might be some time before he returned. The band was to stay where they were camped in Glavenrell. Andris was uneasy, though he wouldn't admit it.

Life in camp was dull without Bellanes. The only thing of interest was training Cabis, the former Sliviite. The man was quickly learning all he could.

Andris was standing sentry duty. This task was tedious; no one came near the camp. He whistled softly, testing his blade on his thumbnail, so distracted he almost missed the rapid hoofbeats. Knife in hand, the big man called.

"Who goes?"

Someone yelled back. "I seek Andris!"

Spring had done her work thoroughly, covering the surrounding branches with thick leaves. Andris could see nothing.

"Your password?" he roared.

"Peace awaits!" came the reply, and King Dahmis burst into view.

"My lord!"

The high king's face was red. "I received a message from Vineda. Bellanes is captured. Gather the band and join my troop. We must ride."

Landen woke to the sound of doors clanging. He raised his throbbing head. He was in a cell. This one had a narrow slit of window showing Archeld's courtyard; a single ray from the setting sun touched the floor with red light. He lay on bare dirt, hands tied behind him, ankles chained to the wall. They had stripped him of most of his clothes.

The Sword of Bellandra is surely my curse. I thought it would allow me to vanquish the sinister tyrant. Instead, it has brought me full circle. Prisoner of Vesputo, and farther than ever from Bellandra's magic.

Thirst had become agony. They'd given him no water for days. But physical pain paled next to the torment of his heart when he thought of Torina. After years of separation, now that they were pledged in love, he was sentenced to leave her, would not see her again until she had finished all her days.

*We will never walk together over the fields of earth.
Never hear the birds in the morning.*

His tired eyes closed. In his imagination, he danced with her, there in the hidden paradise they had made. He could almost smell the wildflowers, feel the touch of her hand.

His door opened. He pretended to be senseless. Water was thrown in his face. His parched lips licked the precious drops.

Vesputo looked down on him. "Enjoying your accommodation?"

Landen thought of Torina by the little spring, smiling.

"I would enjoy killing you," Vesputo said. "I'll spare you if you tell me some things I want to know."

Landen peered at his captor. "You won't spare me, no matter what I tell you." His voice rasped with the effort to speak.

Vesputo opened his hand and put it into the path of dying light from the window. Torina's little ring and Dahmis's emblem lay there in his palm.

"This volcanic stone is quite unusual," Vesputo said, swinging it between his fingers. "It's rumored there are only five of these, each giving the bearer immediate access to the high king."

Landen was silent.

"Now that I have one . . ." Vesputo clasped the stone in a tight fist.

Landen's spirits fell lower. Was his capture to be the means to the high king's entrapment?

"Where did you get this stone?"

When Landen didn't answer, Vesputo continued in a mockingly pleasant tone. "Sworn to secrecy? Of course. There's only one place this could come from. I didn't know you were on such terms with Dahmis."

"There are many things you don't know, Vesputo."

"I know this ring," Vesputo said harshly, fingering the gold band set with a small, shining crystal. "Where is Torina now?"

"I heard long ago that she died here in Archeld."

"Where did you get the ring?"

"She gave it to me when we were children."

"Why?"

"I don't know." Landen wanted to shout his defiance, yell out that he knew who killed Kareed. But if he did, Vesputo would try to compel him to explain. The only person who'd witnessed the killing was Torina. Landen's life was done. He must protect hers.

Vesputo's lip curled. "A man of surprises. Very well. Since you won't tell what I want to know, let me tell you. Torina is as alive as you will be tomorrow."

Landen's mind tossed. *No, he doesn't have Torina. She stayed in the high valley. She's there now. He's only torturing me.*

Vesputo folded his arms. "Tell me where you hid the Sword of Bellandra," he said.

Landen's heart sped till the pulsing blood filled his body with frightful heat. "The Sword?" he gasped.

Vesputo's eyes narrowed. "The Sword. You stole it from me."

"If I had the Sword, would I be here now?" Landen asked incredulously.

He could see Vesputo struggling with some strong emotion. Confusion? Anger? There was a long pause while Vesputo stood over him, the muscles in his jaw clenching. Landen wondered, wearily, if Vesputo would simply kill him now.

But Vesputo whirled, striding from the cell without another word.

The Sword of Bellandra! I put myself in Vesputo's path to find it. But he would never ask me about the Sword if he knew where it was. Why did he think I stole it?

Then Landen recalled that his last trip to Archeld had been for the purpose of stealing a valuable treasure hidden inside a pyramid box.

Lying on the hard-packed dirt of a prison cell, Landen remembered the peace that had come to him during the night, on the wintry plains of Archeld, leaning against the box he'd risked so much to gain. Then he knew what he had done. Tears gathered, trickling across his bruised face.

I had it. I had the Sword.

He heard in his mind the high king's words. *"It belongs to someone else, who is away."* Dahmis had asked Bellanes to steal the Sword on behalf of the exiled prince of Bellandra, never knowing who he was. *And because I thought of the Sword as a mighty weapon, I failed to recognize it when it came to me robed in peace.*

Torina woke with a shuddering start. She was on the ground. A bow lay next to her. A sea of new grass surrounded her.

She tried to remember. When had she fallen asleep? The last she knew, it was night and she was riding through the Archeldan plains, flying down a narrow road in the dark.

Now it was bright day. The sun had traveled half its course. Her horse was nowhere to be seen. The endless grasses of the plains stretched around her, rustling.

Her horse must have wandered off the road to graze. She'd slipped from his back in a stupor brought on by days without sleep. Precious hours were lost. Landen could be dead.

She got to her feet. The ridge of the Cheldan Mountains rose to the east. She was in the middle of the wild plains of Archeld, where almost no one lived. Animals roved here, and in the spring, as now, people didn't hunt them, letting them breed. This was the region she'd crossed during her escape from Vesputo. It had been hard then, riding Amber, the king's horse. Now she was alone.

Torina ordered herself to move. She pointed herself at the western sky. Her tears salted the ground as she began to run.

Chapter 14

Emid sat alone in his room in the training barracks of Archeld, contemplating the formal uniform he was about to put on. He and all his charges were summoned to witness the execution of Landen, for the crime of murdering King Kareed. The public beheading was to be in the early hours of evening. The courtyard would be packed with soldiers.

Once again, Emid was under orders to do something he despised. The lines in his face had grown deeper and deeper in service to Vesputo. He often told himself he did his duty for Queen Dreea's sake and for the absent Torina. If Vesputo's soldiers must be trained, at least he gave them a living memory of their princess. But the years passed by, and word of Torina never came. Perhaps he was wrong to believe she lived. A man like Vesputo would make sure.

Dreea still haunted the halls of the castle, more pious than ever, rarely seen except on charitable missions or state occasions. Soon, it was rumored, Vesputo would marry again and begin a new dynasty.

For over three years, Emid had wrestled with his conscience. His inner voice cried out over and over as he witnessed inroads into the liberties of the citizens of Archeld.

The country was prosperous, yes, but the hardworking people were afraid. Sometimes they disappeared without explanation.

I do what I've always done—train boys to soldier for the king. As if it were still the same land and still the right thing as I know it.

Now, an execution on display.

No one saw Landen commit this killing. Yes, he had motive enough. Kareed killed his father, took away his kingdom, stole the Sword. *But I believe in my soul that he is innocent.*

Emid moved like an old man as he dressed. Sheathing his short dagger, he contemplated turning the blade on himself.

❖ ❖ ❖

Dreea submitted to Amile's gentle hands as they arranged her white hair. The queen's request to miss the execution had been denied. She would be seated on the platform just behind the king when Landen lost his life.

Today the young man Kareed had wronged so deeply waited for death. Dreea wished she could avoid such a sight, but Vesputo was adamant. She was queen. She must attend.

Dreea folded her hands in prayer. She remained in communion with God until a soldier came to escort her. The young man with reserved bearing seemed familiar, though she couldn't place his name.

"Zeon," he told her. She recalled the boisterous youngster who had been one of Torina's childhood companions. Could this grave, controlled man be him? The queen sighed.

She was grateful for his support as he walked beside her. They passed out of the castle into the courtyard jammed with soldiers. The tumult of voices sounded. Clear skies glowed luminous blue above. The bright sun hovered over the horizon.

The crowd parted smoothly for them, and Zeon took Dreea up the steps of a platform. He helped her into a chair and stood next to her. Vesputo was nowhere to be seen.

Dreea looked out at the sea of male faces topping dark green uniforms. They stood grouped in battalions, a formidable sight. She saw Emid, surrounded by boys, close to the front of the mass of men. Beyond the wide walls, curious citizens gathered, not daring to enter the courtyard but wanting a glimpse of the famous outlaw, Landen.

The queen's sight drifted over to where a scaffold had been constructed. To her horror, the prisoner was there, shackled and bound. Dark, curly hair hung unkempt around his haggard face. His guards had naked weapons in their hands. In miserable fascination, Dreea stared at the man who was said to have killed her husband.

He turned haunted eyes to her. He licked cracked lips. He seemed to be straining to speak. Dreea guessed he was so thirsty he was unable to.

"Zeon," Dreea said. "Fetch Emid to me."

Zeon went down the steps of the platform and found the trainer, leading him forward.

"Emid," she said. "That man is suffering of thirst."

"Madam?"

"I order you to give the prisoner water to drink."

"Certainly."

Emid directed one of his charges. Dreea's own throat burned as she waited. The trainer advanced to the scaffold. She saw him get a guard's attention, saw the guard scowl. Emid pointed to her, and the queen gave a royal nod. Emid climbed the scaffold steps. He lifted the water to Landen's lips.

Landen cleared his throat, trying again to speak. What did he have to tell her? The queen leaned toward him as Emid descended, but the noise of the crowd covered his words. All she heard was the roar of many voices.

A horn blared. Vesputo walked through the soldiers toward the platform. Dressed in velvet king's robes, with the crown on his head, he cut an imposing figure as he raised his arms. The horn ceased, the crowd quieted, and Dreea still looked toward Landen.

The prisoner's voice rasped out. "Alive!" she heard him say. Then a guard put a hand on his throat and squeezed.

Alive! Dreea's eyes flew to Emid. The trainer's lips were compressed to a mere line. Had he heard? Was he wondering why this prisoner chose to speak to the wife of the man he killed? Did Landen know something? Was Torina the one who lived? Or was it a prayer for his own life?

"For years, the murder of King Kareed has gone unavenged!" Vesputo called out. He paused dramatically. Dreea tried to think of what to say when he finished his speech. Somehow she must find an opportunity to talk to Landen. As Kareed's widow, she had the right.

"The killer of your king stands before you," Vesputo said.

The crowd murmured. Dreea felt faint. *Vesputo will refuse me. If I poison his moment of triumph, he will poison me. Then who will be left to welcome Torina?*

In anguish, the queen stared at Vesputo's implacable back, imploring God for help.

"The price of treason—" Vesputo stopped, with an intake of breath. He staggered back. His left shoulder sprouted an arrow.

Stunned, Dreea saw the king collapse into his chair, blood darkening the green of his robes.

"Bring me the traitor!" he cried, clutching his shoulder.

In the courtyard, orderly rows of men already converged on an area of the courtyard. The queen could see a boyish figure standing on top of the wall, holding a bow. He fit another arrow to the string just as soldiers swarmed him.

The unknown archer was hustled toward the platform, six soldiers closing ranks around him. His head, under a large, foreign-looking cap, was down.

A doctor hurried up the platform steps. "My king," she heard the man say, "we must get you inside to remove this arrow and tie up the wound."

Vesputo gritted his teeth. "I stay here, to see the face of my would-be assassin and complete the execution."

The doctor motioned Zeon, directing him to brace the king's shoulder. Vesputo groaned as the arrow was pulled out. A deep gash poured blood. The doctor pressed on it.

A new disturbance shook the multitude. Citizens outside the wall shouted, pointing at the road. Dreea could make out a cloud of dust approaching. Soldiers escorting the boy assassin looked around, trying to see through the crush of people.

Moments later, a man with a great scar marring his face rode his horse straight up the courtyard stairs.

"Way!" he yelled. "Way for the high king!" The court-yard soldiers took up the call and gave room, cramming together.

Silence fell, broken by awed murmurs, as a clear path opened between the edge of the courtyard and the plat-form. King Dahmis, in dusty travel robes, his bushy hair streaked with sweat, rode up this aisle. Soldiers bowed as he passed, some cheering him. Soon, the head of his charger drew even with the raised boards of the dais.

The high king seemed to take in everything at a glance. "Wounded?" he asked. "This place smells of treachery, King Vesputo."

Anger threatened the edges of Vesputo's calm. "I did not expect you, my king."

The high king's eyes went to the scaffold, where Landen swayed on his feet.

"I heard news that the warrior Bellanes was detained here," he announced. "I see my news was true."

Dreea stared at Dahmis, thunderstruck.

Vesputo's handsome face went ghastly pale. "Bellanes?" He shook his head. "Impossible!"

"Why are you preparing to execute this man who mas-tered the Sliviites, preventing slaughter and famine?"

Dreea saw confusion and excitement pass through the courtyard like a storm as Vesputo kept shaking his head.

"You know this prisoner as Bellanes?" Vesputo asked.

"Yes. One and the same. This man you have in chains has saved my life and the lives of thousands."

"I know him by another name!" Vesputo disputed. "And by a crime for which he deserves a worse death than I give him. I sought him for years for the murder of King Kareed. His name is Landen."

"Landen?" The high king sounded both astonished and reverent. "The prince of Bellandra?"

Vesputo frowned contemptuously, while soldiers escorting the assassin pushed near the platform.

"What's this?" Dahmis said.

"The one who wounded me," Vesputo answered.

The queen noticed him catch the executioner's eye and move his hand in a quick chop. The man reached for Landen's head to put it on the block.

"Stop!" she called, her voice inaudible beneath the roar of the high king.

"Stop! I forbid you to kill that man! Touch him and you answer to me!"

The executioner hesitated, looking from one king to the other. Vesputo's face was eerily white, while the high king radiated potent command. The executioner stepped back.

Dahmis faced the courtyard. "An attempt has been made on the life of your king! A man stands accused of murdering the former ruler, King Kareed. These offenses must be submitted to justice!"

A noise of approval went up. On the road below, Dreea saw more people flocking. Her head whirled with dizzy relief. *The high king will listen to me, will grant me speech with Landen.*

Dahmis called to the prisoner. "You are Prince Landen of Bellandra?"

The instant silence was formidable. Everyone seemed suspended, waiting for Landen to speak.

"Once I was," Landen said hoarsely.

"King Kareed took away your father, your people, and your kingdom?"

"Yes."

"Did you kill King Kareed?"

Dreea sat forward, heart fluttering.

"No." Landen looked at the queen.

Dahmis spread his arms over the assembled soldiers. "Is there anyone here who knows how King Kareed died?"

"I do!" a voice cried.

Dreea put both hands to her chest. It was the boy assassin who spoke! A soldier clapped a hand over his mouth.

"An assassin to defend an accused assassin? What could you know about King Kareed's death?" the high king asked.

The boy struggled in the soldier's grip. "Let him go," Dahmis ordered. "He can't escape." The soldier released his grasp. "I repeat," the high king said, his deep voice rising, "what could you know about King Kareed's death?"

"Everything," the boy said. Again Dreea's chest lurched.

"Come forward."

The boy moved nearer. Baggy clothes swathed him, the cap hiding most of his dirty face.

The high king blanched. "Vineda?" he said.

For answer, the boy snatched away his cap. Red, abundant hair poured out around unmistakable features.

"Torina Archelda," she said, eyes lifted to her mother.

"Princess Torina?" thundered the high king. "Kareed's daughter!"

Dreea found her feet and ran across the platform, arms outstretched, while pandemonium broke out below. Yells and shrieks echoed from courtyard to road as Torina clambered up the platform steps. The queen folded her daughter in her arms.

"How is this?" the high king boomed. "Princess Torina died years ago."

Torina turned to Dahmis. "No. I left Archeld a fugitive." She pointed to Vesputo. "My father's murderer, Vesputo, took the crown and staged my death."

For Emid, everything slowed. He saw Princess Torina, and just behind her, Vesputo rising to his feet. Even before Vesputo drew the knife, Emid was aware of it. Feeling as if time opened an infinite window for him alone, Emid's sure hand unsheathed his own dagger. All his years of training warriors mounted up inside him. Cool, swift, and deadly, he raised his arm and threw.

Vesputo sprawled on the boards of the platform.

In the same slow time, Emid saw Dreea's hands go to her mouth, and the doctor bending over Vesputo. He saw the rapid dark stain spreading over the left side of Vesputo's chest; the high king inching forward on his great horse, questioning the doctor. Emid already knew what the doctor would say. No one could survive that knife throw.

And Emid felt the weight that had oppressed his life lifting away. He didn't care if he went to prison or if soldiers loyal to Vesputo killed him then and there. He had saved Princess Torina's life. He'd killed the man who murdered King Kareed.

Boys pressed close around him, forming an instinctive

wedge of protection. But no soldiers rushed him. The courtyard was preternaturally quiet, filled with dazed faces. The soldiers stared at the platform where the doctor was shaking his head and covering Vesputo's face; where Torina looked like an apparition in her baggy men's clothes and streaming red hair; where Dreea glowed as if all the angels she prayed to had paid her a visit.

It was the high king who recovered his senses first, turning from the platform to the assembled soldiers and the people massing around the courtyard.

"People of Archeld!" He raised his arms high, fixing the attention of the multitude. "Vesputo, the man you knew as king, is dead! But before you grieve, remember he was never truly your ruler. He gained the crown by treachery, lies, and murder."

He paused, allowing his words to be carried out to the edges of the crowd, murmured from one person to another, till all knew what he had said.

"This is a historic day for Archeld! A young woman has arrived home—the princess you thought dead!"

Torina stood on the platform's edge, untamed hair blowing around her face. Overcome by joy, Emid shouted out. "Welcome home, Princess Torina!"

From all around the courtyard, other people added their voices to his, till an unearthly hurrah shook the air. Looking at the faces of Archeld, Emid saw a quality that had been absent for too long. Happiness. It seemed to him the very air was brighter.

Torina gripped her mother's hand. Dreea behaved like a queen, nodding in stately beauty, waiting for silence to follow the hubbub.

When it was quiet, Torina spoke. "King Dahmis. Bear witness to me as I say, Prince Landen never killed King Kareed. He must be freed."

Emid saw the light in Landen's eyes as the young man looked at Torina, as if two suns let loose all their brilliance. Emid knew love when he saw it.

The high king's voice resounded to the wall. "Free him!"

Landen's guards hurried to remove his bonds. Boys mobbed him, getting in each other's way as they led him, limping a little, to the high king.

"People of Archeld! This is the hero who kept us safe from the Sliviite invasion!"

The soldiers who'd gathered to see Landen beheaded cheered him without restraint. He didn't seem to hear them. From where he stood, Landen reached his hand to Torina. She bent from the platform to clasp his fingers. Emid heard wild shouts reverberating all the way to the sea.

Chapter 15

Next morning, Torina walked with Dreea in the welter of weeds that had been her garden. She bent to a clump of nettles and separated them with gloved hands. A flower poked through.

"So many weeds," Dreea sighed. "I couldn't bear to come here when you were absent."

"Even if the weeds have grown, the flowers never left. This garden will be more wonderful than ever, now that I've come home."

Dreea stroked a green stalk. "I never stopped believing you were alive."

Torina put an affectionate hand on her mother's shoulder. "Hearing your voice on the other side of my door and sending you away—only the threat of harm to you could have made me do it."

"Only strong drugs could have fogged my mind enough to prevent me from breaking down the door."

"When I lived in Desante, I wrote you many letters, never sending them. I burned them just before leaving so they wouldn't fall into the wrong hands. Mamma, you'd have laughed, seeing me living like a peasant, doing everything for myself."

"Thank God you were fortunate and found good people to stay with."

"Oh yes. Fortunate. No word is big enough to describe the kindness I received in Desante. The Dirksons must think I'm dead. I look forward to putting their minds at ease."

"What will they think when they realize they had a princess living behind their farmhouse?" When Dreea smiled, Torina thought her the most beautiful woman in the kingdoms.

"They'll finally have an explanation for why I was ignorant of everything that mattered, such as how to farm and cook! Oh, they'll be surprised. Luckily they all have strong constitutions." Torina grinned.

They were both silent a moment, standing in the sun. "I should thank him," Torina mused.

"King Dahmis?"

"No. Yes—but I meant Vesputo. Without him, I'd still be the headstrong, spoiled girl I used to be. It was Vesputo who taught me the value of many things." She glanced around at the overrun plot. "How little I knew, when I thought it had all gone wrong."

"I understand you, Torina."

Warm sunshine melted across their steps. "Will you go with me to the cemetery? I want to visit Papa's grave. And someone else is buried who needs honor." *Eric.*

"Of course." They walked on.

"What a marvelous young man Landen is, Torina. I still don't quite understand how you came to know each other."

"I'll tell you the story someday, Mamma."

"How brave the high king is," Dreea murmured. "To ride into a crowd of soldiers. As far as he knew, they were loyal to Vesputo."

"Yes. That was brave. It was also very like the king he is."

❖ ❖ ❖

Emid took his seat in the great hall in the castle of Archeld. The polished floor reflected rows of people, festively dressed. Bunches of flowers stood in tall vases. Wreathes hung the length of the long walls.

Near Emid, Landen sat relaxed, dark curls smoothed. Next to him were the other members of his famous band, cleaned up and turned out till they looked uncomfortable.

Queen Dreea and King Dahmis sat on thrones at the front of the hall.

Down the center of the room walked a young woman in soft green silk, her thick red hair twined with flowers. Tears started in Emid's eyes. No veil this time, no concealment. His princess was really here, vibrant as ever. As she passed, she smiled at him.

She knelt before King Dahmis. The king placed a delicate crown on her head. With charming grace, she stood. The high king clasped both her hands in his. His voice carried across the heads of the people. "This is a day for restoring what has been lost! Your princess is found!"

Emid hallooed with all his might, hearing echoes of delight travel the length of the hall. The great room erupted with joyous noise—stamping feet, clapping hands, exhilarated voices. When it died down, King Dahmis spoke again.

"There is another matter before us."

Emid heard rustling as people turned to their neighbors with questioning looks.

"Landen, please come forward," the high king rumbled.

Landen moved with lithe energy from his bench. Everyone stared raptly as he gripped the high king's hand.

"Men and women of Archeld, prepare yourselves. I am about to tell you a story!" the king said. People settled into their seats.

"Once upon a time, there was a coastal kingdom. It stood a few days' journey south of Archeld. The kingdom was small, but rich and very peaceful," King Dahmis began.

Standing by Torina, Landen folded his hands.

"This kingdom was called Bellandra, and its kings and queens kept with them a sacred Sword. Legend said this Sword came to Bellandra from a far island in the deep ocean, an island that could not be found when searched for, but only seen by the pure of heart when they had lost their way.

"Great power rested with the Sword. The power of peace.

"As long as the Sword was kept safe, it was said, the people of Bellandra would also be safe. They put such faith in this that, as generations passed, they forgot to cultivate a vigilant spirit, living instead on tradition alone.

"Nearly ten years ago, the Sword of Bellandra was taken as a spoil of war when that kingdom was conquered by Kareed of Archeld. It has lain unused ever since."

He paused. "It has been in my keeping for some time now, recovered by a warrior of Bellandra, a man with the heart for peace." The high king pointed to Landen and stopped speaking. He bent behind Dreea's throne, raising a large, pyramid-shaped box that Emid recognized. He set it down next to Torina.

"Landen," the princess said, touching the box. "This belongs to you." Her voice brimmed with happiness. "My mother and I give back Bellandra to you, with apologies and gratitude. Apologies for your suffering, and gratitude that we have come to know you."

Landen took her hand, kissing it. "Thank you," he said simply.

He knelt reverently beside the pyramid. Slowly he ran his hands over its contours, while the gathering of people watched, entranced.

Then with swift strength, Landen broke the locks. The box fell open. He lifted out a sharp and iridescent Sword. Luminous light sparkled on its shaft, dancing forth to merge in a shimmer of rainbows. Gazing at it, Emid felt love overwhelming his heart, as if all the love he had ever known in his life gathered into a single beacon.

The moment spilled waves of harmony, till everyone was smiling. One of Landen's companions, a hideously scarred man, looked ready to burst into song. Next to him, a huge man buttoned into a tight white shirt beamed.

Torina reached behind the throne, pulling out a beautifully crafted scabbard. She buckled it around Landen's waist.

"So you can carry it with you," she said.

Landen sheathed the Sword. Signaled by King

Dahmis, musicians struck up a lively tune. People rustled toward the doors, talking and laughing.

Emid made his way toward Torina. She was looking into Landen's face. She seemed not to see anyone else. As Emid watched them together, he was taken back to the little glade on the forested hill, where two royal children played at archery.

Perhaps I knew it then. Certainly, I know now. Destiny placed them next to each other.

"What is your future, son of a king?" he heard Torina say.

Landen smiled. "Ask your crystal, daughter of a queen."

She traced his eyebrow with a finger. "My crystal never tells me what I can see with my own eyes."

Standing nearby, Queen Dreea and high king Dahmis regarded the couple.

"Those two are carved from the same tree," the queen said.

"By the same blade," the high king answered, and offered her his arm with splendid dignity.

Acknowledgments

Grateful thanks to the following people: my parents, for teaching me to love reading; my husband, Tim, for his steady love; sisters Bridget and Peggy, and friend Mary Ann, for believing in this book; the many dear friends who make my life so interesting; Ben Sharpe and Regina Griffin, for their astute input while editing this book; Sophie Hicks, my agent, and Holiday House, publisher, for their wonderful work on behalf of this story. Special thanks to David Fickling.